# With Violets

# With Violets

Elizabeth Robards

Five Star • Waterville, Maine

First Edition
First Printing: January 2005

Set in 11 pt. Plantin by Minnie B. Raven.

Printed in the United States on permanent paper.

**Library of Congress Cataloging-in-Publication Data**

Robards, Elizabeth, 1964–
　　With violets / by Elizabeth Robards.
　　　　p. cm.
　　ISBN 1-4104-0222-3 (hc : alk. paper)
　　1. Morisot, Berthe, 1841–1895—Fiction.
　2. Triangles (Interpersonal relations) — Fiction.
　3. Manet, Edouard, 1832–1883—Fiction.
　4. Women painters—Fiction.　5. Brothers—
Fiction.　6. France—Fiction.　I. Title.
PS3620.H684W57 2005
　813′.6—dc22　　　　　　　　　　2004043304

This book is dedicated to my grandmother,
Wiladean Barnett,
who will always be my lucky star.

# Acknowledgments

This book wouldn't be in your hands if not for Russell Davis, the most wonderful editor in the world. Russell, thank you for asking me what I really wanted to write, then making it possible for me to pen the book of my soul.

Deepest appreciation to Peter Pettegrew, a modern-day Impressionist master. Pete, thanks for painting the gorgeous landscape on the cover of this book, for sharing your vast knowledge of the painting process, and for the long-term loan of your Impressionist library.

A million thanks to my fabulous agent, Michelle Grajkowski, for her steadfast support and undying enthusiasm. Michelle, thanks for riding the manic tides and bailing the emotional waters of hurricanes Charley, Frances. How did I get so lucky to work with you?

To my parents, Jim and Lynn Robards, and our friends, Albert and Michelle Bodier—thanks for a wonderful time in Cannes.

To Jay Robards for all your support.

Teresa Brown, Elizabeth Grainger, and Catherine Kean—three very talented writers and the most excellent critique partners a gal could hope for. Ladies, thanks for taking time away from your own work to lend your expertise to this book. I don't know what I'd do without you. Special thanks to Elizabeth for her help with the French language and translation of Berthe Morisot's correspondence.

Special thanks to Deborah Pfeiffer—tremendously gifted writer and editor extraordinaire—for the "get out of deadline free" card. Debbie, you saved my life!

Kathy Garbera and Mary Louise Wells (two more exceptionally talented writers)—your support, friendship, and humor make my life very rich.

One of my key sources in researching the lives of Morisot and Manet was *Berthe Morisot: The Correspondence with her Family and Friends*, compiled and edited by Dennis Rouart. I deeply appreciate the book's contribution to the story.

And finally, love and thanks to Jennifer and Michael. You make my life complete.

# Chapter One

## Paris–1868

*They will become painters. Are you fully aware of what this means? It will be revolutionary—I would almost say catastrophic—to your bourgeois society. Are you sure you won't curse art, because once it is allowed into such a respectable and serene household, it will surely end by dictating the destinies of your children.*
*—Joseph Guichard*

I'd seen him in the Louvre. We'd exchanged glances. Polite nods. Single words. No more. It wasn't proper, because we'd not been formally introduced.

I could not help but notice him. His fine clothes and fair hair set him apart from any man I'd laid eyes upon. He commanded attention and compelled the beholder to drink in his being. A masterpiece who spoke to the soul.

Our meeting happened weeks later, as I copied the Rubens with my friend Rosalie. I heard men's voices sounding behind us. Indiscernible; only tones and inflections; patterns of speech echoing a symphony of color in the empty *musée* gallery. One timbre dark and rich as umber shadows. The other vibrant as vermilion.

I did not turn around. I'd memorized his voice, his gestures, as he copied the Italians and the Spanish. The manner in which he attacked his brushwork—Painting. Stopping. Retreating. Studying. Stepping forward to begin

9

again. Then, as if he sensed me watching, he'd abandon his dance and glance up, his gaze snaring mine like a mesh net. He'd smile. Nod. Before I could summon the grace to look away, he was lost again in Tintoretto.

I should have felt ashamed for staring, but I did not. How odd that propriety chose that moment to drop her weighty baggage, prohibiting a glance at him as he approached.

The murmur of voices stopped. All was quiet save the rhythmic tap, tap, tap of shoes and walking stick on the parquet floor. The conversation resumed not ten meters behind me, muted by veiled whispers.

Rosalie painted in oblivion. How I envied her calm.

Chewing the wooden end of my brush, I fixed my gaze upon the bare breast of Rubens's water nymph, determined not to falter in the face of this contingency.

I'd worn my green dress, although it was covered by a frightful gray painting smock. I did not remove the cover-up. Nor did I preen and primp like an idiot. I acted natural, as if his footfalls were not stopping behind me.

Rosalie murmured. The sound washed over me in cobalt waves. I plunged the tip of my brush into the vermilion, swirling it around so the lovely brashness coated the bristles. I dabbed at the water nymph's nipple.

"*Bonjour, Mesdemoiselles.*"

I tightened my grip on my palette.

In my peripheral vision, I saw Rosalie whirl around. Too anxious. "*Bonjour, Monsieur* Fantin."

Moistening my lips, I kept my gaze upon my canvas, waited five beats, and turned, as if I'd just realized we were no longer alone.

"*Bonjour.*" My voice, cold and thin, was lackluster shades of gray.

"*Mesdemoiselles,* may I present *Monsieur* Édouard Manet."

I pressed my thumb into the edge of my palette until my hand tingled.

"*Monsieur* Manet, I give you *Mesdemoiselles* Rosalie Riesener and Berthe Morisot."

"*Bonjour.*" He bowed, quick and proper, over his silver-tipped walking stick. "I am quite familiar with *Mademoiselle* Morisot's work. I have often enjoyed it at the Salon. I am a great admirer."

His words resonated in the *musée*'s great gilded hall. An admirer? He knew of me?

Did he jest?

His smile appeared genuine, but if I pondered his words too long, I sensed a hint of mockery in the upturned corners of his mouth.

"*Merci.*" I fought the urge to retreat. I was not practiced at conversing with men. Words never came easily. My mother berated this fault, fearing people might think my silence proud or sullen. Alas, much to Maman's dismay, I would've preferred to remain mute than spew nonsense.

So you see, it was best the meeting came as a surprise, that *Monsieur* Fantin gave me no notice of the introduction. For I was of a mind to create monsters in my head. Not that I thought *Monsieur* Manet a monster.

*Au contraire.*

Although, the sheer magnitude of his persona frightened me as much as it thrilled me. I admired his freedom, his sincerity, his willingness to explore and express what was real, what was true. He was at once terrifying and glorious. And breathtaking.

A master.

He stepped closer, walking around to the working side of

11

my easel. "What have we here?"

My throat tightened, and I thought I understood how Eve felt in the garden when she realized the full magnitude of her nakedness.

It was just a painting—Rubens's *Queen's Arrival at Marseilles.* I tilted my chin to meet his gaze.

His eyes searched my face, and his lips curved into a smile. "Beautiful."

*Mon Dieu,* he was bold. I'd heard tales of his exploits, but who was to know how much was embellished? He was not a bohemian. For all appearances, he was a proper gentleman, if not a dandy.

My gaze shot back to the water nymph's lush form. I knew he was watching me, a casual assessment. Yet, I sensed the man was capable of consuming all in his possession.

If I were prone to blush, it would have happened at that precise moment. Thank heavens my body did not make a habit of betraying my emotions. Of all my strengths, I was grateful for containment.

I took a deep breath. The smell of the paint calmed my nerves. I touched the tip of my brush to the ochre paint, intending to deepen the shadow under the nymph's breast, but as the brush stroked the flesh-colored curve, the vermilion bled through. The resulting orange-tinged streak resembled a gruesome, bleeding gash.

*Monsieur* Manet's mouth pressed into a straight line. "Why do you mix those colors?"

A claustrophobic tingle coursed through my limbs. "*Monsieur* Manet, I beg your pardon, but I cannot work with you peering over my shoulder."

"Excuse me, *Mademoiselle.* I, too, could not work with onlookers hovering."

If I offended him, he was too much of a gentleman to make issue of it. I thought he would bid me *adieu* and take his leave. I felt sick at the thought of confessing to Maman I made the acquaintance of the great Édouard Manet and succeeded in affronting him in less than a quarter hour.

Yet he lingered. "Perhaps I might offer one suggestion?"

I said nothing, which he must have mistaken for acquiescence. He stepped closer; our bodies were a breath apart. As bold as you please, he plucked my brush from the palette. Long, clean fingers swept my thumb. A tingling glow spread across my breasts and throat, and I stepped back to create space between us.

Unaffected by the familiar contact, he loaded paint onto the brush. I was relieved he did not look at me. If so, I feared he might have seen a gaping idiot staring back, a girl rendered stupid by the touch of a man.

Rosalie and Fantin abandoned their conversation and observed Manet at work. Awestruck, I watched him heal the wound I'd inflicted. Rubens could have scarcely done better.

I'd studied the painting for weeks. Yet as I watched him transform my blunder into perfection, it was as if I saw it for the first time.

Rosalie sent me a quizzical glance.

But I did not stop him from altering my work. How could I make her understand when I did not?

In the presence of the old masters, with the gaze of the water nymphs raised to the heavens, and a disapproving Maria de' Medici staring down upon us, I must have resembled a wide-eyed girl consumed by the power of genius.

He finished. Thrust the brush toward me, looking quite pleased with himself.

I reached out to reclaim it, but he did not let go. To my

horror, he gave it a little tug, and pulled my hand, brush and all, toward him. His eyes sparkled like two shiny gray pools.

"Yes. Beautiful, indeed," he muttered.

My mouth went dry. "*Monsieur,* you are bold to take such liberties. I am not your student."

"*Mademoiselle,* I do not take students under my wing. I am far too busy with my own work to accept the responsibility of fostering creative whims. Even if I did, you are much too accomplished and your reputation far too superior for me to make such base assumptions. Please forgive me if I have offended you."

Still holding the brush, he took my hand in his and bowed. This time there was no playful tug. Just my small hand consumed by his, rugged and large.

His skin, touching my skin.

Bold.

Pure.

Honest.

A strange sensation wound its way down my spine and blossomed in my belly. I drew my hand from his and placed it on my middle, trying hard to breathe. It was as if someone cinched my corset so tight it killed my breath. A fever brewed and spread to my face and extremities, pooling in delicate places of which proper ladies did not take notice.

"*Mademoiselle?* You do not look well. Sit down, please. Let me help."

His hand was at my elbow. I let him escort me to a wooden bench in the center of the gallery.

"Berthe?" Rosalie knelt in front of me, the cool backs of her fingers pressed to my cheek. Her touch helped me focus and reminded me of all I'd heard about the purported effect the illustrious *Monsieur* Manet wreaked on the fairer gender. How his quick mind and clever wit captivated both men and women.

I was furious with myself for acting like such an imbecile. *Je ne suis pas une femme légère.* I was not a silly woman. I should've been immune to such base nonsense concerning a man who surely had as many mistresses as controversies swirling about him.

"I must have caught a chill." Yes, that was it. "Rosalie, we should call it a day. I am exhausted."

"I will gather our belongings."

I sat for another moment.

"Please allow *Monsieur* Fantin and myself to see you home."

"That is unnecessary." I stood, feeling stronger.

"*Mademoiselle*, it is our duty," said Fantin.

I shook my head and silenced him with a wave. The last thing I needed was to arrive home with two men in tow. That would make it impossible to salvage any shred of dignity.

"As you wish," said *Monsieur* Manet.

He and Fantin exchanged a glance. I walked to my easel to relieve dear Rosalie of packing my paints.

Manet lingered as I wiped the wet paint from my palette, taking care not to get the remnants on my hands. I wrapped the wooden board in a cotton cloth.

"I fear I am leaving you with a most unfavorable impression," he said.

"No. I am exhausted. For that, you cannot blame yourself."

"Then you will give me another chance to improve your opinion?"

I did not answer him. I dropped the brush into my bag, then slipped out of the gray smock and smoothed the bodice of my dress.

His gaze traced my motions. "Very well, then."

"Very well."

He nodded to Fantin. *"Au revoir, Mesdemoiselles."*

*"Au revoir, Messieurs,"* said Rosalie.

The two men walked away. As they reached the gallery door, Manet turned back to me and tipped his cane. "To second chances, *Mademoiselle.*"

# Chapter Two

*There are certain people whom one loves immediately
and forever.*

*—Unknown*

"I cannot believe you met him," my sister Edma lamented
as we painted side-by-side in our studio. "The one day I do
not go to copy, Fantin brings Manet around for introduction. I shall never forgive him."

If she'd expressed her displeasure over missing the introduction once, she'd bemoaned it a million times since I'd
met Manet not even twenty-four hours prior. Edma and
Maman hung on every word, begging for details until they
were satisfied they'd drained me of all I might offer.

Usually, Maman accompanied my sister and me to our
copying sessions, but that day Edma chose to forgo the
Louvre in favor of receiving Adolphe Pontillon, who'd
called on her more often than I cared to face.

Given a choice between art and romance—Well, to
Maman there was no choice when romance was in the picture. She and Edma stayed home to entertain Adolphe. I
went with Rosalie for the morning.

I did not know who was more distraught over missing
the excitement. But at least my mother dismissed her disappointment with a simple, "To think of all the hours I've sat
in that wretched *musée*. I turn my head for a moment and
*voila*."

Maman and Papa were good sports. While most parents

insisted daughters of marriageable age approach a hobby, such as painting, as nothing more than a fleeting fancy, mine indulged.

"The talent you and your sister possess brings your father and me great joy. Not as great as the day you shall marry, but in the meantime, it shall suffice."

I knew there would come a day when she and Papa expected me to lay down my brush and give myself in marriage. Fortunately for me, Edma's blossoming relationship with Adolphe deflected attention from my lack of interest in the men who came courting.

In the studio, Edma let loose yet another misery-laden sigh. I blended emerald into the leaf of the still life I painted. "I cannot help it if you had better things to do yesterday than attend to your copy studies."

She rolled her eyes. For a moment we painted in silence.

"How is Adolphe?" I asked.

"Fine. Is Manet very tall? You did not mention his height."

"Edma, this has grown tiresome. You have spoken of nothing else this morning. Tell me about your visit with Adolphe."

"There is nothing to speak of where Adolphe is concerned. It is all so very dull. My whole life is dull. You could at least humor me. When you tell me of the meeting, it makes me feel as if I shared the experience. I should think you would realize that, but no, you hoard him all to yourself."

I *was* hoarding a few details. One in particular: that despite Rosalie's presence, it seemed he saw only me. I was happy for it.

I could not tell this to Edma or Maman. It would've sounded foolish. So I held back this delicious detail. Something to savor. Like a child with a stolen sweet, I could enjoy the private thought as I lay awake retracing the meeting in my head.

Second-guessing every gesture. Every smile. Every word.

His hand on mine.

In my mind, I moved toward him without hesitation. We stood so close I felt his breath on my cheek, my ear, my neck—

"Are you listening to me?" Edma huffed and scooted her chair away from her easel. The legs sounded the impatient growl of wood raking over wood. But she did not stand up. Instead, she leaned into the portrait and worked with staccato jabs.

"Perhaps now you shall be more interested in your copy work at the *musée?*" I arched a brow at her in a way that always made her smile. She frowned, but then her scowl gave way to a wicked smirk.

"*Oui,*" she said. "Perhaps we both have gained a greater appreciation for what the masters might teach us."

We laughed together. Her rising spirits buoyed me.

"In fact," she said, her eyes bright with a fresh scheme, "let's visit the masters now. Come, Berthe, let's go."

This suggestion, or perhaps her exuberance, made me feel as if I were walking down a steep staircase unsure of my footing. I inhaled—the scent of paint, and oil, and hydrangeas. My stomach pitched.

"Lunch is almost ready. We shall go Friday."

"But today is Wednesday. That is two days away. I want to go today."

"Edma, think. Do you believe he lives at the Louvre day and night? We have no guarantee he will be there. Besides, I do not wish to appear anxious. A few days' absence shall suit us."

"It will not suit *us*. You are only thinking of yourself. It is not fair."

"No, my dear, dear Edma, what is not fair is your having a tantrum over something so minuscule."

She stamped her slippered foot. Her dark, upswept hair offset her flushed cheeks. She looked so childlike with her pink dress peeking out from her open painting smock. Paintbrush in hand, her arms dangling along the sides of her chair, and she pouted.

I chuckled. I could not help myself.

Edma glared at me and flung her brush onto the paint-splattered table that stood between our easels. It sounded like a carillon as it struck the grouping of glass jars—some holding pigment and brushes, others half-full of linseed oil—finally resting among the mélange of sullied palettes and stray paint tubes.

She stood.

I turned back to my still life and blended a perfect highlight on the flower petal. She plopped down onto the brown divan along the wall behind me. The old piece of furniture *poofed* and creaked under the stress.

*"Hmmph."*

I saw the action so clearly in my mind's eye, a most unrefined expression of displeasure reserved for the rare occasion my sister and I disagreed. Three hundred and sixty days of the year we got on famously. When we didn't, even the smallest issue seemed catastrophic.

It hurt me to know she was angry. But it paralyzed me to think of facing him again so soon.

Too eager for the second chance of which he spoke.

The odd swirling sensation returned to my belly. It curled my toes inside my slippers. I squeezed them hard to counteract the wooziness. At least this time the feeling did not take me by surprise.

I turned in my chair to face my sister, who sat on the divan with her elbows resting on her knees, her chin on her palms, a scowl fixed on her pretty face.

"Do not pout, Edma. If you must go to the Louvre, see if Maman will accompany you. If Manet is there, you may hoard him all to yourself."

"Accompany you where?" Maman's voice, as crisp as a primed white canvas, called from the doorway. She breezed into the room, clutching a letter. The pale blue of her dress in harmony with her silver hair. She looked from Edma to me. "Is everything all right?"

Edma snared me with her eyes. Her glance was a warning. Her eyes were two poison darts.

I said to Maman, "We were just discussing technique."

"*Oui.*" Edma glowered. "I was telling Berthe her *perspective* is all wrong. The flower—" she frowned at me, "she is much too big for her vase."

Maman walked over to my painting. She studied it, then turned back to my sister.

"It is charming. I see nothing wrong." She frowned. "Sit like a lady, Edma. I have brought you up better than this. You are peevish today. What ails you?"

Edma scooted to the edge of the divan and sat rod-straight. She did not answer nor did she try to hide her displeasure.

"Perhaps this will cheer you." Maman waved a crème-colored note. "*Madame* Auguste Manet has invited us to supper tomorrow evening."

The name Manet crashed like cymbals in my mind. Light-headedness seemed to lift me up and render my body numb. Edma sprang to life and hurried to Maman's side.

It took a moment for the implication to register: *Madame*

Auguste Manet, his mother, may have sent the note, but the invitation had *Monsieur* Édouard Manet written all over it. So this was how he planned to impress me. On his own turf.

I should've guessed as much.

"One day's notice?" Maman looked at me, and I felt myself settle back into my body. "Does he think we are so unpopular we have no other engagements?"

I opened my mouth to speak, but Edma cut me off.

"We do not have plans. If we did, I should think we would cancel them. It is not every day we receive such an invitation."

Maman held out the letter. It seemed a briar rose that needed careful handling or it would prick me. With my forefinger and thumb, I took it from her. Edma appeared at my side grinning, a sheepish gesture of reconciliation. Her shoulder pressed against mine as she leaned in for a better look. The note, sturdy black script on steadfast crème cardstock, said:

*Please come for dinner; forty-nine rue de Saint Pétersbourg; Thursday evening, seven o'clock. Regrets only.*

Regrets.

Was regret what I feared? Regret that I would discover him mortal? That the champion of all that was shocking and real would be proven merely a man?

"We will go?" I asked Maman.

"I suppose. Since your father is away, it will give us something to tell him when he returns. And I should be delighted for the opportunity to ascertain if your Édouard Manet is as charming as you claim."

My stomach fell like a rock dropped into deep water.

Edma grabbed my hands and pulled me up from my chair. She turned us about in circles, crushing the invitation in her grasp. The corner of the stiff paper cut into my palm.

Why worry?

Courting men were all the same—all charm and very little substance. Each with expectations for me to favor him above my painting. Each demanding a compromise. I'd never met a man who outshone the promise of the next image that would court me, tease me, seduce me. Until I laid it down upon my canvas and had my way with it.

Why would Manet be different?

Edma and I stopped spinning, but my mind continued to whirl. The paintings, hung one upon the other on the studio walls, danced around me as I tried to regain my equilibrium. I glanced down at the crumpled note in my hand, and the world shifted under my feet.

In a boudoir perfumed with *Violettes de Parme*, Edma and I chattered and shared confidences. Giddy worries. Sudden panics. Trepidations born from ridiculous designs.

"When Fantin called yesterday, he told me Emmanuel Chabrier played Saint-Saëns's *Danse Macabre* last week at the Manets' soirée," Edma said, breathless. Her eyes sparkled as she brushed my hair. She paused and studied me in the glass. "What will be your first words to Manet?"

In my mind, I'd rehearsed the scene a million times, but put to the test, I could not recall a single syllable.

"I suppose I shall say, *'Bonsoir, Monsieur.'* "

She clucked her tongue. "That shall set his heart aflame."

"If so, he is too easily impressed."

Edma set down the brush. I knew she could see through my guise. I picked up the silver hand-mirror with trembling

23

fingers and studied my reflection.

I closed my eyes, drew in a shallow breath and set down the mirror. Crystal crashed. My eyes flew open, and I caught a perfume bottle just before it rolled off the dressing table. The stopper came loose and liquid splashed on my hands. The sweet scent of violets flooded my senses and calmed my rattled nerves.

Edma giggled.

I could not help but laugh with her. Dear, sweet Edma, the one who knew me so well, sometimes better than I knew myself.

We tied laces, cinched corsets, smoothed folds and straightened bonnets; the mood was lighter than it had been in days. Hiding my desire like a gold ring tucked away inside a delicate ivory box, I perfumed my dreams with what remained of the spilled violet water and stilled my unsteady hands with the sweep of satin gloves.

Finally, when there was nothing left to do save leave for the soirée, I checked my reflection in the hand-mirror one last time. The pretty trinkets on my dressing table shimmered in the half-light. One careless gesture would send the *bibelots* smashing to the floor.

As I returned the mirror to the table—a slow, deliberate gesture—my hand did not shake.

# Chapter Three

*Entering the hall, she meets the wife . . .*
*Words stick; does not manage to say anything.*
*Presses hands together; stands hesitating.*
*Agitates moon-like fan, sheds pearl-like tears.*
*Realizes she loves him as much as ever,*
*Present pain never come to an end.*
*—Anonymous, China—The Rejected Wife*

We traveled in the cold rain from our home on *rue* Franklin to the soirée on *rue* de Saint Pétersbourg. The foul weather did not dampen my spirits. Yet it took but three hateful words to ruin my evening: *Madame* Édouard Manet.

He was married?

It didn't make sense.

Inside the lavish drawing room, the distant rumble of thunder sounded as I gaped at the profile of the fat, dowdy woman playing Chopin on the piano. Her hair, parted in the middle, was pulled back in a severe chignon. The style emphasized a round face that seemed to have swallowed her chin and redistributed it in three tiers of gelatinous flesh that danced as she pounded the keys. Her upturned nose was too small for her masculine face, and in conjunction with her pursed, thin-lipped mouth, she looked as if she smelled a fetid odor. All broad shoulders, bosom, and tree-trunk waist, she was a sausage stuffed into gray silk.

Édouard Manet was *married?* This was his *wife?*

I glanced around the room and wondered if I'd heard

*Madame* Manet, *mère,* incorrectly.

Edma leaned in and pinched my arm. I wanted to scream, but I did not.

*Madame* Manet, *la mère.*

*Madame* Manet, *la vache.* She was a cow.

Unfathomable. I thought a man whose very existence was built on aesthetics, a dandy in his own right, would surround himself with beauty in every facet of his life. There had to be something more to this relationship than met the eye.

"Suzanne is a very gifted pianist." Our hostess paused as if to let us appreciate the melody drifting from the instrument. *Madame* Manet, *mère,* was petite with dark auburn hair and large, worried blue eyes, which swam like twin oceans across her angular face. Her narrow shoulders sloped under her black mourning dress, and her mouth turned down at the corners, giving an air of displeasure even when she spoke of the positive.

As she talked, my gaze drifted across the line of gilded crown molding to a large portrait suspended by a maroon cord. Hung in front of the mirror above the fireplace's intricate carved mantelpiece, the painting was of *Madame* Manet and a handsome gentleman, who must have been her late husband, as I could see a marked resemblance to Édouard.

My gaze fell to the lush deep-red Turkish rug that stretched the length of the parquet floor. Reflected in the mirrored walls, the lavish room seemed aflame in tones of gold, white, and red.

The tempo of the song increased, and I glanced back at Suzanne. Her pudgy hands flew over the keys.

*Je ne comprends pas.* I did not understand. How could a man with such an eye find anything beautiful in this woman? It irritated me.

Suzanne pronounced the final weighty chord. Two men standing near the piano applauded. She smiled demurely and began another song.

"The great composer Franz Liszt encouraged Suzanne to come to Paris from Holland to pursue her music," said *Madame* Manet. "She and Édouard moved in with me once they were married."

The comment buzzed like a gnat I longed to swat.

"Was she the success *Monsieur* Liszt predicted?" Surprised by my irreverence, I could not look at Maman.

*Madame* Manet lifted her lorgnette as if peering through the veiled meaning of my words to the heart of the insult.

She tilted her head to the right. "But of course she was successful, *Mademoiselle*. She married my Édouard."

Thunder erupted. Edma giggled a nervous little laugh. I was sure she intended to cover my rudeness by treating the exchange as folly.

I suppose I deserved the verbal slap, but I did not need my sister making excuses for me, spoken or implied. The stuffy room closed in on me.

It was on the tip of my tongue to ask for the return of my mantelet so I might bid the good *Madame* Manet *adieu,* when I spied him across the room, standing just outside the far interior doorway: an apparition under the chandelier's flickering, yellow candlelight.

From the tip of the knotted tie peeking out from his tweed vest and buttoned-up waistcoat, to the smart line of his trousers, he was a startling sight to behold.

Suzanne shifted into Beethoven's *Moonlight Sonata.* Not as difficult as the Chopin, but I surrendered to its beauty. She played it flawlessly. No doubt showing off her range.

How long had he watched us? Had he read the affront in his mother's body language after my gauche comment?

The pull of his gaze promised to monopolize my attention, but I resisted. I did not care to flirt or be flirted with by someone who was otherwise attached. What was the point?

I focused on an arrangement of six landscapes hung on the wall between him and the piano.

Again, thunder roared outside, a clap loud enough to command attention away from Suzanne's droning music. Everyone started, but her rhythm didn't break. She did not even glance up at the newly arrived guests in the entryway.

Édouard moved toward us. I folded my hands into the pleats of my skirt so not to fidget. It was a foolish notion to think I could travel home alone in such weather. If I mentioned it, Maman and Edma would not hear of it. And I could not bear to spoil their evening.

"*Madame* and *Mesdemoiselles,* welcome." He took my mother's hand and bowed.

"Ah, Édouard," said *Madame* Manet. "Please entertain the Morisots. I must greet our new guests."

Manet straightened. "With pleasure."

His mother ambled off toward three men, two of whom I knew: Alfred Stevens, who'd painted my portrait; and a waterlogged Fantin, who looked as if he'd blown in with the storm. He spied Edma and turned the brightest shade of red I'd ever seen.

The third, a rather sour looking man, emitted all the joy of a wet cat. He seemed quite disgusted as he roughed rain from his beard.

"I am very happy you would brave such weather to join us," Édouard said to Maman.

She tittered and purred an appreciative greeting, but by that time his eyes were fixed on Edma.

"Who is this captivating young woman?"

Edma swooned. Like clay waiting for his warm hands.

I wanted to pinch her like she'd pinched me earlier. Luckily, Maman took charge. *"Monsieur* Manet, this is my daughter, *Mademoiselle* Edma Morisot."

*"Enchanté."* He bowed, but did not take her hand.

I was glad. And even happier when his attention shifted to me, his gray eyes like the stormy evening sky.

"You have already made the acquaintance of my youngest daughter, Berthe."

"Of course." He neither bowed nor took my hand, but his gaze was a warm embrace. "I have been anticipating this evening, *Mademoiselle*. All day I could think of little else."

The odd funneling sensation swirled in my stomach. I was struck dumb. Maman stiffened, and I felt the air around her tense. From the corner of my eye, I saw movement. *Madame* Manet ushered the new arrivals to our huddle. I was relieved for the diversion.

It was good to see Fantin and Stevens, who shifted a brown paper package from under his arm to his hands. The familiar faces took the edge off the evening. Buoyed by their company, I relaxed.

The third gentleman was the artist Edgar Degas. I knew of him. I'd even admired his delicate pastels, but before this evening I'd never had the pleasure of his acquaintance.

*"Mademoiselle,* your portrait is finished. It is beautiful, if I may boast." Stevens hesitated an instant, then handed Édouard the package. "This is for you."

Manet tore away the paper, revealing a small gilded frame. Perhaps something Stevens painted as a gift for the occasion. Édouard's mouth tightened and his jaw twitched.

*Madame* Manet glanced at it. Her eyes widened and she seemed startled, even taken aback. Then she blinked and snapped into action.

"*Allons. Allons.*" Come along. Come along. She motioned Maman, Edma and me to follow. "The eligible ladies must make the acquaintance of my younger, *eligible* sons, Eugène and Gustave."

As we exchanged formalities, Édouard's gaze was fastened to me the way eyes in a portrait seem to follow one around a room. Suzanne played on without looking up, and *Madame* Manet pointed out a young man lurking on the far side of the piano. I'd not noticed him until now.

"Léon is Édouard's godchild. Suzanne's brother." She spat the words as if they left a bad taste in her mouth, but I was beginning to realize it was just her manner.

The boy stood quietly, leaning on the piano, reading music over Suzanne's shoulder. He turned the pages for her. The two appeared content in their musical world, side-by-side in companionable silence, undaunted by the milling, chatting guests, who'd made themselves quite at home by the time the dinner bell sounded.

Our hostess clapped her hands. Everyone quieted and Suzanne stopped in the middle of a stanza.

"Dinner is served. Please, let us go into the dining room."

Degas and *Madame* Manet led the procession. I thought it sweet when Édouard offered his arm to Maman.

He was not living up to the image of the rebellious rogue who painted naked women for the shock value. I was not sure if the discrepancy in character—or the enhancement thereof, depending on one's viewpoint—disappointed or charmed me.

Édouard Manet was proving to be a gentleman through and through.

Mannered.

Sophisticated.

Attentive.

Although, not so dutiful to his wife. I'd not seen them exchange so much as a glance all evening. She might as well have been a hired musician for all the attention he paid her. He might as well have been a single man. But he was not. He was married. Far be it for me to have questioned the strange ways of man and wife.

"May I have the pleasure?" Eugène extended an arm. I slipped my hand through it, and we fell in line behind Edma and Gustave. I glanced back and smiled at Fantin, who trailed alone behind us, whistling, hands clasped behind his back.

"Oh, do come here." I offered him my free arm, then cast a questioning smile to Eugène, who did not seem the least bit put out by my gesture.

Ahead, Stevens escorted Suzanne. It dawned on me that we'd been introduced to everyone except the one I was most curious about. How peculiar *Madame* Manet would make such an effort to sing her daughter-in-law's praises and not present her once she'd finished her musical performance.

Suzanne took her seat at the extreme opposite end of the table from where Eugène deposited me. *Madame* Manet graced the place of honor at the head of the table. Degas was to *Madame* Manet's left, Suzanne's right, and sat angled away from the younger woman, his full attention trained on our hostess.

As we awaited the first course, Stevens, Gustave and Fantin engaged Edma in conversation. Poor Fantin, it was evident he was quite smitten with my sister, but seemed incapable of expressing himself.

Eugène vied with Édouard in monopolizing Maman's attention.

And there sat Suzanne, alone in the midst of the crowd,

as if mute without the voice of her music. There was no doubt as to which *Madame* Manet was the lady of the household.

A manservant ladled the soup. Suzanne stood and whispered something in her mother-in-law's ear. *Madame* Manet scowled and nodded. Suzanne took leave.

The room was alive with merriment, and no one seemed to notice her departure. I suffered a pang for her. I knew how it felt to be alone in a crowd. Perhaps somewhere deep down, on a base level, Suzanne and I were not so dissimilar.

My gaze drifted to Édouard, who nodded at something Maman said. His gaze snapped to mine as if I'd called his name. My breath caught, and empathy for Suzanne sputtered and died like a snuffed candle.

We dined on the sumptuous feast under the champagne glow of candlelight: potage Saint-Germain, grilled red mullet, lamb chops on a bed of asparagus, roasted woodcock, truffle salad, ice aux fraises, camembert, ripe berries, grapes and walnuts.

The delicious aromas and diffused colors—all contrasts and shadows—swirled around the room, weighing heavy and intense on the night, bathing it in the smoldering warmth of a humid summer sunset, despite the cold rainy night. The food was superb, yes. But just as the heat of summer stole my appetite, the evening's excitement robbed me of my enthusiasm for food. What I craved was the delicious company, the energy of this magnificent evening.

Maman was in prime form, entertaining Édouard and Eugène, reveling in the attention they lavished upon her. I enjoyed sitting back amidst the hum of conversation and watching.

Maman dabbed at the corners of her mouth with her

napkin. She touched Édouard's arm. "Tell me about your work."

"What would you like to know beyond that I paint pictures that enrage the critics? Have you not read the vile things they publish about me in *Le Figaro*?"

Maman's hand fluttered to the brooch at her neckline. "Indeed, I have seen your name in the press." She sipped her Bordeaux. "Not always in a favorable context, I dare say."

Édouard shrugged. "I am in the fortunate position to live well without the necessity of selling my paintings. The critics and their tiny minds are of little consequence to me."

"Ah, to be in such an enviable position." Stevens raised his wineglass to his lips and emptied it. "You can afford to paint your brazen naked women because you need not kowtow to the establishment with the rest of us peasants."

"If you do not like the way the Academy runs things," said Degas, "do something to change it. Do not sit and whine."

"Wine? Yes, please, I would love more wine." Stevens held out his glass to Degas and laughed. "Oh, I see, you do not mean wine." He gestured to the carafe. "You mean do not *whine*. Silly me."

Degas frowned, and I wondered if the dour little man possessed a sense of humor. I found Stevens's antics quite funny.

Édouard leaned back in his chair, looking amused.

"Rather than playing the buffoon, it would behoove you to take a stand against the academicians who dictate the direction of art. Their views are criminal."

The manservant filled Stevens's glass. He lifted it to his lips and drained it in one gulp. "I am not of the means to paint a nude strolling the Champs-Elysées for the shock value."

"I am not merely painting to shock," said Édouard. "We must be of our time and paint what we see."

"Even Napoleon III hasn't been influential in changing the minds of the old Academy stodgers," slurred Stevens. "I depend on the Salon, and it would be the end of me if I alienated the establishment."

"And we all know how Napoleon handled the Maximilian affair. Pulled out of Mexico and left the poor emperor to the gun." Degas sneered. "He only runs with a cause until it no longer suits his purpose. If you are content to do nothing to change the Salon, then you are worse than he."

*Madame* Manet gasped, tapped her wineglass with her fork.

"That is enough. I will not have political talk at my dinner table. If you must argue such matters, save it for your cognac and cigars."

I could appreciate both Stevens's and Degas's points. The Academy had a firm grasp, dictating the direction of modern art. Many, myself included, believed they needed to move forward, away from the staid mode of history painting. We were more than halfway through the nineteenth century, yet art did not reflect the times. But who was so bold as to rap the knuckles of those who held an artist's fate in their fat fists?

I watched Édouard as Maman spoke to him: free and unself-conscious. I gazed at him in awe of his unpretentious freedom, his ability to just be.

He'd taken a stand against the status quo with his paintings. In turn, he'd suffered a brutal beating when the Salon shut him out. It was that rebel quality coming from someone who, for all appearances, resembled the perfect gentleman that I found rare and exciting.

And I must admit *très séduisant*—very seductive.

Ahhh, to be so liberated to even utter such a forbidden word as *"séduisant."*

"Pardon, *Mademoiselle?*" His eyes were a soft caress. "I hope tonight's conversation has not offended you."

"*Monsieur* Manet, I am not easily shocked. I should think art a most inappropriate profession for someone with a delicate sensibility."

"*Très bien.*" He leaned closer, resting his chin on his palm. His elbow touched my dessert spoon, sending it askew. I wanted to straighten it, set it back in its place, but I did not.

He reached over and teased the silver handle with a manicured finger, leaving it out of line. Then started to say something, but stopped.

"*Comment?*" I sipped my wine, watching him over the rim of my glass.

He hesitated. I could see the great wheels turning in his mind as his gaze dropped to my lips, then back to my eyes. What I imagined him thinking frightened me. I dropped my gaze and it landed where his shirtsleeve pulled away from his wrist. I glimpsed the hair on his forearm, curly and golden downy in the candlelight; the subtle masculine line where the hair stopped and the skin grew pale and smooth. I wanted to touch him there, to judge for myself if, as promised, the texture of hair and skin held the very essence of masculinity.

I shouldn't have noticed such things, in his wife's home, at his wife's table.

But it was not his wife's home.

Nor her table.

Even so, he remained a married man.

Unattainable.

Forbidden.

The trill of Maman's laughter sliced the air. She was captivated by Eugène's conversation, and I glanced back to Édouard and found him watching me.

"Do tell me what thoughts go through your mind to provoke such a look." His voice was honey, tempting me to taste that for which I should not have hungered.

I toyed with the idea of speaking my thoughts. Right there with everyone around us, I wanted to offer a coy smile, stroke his naked wrist and tell him *that* was what brought such a look to my face.

I shook my head. "You would think me impertinent."

"I should never think so."

I leaned in a bit.

"Perhaps . . ." I bit my lip. "Perhaps I shall tell you sometime. Once we know each other better."

Warmed by the wine and soothed by the faint sound of the falling rain outside, a breathless sense of pleasure spread through me.

"Then, beautiful *Demoiselle,* I hope we shall know each other better." He placed his hand on mine. "Very soon."

He smiled, and I was moved by the same force that coaxed the earth around the sun. I didn't know who was rotating around whom. We seemed to float up and out of the room, away from the party and pointless polite conversation. I was gripped by the overwhelming need to touch him, to press my hands to his cheeks, to let his warmth course through me.

He refilled my wine goblet with Bordeaux from the decanter on the table, raised his glass to mine. *"Très séduisant. "*

The crisp ping of crystal sounded a personal symphony. For an instant I felt unsteady, as if I were gazing through the cheval glass at the male image of myself. It was nonsense, but somehow in that instant, I knew him intimately. Deeper than the cutting rubbish published by critics. Beyond the surface glances to a pure dimensional void of space or time.

"Just ask her, Édouard." A deep voice from the opposite end of the table sliced through our private universe.

I felt myself freefalling and crash-landing in the midst of the silent room. All heads turned toward us.

It was Stevens who spoke. He wiped his mouth on his sleeve. "The poor fellow has been in misery over *Mademoiselle* Berthe. That's why I brought him the painting." He slurred the comment to no one in particular and chuckled.

*Madame* Manet gasped.

The painting that set her on edge before dinner? *Mon Dieu.* I'd done nothing to cause *Monsieur* Manet misery—A clap of thunder erupted, as if we'd angered the gods.

In my peripheral vision, I saw him leaning on his elbow, his clenched fist pressed to the bridge of his nose.

"My dear miserable friend," Stevens said. "She is right there at your fingertips. Just ask her."

# Chapter Four

*Our words must seem to be inevitable.*
*—William Butler Yeats*

"You insult my daughter and offend me with your crass insinuations." Maman shoved back her chair and stood up from the table, wobbling a bit, glaring first at Stevens, then at Édouard. "Do you think Berthe a common model? Like your Olympia?"

Maman didn't wait for an answer, but gave a curt nod to *Madame* Manet. *"Merci, Madame. Bonne nuit."*

Édouard got to his feet. For a moment I thought he would not let her pass. The two squared off, Maman glaring, Édouard imploring her to stay.

*"Madame,* please, your daughter is very beautiful. I wish to paint her portrait. That is all *Monsieur* Stevens was trying to say, although quite poorly, I must admit. He meant no harm. There was no insult behind his drunken jest. Right, Stevens?"

The man slumped down in his chair like a rueful, naughty child trying to render himself invisible. He shrugged. "Of course. I meant no harm. Please forgive me, *Madame, Mademoiselle."*

With all the commotion stirring around me all I could think was: Édouard Manet wanted to paint me. All I could do was sit leaden in my seat, hands in my lap, trying to breathe. Stevens painted my portrait, yet somehow this was different.

I didn't know whether to hug Stevens or strangle him for laying the unmentionable wide open on the table for all to see. I stole a glance at Edma, who looked captivated by the fiasco.

Degas frowned and studied his fingernails. "I do not understand the fuss. I don't see any harm in Manet painting her. She knows she is a painter, not a model, even if she does afford her colleagues the favor of her likeness every so often."

Maman let loose a little cry and threw up her hands. "I am now quite sure I regret giving *Monsieur* Stevens permission to paint my daughter."

She pushed past Édouard and stormed out of the room. He followed, as did Edma and I.

"*Madame,* please. Be reasonable."

"Reasonable?" I feared Maman might slap him. Instead, as bold as you please, she strode over and snatched up the gift Stevens presented to Édouard.

White-knuckled and shaking, she gripped the gilded frame. Her face turned an unhealthy shade of ash.

"Maman?" I murmured.

Edma and I rushed to her side. From the look on her face I feared she might faint dead away. Then I saw for myself what had offended her.

Stevens's painting.

Of me.

It was not the likeness that was so horrid. It was how he'd inscribed it. The words were painted on the canvas bold and black, right above my head: *To Monsieur E. Manet.*

My mother's face flashed like the lightning storm outside. "My daughter's image gifted like chattel to a man whose acquaintance I have just made this evening? A married man." She signaled a manservant for our wraps and hats. "Unforgivable."

*Madame* Manet appeared at her side and slipped the frame from Maman's hands. Eugène whisked it away. *"Madame. . . ."* Her voice, low and discomfited, trailed off as if she were at a loss for words.

Gustave placed a tender hand on his mother's shoulder.

It was what Maman did not say that screamed loudest: *Your son is a man whose radical politics and reputation for the risqué trail after him like the stench of a leper. I do not wish my daughters infected by him.*

A bouquet of purple hyacinths and a note arrived the next morning.

When Amélie presented them to Maman, Edma and I were sitting on the divan in the drawing room with sketchpads in our laps. Maman rested in her chair by the window and read the letter with a face as blank as untouched paper.

Cradling the blossoms, Amélie stood behind our mother and gave us a knowing smile.

An arched brow.

A nod.

Edma elbowed me and mouthed, "From him."

I bit my lip as my gaze flickered to Maman. But she was still scrutinizing the note through her lorgnette.

Amélie shifted the flowers for Maman's inspection. Their pleasing scent filled the room, and I inhaled the sweet expression of Édouard's regret.

Hyacinths—the flower of repentance, a symbol of atonement for one's misdeeds.

Maman scrutinized the bouquet through her glasses, but did not accept it.

After a moment's hesitation, Amélie retracted the

flowers. "I beg your pardon, *Madame,* the courier awaits your answer."

Lips pursed into a tight rosebud, my mother lowered her looking glass and thrust the card at the maid. "The answer is no. Return the flowers."

Edma gasped.

My heart twisted. "No? Maman!"

I scooted to the edge of the divan. The sketchpad fell from my lap as I hovered in a half-seated, not-quite-standing pose.

"They're beautiful." My voice was a squeak. "Please do not send them away. We . . . we could use them in the studio, arrange them into a beautiful still life."

My mother looked right through me. The same way she did when we boarded the carriage last night. Even if she struck me, it would not hurt as much as her quiet rage.

My knees gave way and I fell back into the cushions.

Oh, she said she didn't blame me. She'd proclaimed the fiasco Stevens's fault, belittled his disregard for proper decorum.

"Right in front of *Madame* Manet," she'd said in the carriage. The black of night cloaked her disgust, but I knew the look. She wore it like a decorated soldier wounded in battle.

As I counted the clip-clip-clop of the horse's hooves muffled by the squeak and rattle of the carriage, she ranted, "Right in front of Suzanne, as if she were not the wife. As if she would not care that her husband might be 'languishing in misery' over another woman. Unnnnnn-thinkable." Maman dragged out the word, her voice an octave higher than its usual pitch.

I stared out the window for the duration of the trip, relieved I could not see her face. Or perhaps I was glad she could not see mine.

"It is a good thing your father was not with us to witness such a slight against his own flesh and blood."

A small *oomph* punctuated her words as she threw herself against the seat back. Finally, it seemed the rant flushed her bile. The rhythmic sway of the carriage carried us home through dwindling rain and lulled her into heavy stillness.

I knew she blamed me, even if she did not realize it herself.

I was twenty-seven years old and long past marriageable age. Even worse, I was a painter, a sympathizer of the disgraceful cretins who'd passed my portrait back and forth like a bawdy joke, an illicit amusement.

Pornography between married men.

If word of last night's incident got out, my chances of finding a husband would narrow even further. The only reason it gave me pause was the potential repercussions Edma might suffer.

She was changing, starting to come around to Maman's way of thinking with interest in Adolphe Pontillon. A navy man. A sensible man with whom she could make a life and have so many *bébés* they would fill her world and edge out everything except proper life.

Sometimes I felt as if there were another Berthe living deep inside me. She was not the dutiful daughter, nor the quiet artist who dallied in paint for amusement, willing to forgo it for matrimony. This Berthe hoped word of Stevens's prank would spread like syphilis through the brothels. The thought of forcing herself into a charade of convention made this Berthe feel like a caged beast. She'd rather die than be sentenced to such a dull life.

I was afraid of this Berthe because I tried to be good. I tried to do what Maman expected of me, but more often than I cared to admit, the other Berthe lurked in the shadows of my heart, threatening to consume propriety.

"I am sure the courier will not wait all day, Amélie," Maman snapped. "Tell him to take these back to the person who sent them."

The maid hesitated, slanting a glance at Edma. What had I missed?

Maman frowned and clapped her hands.

"*Tout de suite,* Amélie!"

With a swoosh of skirts, the maid rushed out of the room.

"But Maman," I protested.

My mother got to her feet and brushed past me without a glance. She'd not been gone ten seconds when Edma grabbed my hand and pulled me up and off the divan.

"Come. Fast."

In the foyer, we nearly collided with an ashen-looking Amélie, standing with the flowers clutched to her breast, her back pressed against the wall as if she expected Maman instead of us. Her gaze darted around, then she thrust the note and flowers at me. Amélie tried to back out of the room, but Edma grabbed her wrist.

"No, Amélie, stay." My sister's words pinned Amélie to the spot. "Ask the boy to wait while we write a reply."

My heart thudded. "Reply? What shall we say?"

Edma threw her hands into the air. "We cannot send him back empty-handed. We must say something."

Amélie disappeared through the front door to detain the messenger. Edma grabbed the note from my hand and opened it, and we huddled together to read it.

*Dear Madam and Mesdemoiselles,*
*I am mortified by last evening's unfortunate turn of*

*events. I wish to call on you this afternoon to convey my most sincere apology.*

*Yours respectfully,*
*Édouard Manet.*

A humble request for forgiveness.

I buried my face in the sweet-scented blossoms and inhaled until I felt my sister tug at me again.

"Come. We must work fast."

We paused at the entrance to the drawing room for a cautious glance about the place. To our good fortune, we saw no sign of Maman.

Edma tossed the card on the desk and set about foraging in the drawer for a pen.

I set down the flowers and picked up the crème-colored linen card. I traced the top fold with my nail, teasing my way around the wax seal and down the side until almost as if by its own will my finger slipped inside the note to rest between Édouard's words. I did not open the card, but I could see the ghost of his script through the paper and somehow that was enough. I ran the tip of my finger on the underside, along his writing, caressing each word. My finger pushed against the upper fold.

"Put that down." Edma snatched the paper from my hand. The crisp edge sliced my finger, leaving a clean, white gash.

I gasped and pressed the stinging flesh to my lips. The moisture intensified the discomfort.

Edma turned Édouard's note face down on the desk. She dipped the pen into the inkpot and glanced up at me. "What shall we say?"

"Do not write on his note. Use a fresh sheet of stationery from the desk."

"We cannot do that. Maman has only four sheets and she will wonder what happened to the missing paper."

I bit down on the wound instead of answering her. The metallic taste of blood filled my mouth. "Do not write on his note. Take a fresh sheet from the desk."

"Maman has only four pages left. You know how she keeps track."

I frowned and wiped my wet finger on my blue skirt.

She scowled and thrust the pen at me. "Here, if you don't like my suggestion, do it yourself. This is for your benefit, not mine. It should come from you. But hurry."

The reality behind her words startled me, as if someone lit a candle in a pitch-black wine cellar.

Still, I took the pen. A drop of ink splattered onto the desk, near the paper. My sore finger throbbed against the pressure of my grasp.

Edma fidgeted and worried the lace collar of her yellow dress. "If we invite him today, Maman will be furious. It will not be fair to subject him to her mood." She glanced toward the door. "Another day. Tomorrow perhaps?"

"Amélie?" Maman's voice sounded in the hall just outside the drawing room. Edma and I jerked upright.

The flowers.

I yanked open the desk drawer and swept the blossoms inside, nearly clipping my sister's fingers as she dropped Édouard's card among the contraband.

The scent of hyacinth lingered and the drawer's slam seemed to echo as Maman ambled into the room. We must have looked a guilty sight, standing shoulder-to-shoulder behind the desk for no apparent reason.

Maman scowled. "What are you doing?"

At the same time Edma said, "Nothing," I started to explain, "We are studying the angle of the room to use for a charcoal drawing."

Unaccustomed to lying, I dropped my gaze. Two stray purple petals lay atop the desk. They must have fallen as I swept the flowers out of sight. Bending forward, I covered the errant blossoms with my hand. I also hit the wet ink spot.

Maman watched us for a moment. She shook her head as if she'd resigned herself to the strange ways of the younger generation. "Where is Amélie? That girl is treading a thin line today."

Amélie. Oh, no. My heart thudded. Maman would have a fit if she found her with the courier so long after she'd told her to send him on his way. How would she explain the absence of the note and flowers? Given Maman's mood, Amélie's thin line might break in two.

"Amélie!" Maman headed toward the foyer.

I squeezed my eyes shut and sent a silent prayer that the girl would think fast enough to formulate a plausible excuse for loitering. I grabbed Edma's arm, and we braced ourselves for Maman's explosion.

But there was none. Only the sound of her calling for the girl in a shrill and distressed tone.

"Amélie!"

"*Oui, Madame?*" Amélie's voice sounded from the kitchen, the opposite direction of the foyer.

Smart. She'd reentered through the back. The ingenious girl had pulled it off. I'd thank her later.

I hoped she'd convinced the courier to wait for the note.

I dared not look at Edma's face until Maman was out of the room and well on her way to the kitchen. I noticed I'd transferred the ink stain from my hand to my sister's sleeve. But there was no time to worry about it.

Edma jerked open the drawer. I grabbed Édouard's note

46

and penned: *Please come Tuesday at four o'clock.*

"Tuesday next?" Edma protested. "That's four days away. Tomorrow."

"Too soon. Maman will never receive him."

We heard our mother's voice in the hall again. Then Amélie's voice, louder than usual. "*Pardon, Madame,* just a few more questions regarding luncheon?"

Maman's footsteps retreated.

Brilliant girl.

My heart was in my throat, but I managed to choke out, "Edma, hide the flowers and distract her until I get back."

I hurried down the hall on light feet so the sound of my slippers would not give me away. Icy currents coursed through my veins. I held my breath and prayed Maman would not see me as I entered the foyer. Once safe in the entryway, I eased open the front door, then pulled it to a soundless close behind me.

Stepping from the foyer into the windy brightness of the day, it took my eyes a moment to adjust. I hurried down the stone steps, across the walk and out the gate, where I almost collided with a boy chasing his little dog down the street.

I righted myself. Reflex made my hand fly to my head to secure my hat. But I wasn't wearing one. Nor was I wearing gloves, I realized, as a handsome couple strolled by arm-in-arm. I felt naked standing on the city street in my housedress, my head bare. A gust of wind urged my hair out of its chignon.

The man and woman were not neighbors, *Merci Dieu.* In fact, I'd never seen them before. But, my, how right they looked walking together in the gentle warmth of the morning sunshine, oblivious to my near mishap with the boy, unaware of all but each other.

As they passed, I glimpsed a nuance in the woman's expression, a mixture of aloof pleasure and worldly knowing, a subtle power in the tilt of her chin. I followed their movement as they continued down the *rue* Franklin until the sun silhouetted them. The bright light burned my eyes.

The sun's glow reflected off windows and metal rooftops, belying the storm that savaged us the night prior. It struck me that fate was no more than a storm that blew through, upsetting everything in its path until a random change of course propelled it in a new direction, leaving us to pick up the pieces.

Movement out of the corner of my eye drew my attention to the manservant from last night's soirée. Slouched against the stone wall, he looked much younger than he appeared the previous evening, a boy who'd barely stepped through the threshold of manhood. He straightened when he saw me and tipped a quick nod.

I held out the note. "Please deliver this to *Monsieur* Édouard Manet. *Merci.*"

He reached out to take it from me. The light captured the ink stain that sullied my palm. My gaze flickered to the note and my writing, scrawled as dark and bold as a dirty secret exposed to the world.

In a dreamlike slow motion, he took possession of the letter. I glimpsed a flicker of amusement in his eyes, and it seemed I could almost read his thoughts: flowers from a married man to a woman not his wife; notes with sweet sentiments flying back and forth. Fodder for folly.

I was not the first.

Instinct screamed for me to repossess the note, but by that time he'd already thanked me and turned away.

I should've gone after him or at least called, "Tell him no. The answer is no."

But Maman appeared at the gate.

"Berthe, what are you doing out here?" Her initial surprise settled into angry lines across her forehead.

Panic, like pin pricks, coursed through me as I looked from her to the courier who was growing smaller as he made his way down the *rue* Franklin.

"You're flushed," Maman said.

She reached for my cheek, but I drew back. Her eyes flashed. "What is the matter with you? What in heaven's name are you doing out here all alone? No hat. No wrap. Really, Berthe."

Edma peered at me over Maman's shoulder. I glanced from her wide, guilty eyes to my mother's, narrow and accusing.

"I needed. . . ."

Wide and guilty.

"I thought. . . ."

Narrow and accusing.

"I needed . . . air."

"Why did you not go out into the garden instead of coming out here like this?"

Too shaken to speak under the pressure of her scrutiny, I shrugged and glanced down the street. The messenger was gone. I tried not to gulp air in greedy, unladylike breaths.

"Come inside at once." Maman stepped aside to afford me room to pass. As she followed Edma and me up the walk to the house, she muttered the entire way. "Since last evening both of you have behaved most strangely. All the more justification to avoid *that man*. Yes indeed. Controversy breeds controversy. That is what I have always believed—Edma!"

At the top of the steps, Maman grabbed my sister's arm. "Is this ink on your sleeve?"

I glanced at the black stain on Edma's yellow dress. I closed my dirty hand and hid it in the folds of my skirt.

The next thing I knew, Maman threw Edma's arm away from her as if the sight disgusted her. "Please go for a walk or go out into your studio for a bit. My nerves cannot tolerate the two of you. But change your dress first, Edma. You look like a filthy street urchin."

Still muttering, she pushed past us and climbed the steps to the front door.

Edma and I stood on the walk staring at each other until our mother disappeared inside.

We were not used to deceiving Maman. My sister did not have to say a word for me to understand what she was thinking. If impulse was the devil's temptress, we were her pawn. Now we had four days to explain to our mother what we'd done.

# Chapter Five

*Nobody ought to look at paintings,*
*who cannot find a greater meaning than*
*the artist has actually expressed.*
　　　　　　　　　　　—*Nathaniel Hawthorne*

Anticipating Édouard's arrival Tuesday made time stand still. For four days, the hours lingered like life in a dream-spun impression that could not live for being confined to the canvas. The days dawned and faded, sketching vignettes so similar one fell into the next as colorful glass in a kaleidoscope shifted shape by traveling in a circle.

Tuesday, the stillness broke like the kaleidoscope smashed to the floor; all the shards flew free.

Edma and I had not told Maman of Édouard's impending visit. We were still searching for the proper words, when Maman found the hyacinths we'd hidden in our studio.

I was sitting on the terrace when I looked up and saw her clutching the withered flowers like a ghost bride haunting the altar of her abandonment. I should have taken it for a harbinger of what was to come, but I was stunned into a strange heightened awareness. The jasmine was blooming on the terrace. The bush drooped with the weight of the blossoms, as if its perfume were so heavy it caused the plant to pitch forward. I think I'll always associate the scent of jasmine with Maman's rage. Strange it would not be the hyacinth, but they'd started to fade. When she threw the wilted bundle at my feet, several dried petals lifted on the breeze and rolled like tiny tumbleweeds across the terrace.

"What are these?"

The vibrant purple had dulled to a stormy gray. The old, withered stalks looked like the protruding veins on my mother's wrinkled hands.

Maman was always in a nasty mood when Papa was away. He wasn't due back until the following day. Her expression warned she might slap me if I did not answer her *tout de suite.*

"They are flowers."

She gritted her teeth in a grimace that looked equal parts disgust and impatience.

"I can see that, you stupid girl. Where did they come from?"

Stupid girl? I was stunned into silence. My mother never spoke to me in such a manner. Never called me such horrid names. She hovered. I stood up to meet her.

She was so close I could feel the moisture of her breath as I stood there, a good head taller than she. My mother did not cower. She stared up at me, demanding an answer.

"They are the flowers delivered from Édouard Manet."

Maman slapped me hard across the left side of my face. The blow smarted like a thousand nettles, but I would not let her see how much it hurt.

A wry smile pulled at the corners of my mouth. "Édouard Manet is calling today at four o'clock."

I believed she would strike me again, but she wavered. *"Je ne comprends pas?"*

"What don't you understand? I invited him and he is coming."

The sun disappeared behind a cloud. The breeze picked up, and the air chilled.

Her gaze was a gauntlet thrown between us.

"You shall send him a note telling him he is not welcome in my home."

"He thinks you are the one who sent the invitation. I wrote it on the back of the note he sent Friday, and I did not sign my name. If we rescind the invitation, it shall reflect poorly on you."

Much to my relief, my voice didn't shake. Maman stared at me for a long moment. I could almost see the thoughts calculating in her head.

She prided herself on being a superior hostess. It stemmed back to Papa's prefect days, when she'd refined entertaining to an art.

"Were you planning to tell me or were you going to let him surprise me?"

"I was going to tell you, Maman. When the time was right."

She laughed. The sound was like bitter lemon. I wondered where Edma was and how she'd managed to disappear at just the right moment. I didn't blame her. The largest part of the onus lay upon me.

Maman did not speak to me again until Édouard arrived. I found my sister hiding in the kitchen. She heard Maman yelling at me on the terrace and hid out with Amélie. I considered berating her for such cowardice, letting me bear the brunt of our mother's anger, but it wouldn't have changed anything.

Amélie left to prepare for our guest. Edma and I sat quietly; sad that Maman was cross at us, but relieved. It was as if the curtains had been thrown open, permitting light to bathe a dreary room.

Our mother, the gracious hostess, would receive Édouard. She'd hear what he came to say. He'd be in the carriage on his way home before he realized he was never welcome in the first place.

"He wants to paint you." Edma shrugged. "Is Maman afraid you'll turn into his new Olympia right before her very eyes?"

Olympia—scandal's own mistress. It was rumored that Victorine Meurent, the beautiful woman who posed for Olympia, was Édouard's mistress at one time. She left him. For years he painted no regular model. I didn't realize he was searching for a replacement.

I couldn't help but picture myself as Olympia, wanton and mocking, sprawled in serene impudence, with a thin black ribbon around my neck and a small slipper on one foot. The other foot, brazenly bare, tucked beneath the sole of my shoe, toes teasing, hinting at hidden promises yet to be discovered. If Maman knew my thoughts, she would have locked me away for the rest of my life.

"*Mademoiselle* Berthe, your mother wishes you to join her in the drawing room."

Amélie's voice shocked me back into reality. Edma grabbed my hand.

He'd arrived.

Blood rushed in my ears. Perhaps that was why I hadn't heard his knock.

Edma rose to accompany me.

"*Pardon, Mademoiselle* Edma. *Madame* wishes your sister to go alone."

Edma's mouth fell open, but she didn't protest. As I walked to the sitting room like a woman doomed to the guillotine, the other Berthe chanted with each step I took toward Édouard.

*Olympia, who looks the world in its naked eye without a blink of shame.*

Was that how I looked Thursday night as Stevens goaded Édouard to ask me to sit for him?

*Olympia, the mistress odalisque.*

Was that how I looked hesitating in the drawing room doorway as Édouard stood to greet me?

There were certain places in Paris I went to seek refuge. I loved to walk along the *quai* near the Louvre. There was something soothing in the way the buildings rose up near the river Seine, like tall, stately sentries standing watch over the long, straight line of old houses with their irregular rooftops and stone balconies jutting like drooping eyelids off melancholy faces. It was my sanctuary. I always felt as if no harm could come to me there.

Seeing Édouard in the drawing room, I wanted to grab Edma and run to my haven near the Louvre. Alas, it was impossible, so I tried to think pretty thoughts that would calm me: the boats moored along the river dipping and nodding without a care; the rhythmic song of the water slapping the embankment; Suzanne not accompanying her husband on this visit—

That was not a pretty thought, and I knew I should not dwell on it. Even if it was the truth.

I tried to clear my mind, but Édouard looked stunning. I didn't know if it was the way his navy frockcoat turned his gray eyes a shade of deep blue or if it was the pull of his presence that attracted me, but as he took my hand and bowed, I found myself at a loss for what to say or do.

"*Mademoiselle,* so nice to see you again."

I looked to Maman for direction. She motioned me to sit next to her on the divan. I was glad because, despite her earlier rage, she felt safe, and I hoped somehow it meant she'd forgiven me.

"Maman sends her regards," said Édouard after taking a seat across from us. His silver-tipped walking stick lay on the floor next to him. His elbows were propped on the arms of the chair. He steepled his long, slender fingers as he spoke. "She wanted to come, but I told her it would be best if I came alone."

Amélie set a tea tray on the table between us. Maman nodded for me to pour the tea. The room was so quiet, I prayed my hands would not shake and cause the cup and saucer to rattle.

I managed to complete the task without disgracing myself and handed him the first cup.

He accepted it and said, "*Mademoiselle,* I deeply regret what happened Thursday night. It was a disaster. A disgrace. *Monsieur* Stevens and I meant no harm to your good name."

Édouard looked me square in the eyes. His words resonated in earnest, an agitated swirl, as if a swarm of bees took formation in my belly. A few seconds passed before I realized I was still holding onto his saucer.

I let go. A small wave of tea splashed over the top of the cup.

Édouard pretended not to notice and turned his attention to Maman. "If necessary, Stevens will call to apologize himself."

"That won't be necessary." Maman looked pale and drawn. "*Monsieur* Manet, before Berthe joined us, you mentioned you just returned from Boulogne."

Édouard sipped his tea. He lowered the cup to the saucer, resting it on this knee. "I have indeed. In fact, my mother, Suzanne and Léon are still there."

So that explained it. It was not practical for his wife to come. I was not sure if justification for her absence made me feel better or worse. But, there it was . . .

"They will stay for the rest of the month, but I will travel back and forth between Paris and Boulogne. I must work, and it is impossible to paint with the family in close proximity. Besides, Boulogne would not work for my next project." His gaze flicked to me, then back to Maman, who watched him, sizing him up as a judge decides the fate of a criminal.

"What is this next project, *Monsieur?*" she said.

"Earlier this week, I was out for a stroll and happened upon the most interesting sight. It was a vision. A woman sitting high upon a balcony fanning herself. It reminded me of a Goya painting I saw in Spain in 'sixty-five. It was breathtaking. Are you familiar with his work?"

I nodded. "I once admired an engraving of his painting in a book."

"It is a masterpiece." His eyes were full of wonder. He opened his mouth to speak again, faltered, then blurted, "What Stevens said is true. I have long desired to paint your daughter's portrait, *Madame*. I would be most humbled and most appreciative if you would allow her to join *Mademoiselle* Claus and *Monsieur* Guillemet in my own re-creation of Goya's balcony composition."

He strung the words together in one breath, as if pausing might rob him of the opportunity to finish. It was all I could do to keep from gasping. I stared into my teacup as the three of us sat in thick silence. The grandfather clock ticked a full twenty-five beats before my mother said, "Berthe has quite a mind of her own. The decision is hers."

Maman would not look at me. She sipped her tea and stared at a spot over Édouard's right shoulder.

"*Mademoiselle,* you would come into my studio first as a colleague, second as a model." He turned back to Maman.

"I use that term with all due respect, *Madame*."

Overwhelmed by the sick feeling that Maman was pushing me into my own trap, making me pay for my defiance, I could not answer.

Inside me two women warred: Propriety, the obedient daughter, the proper lady, quiet and contemplative; and the impulsive woman I scarcely recognized—the ugly creature prone to being swept away; she was not so compliant, discreet or pensive—an Olympia of sorts.

In Olympia's shadow, Propriety could not find her voice. This delighted Olympia. So did the thought of being Édouard's model. Yes, the prospect delighted and aroused her.

Olympia pushed me along the knife's edge to manipulate Édouard's delivery to me this afternoon. It was Olympia who made me say, "I would love to be your model."

# Chapter Six

*I know your heart which overflows*
*With outworn loves long cast aside*
*Still like a furnace flames and glows,*
*And you within your breast enclose*
*A dammed soul's unbending pride;*
*—Baudelaire, Les Fleurs Du Mal*

No sooner had Édouard invited us to his studio on Thursday to begin the painting and taken his leave, when Maman's anger swept through like a mistral, menacing all in its path.

"You are a disgrace to yourself and your family."

I should've expected her anger. On a deeper level, I knew it was coming, yet I was too afraid to face it or to brace myself for the inevitable: that she would fly to pieces after I'd betrayed her twice in one day.

She'd seen him to the door, leaving me in the drawing room alone. Once the front door clicked shut, I rose from my seat on the divan and made for the sanctuary of my studio.

But I was too late.

Maman cornered me. "You sit right there and listen to me." She thrust her finger in my face and backed me to my place on the divan. "You will not humiliate this family."

The force of her anger seemed to vibrate the house, but soon I realized only her voice shook. I could have more easily weathered another slap across the face or would have preferred her to drag me by the ear and throw me out into the street at Édouard's feet rather than face the realization of how much I'd hurt her.

It was not what I'd intended. Feeding on itself, the circumstance took on a course of its own. The reality was a physical ache that manifested itself in the pit of my stomach, a by-product of the lump lodged in my throat that would not allow me to speak despite the words raging in my head.

*You gave me the choice, and I took it.* I wanted to say this, but I didn't. The situation was bad enough without flippant comments.

"I suppose you think you know what's best?" She was screaming at me. "You know what you are doing? How are you going to explain this to your father . . . ?"

I tried to answer, but my attempt to speak against her barrage of questions was as useless as trying to walk against the mistral's winds. I let her blow.

"What are you trying to prove?"

I did not answer immediately. She must have thought I was mocking her with sullen silence.

"Answer me when I speak to you! I asked what you were trying to prove?"

I cleared my throat. "I was not trying to prove anything, Maman."

Heat flamed my neck and ears. I hoped she would not notice. She shook her head, disgust skewing her small features. "He's a married man, Berthe. You're a single woman. Have you become so blinded by selfishness you have forgotten it is not your own reputation at stake here?"

I knew it was not my future over which she fretted. It was Edma's relationship with Adolphe. The one bright spot she'd pinned her dreams upon; more hope than I'd given her.

"Maman, I do not know what you mean. Married or not, I have no ill intentions. I simply want to learn from *Monsieur* Manet."

"Learn? Learn what? You do not need another painting teacher."

"I am not looking for a teacher as much as I am looking for the inspiration I might receive by just watching him work."

"Ridiculous. Your father and I have invested far too much money in your lessons with *Messieurs* Guichard and Oudinot. If you must seek inspiration elsewhere, we are not getting our due from them."

She threw her hands in the air and talked as if someone else were in the room. "We spoil her. That's the problem. I should not be surprised that she turned out this way. But I am surprised." She turned back to me. "Surprised and shocked and saddened. Because with all we've given you, all the leeway and latitude, you've become a person I don't know anymore."

The lump that blocked my words blew like a champagne cork.

"How can you claim you do not know me, Maman? I'm your daughter. I'm an artist, just as you and Papa have encouraged me."

Maman flinched, almost imperceptibly, but I saw her react to the sting. Then she refocused her piercing glare on me.

"Your father and I have encouraged you to be a proper lady."

I should've let it go. I knew better, but my ire was like a door forced open under pressure. No matter how I tried to bar it shut, bile manufactured by the talk of my place in this world grew until it oozed out between the façade's cracks and crevices, until the door swung open and everything spilled out.

"Proper? As if it were my life's purpose? It is not my fault I was born a woman."

My mother stared at me for a moment, cold and disbelieving. When she spoke, her voice was low and uneven, as if I'd wrung from her all the energy she possessed.

"Berthe, we've afforded you advantages many a young woman would delight in. Luxuries. The best clothing, the best upbringing, the best possible position to meet a man who will ensure your future. Many respectable young men call, yet you push them aside, when all you need do is—"

"What? What should I do, Maman? Sit upon the sofa waiting for a proper man to give me permission to live? If that is so, it is a dull existence. If that is all you want for me then, why, Maman, did you raise me to think? Why did you and Papa encourage me to have an opinion?"

She closed her eyes against my words. I knew I'd delivered the fatal blow in our verbal jousting match. Although all the bile had drained from me, I felt worse. It was as if the bond between us that once seemed immovable had splintered. Panicking, my mind reeled, searching for a way to mend the fracture.

"I'm sorry, Maman. I never meant to . . . I never meant to disappoint you."

I was sincere. But she did not answer me. She turned, leaving me alone with my words reverberating in the air.

Two days later, Maman accompanied me to Édouard's *rue* Guyot *atelier*. Would we have gone to his studio if Papa had not returned home the next day? He didn't mention the incident with Édouard, but I knew she told him. How else would she have explained why she wasn't speaking to me after our argument in the drawing room?

I was sorry to give Papa such a stressful homecoming. I'd missed him. Our house was not the same without him, and my mother grew so tense.

I believed it was he who was to thank for Maman's accompanying me to Édouard's. Papa was a strong man. A practical man. He looked beyond society's silly, superficial dictates to the matter-of-fact. The fact that I could learn something from Édouard.

*Ah Papa.* I don't know what I'd have done without him.

Maman and I arrived late, or at least later than Fanny Claus and *Monsieur* Guillemet, the other models Édouard engaged for the painting.

*"Bonjour, bonjour!"* Édouard answered the door with a warm greeting. Maman was cordial, but aloof—for my benefit, I was sure—as he took our wraps, and made introductions.

Tall and distinguished, *Monsieur* Guillemet bowed with a flourish and worked a bit too hard to charm us. I hoped it would melt Maman's icy formality.

Édouard presented Fanny Claus, a young violinist and friend of his wife, Suzanne. Apparently, she and Suzanne often played duets at the Thursday night parties at his mother's house.

The demure Fanny Claus nodded. I was disappointed when I realized we'd both worn white dresses for the occasion. They were of vastly different styles; still I worried that the monochromatic sameness would not work for Édouard's painting, and he'd require one of us to change. But he'd be the one to decide, I thought, eying the short, puffy Fanny Claus.

I would not go so far as to call her fat, but she was an unredeemingly plain girl. She had no neck to speak of and a long, pallid face with close-set black eyes that gave the appearance of two raisins pushed into rising bread dough. The simple white frock did nothing for her complexion.

"May I offer you some tea?" Édouard asked. "Or perhaps a cup of chocolate?"

"Tea would be lovely." Maman turned her back on me, to talk to *Madame* La Rue, Fanny Claus's chaperone, a formidable-looking woman wearing a matronly navy blue dress with a high, rounded waist and fitted sleeves with epaulettes.

I looked at the paintings hung on the far wall. So many it was difficult to take them all in. Portraits, still-life scenes, fruits, flowers, vegetables hung haphazardly one atop the other . . . even more tucked in a little nook around the corner of a partition.

"*Mademoiselle,* what may I prepare for you? Tea, chocolate?" Édouard stood behind me, blocking my exit from the small alcove.

"Nothing for me, *merci.*"

"Are you sure there is nothing with which I might tempt you?"

His voice was a velvet cloak inviting me to abandon all apprehensions and allow myself to be wrapped up in it. It stole my breath and sent my stomach into tight spirals. Until something flared inside and challenged me to call his bluff. "Beyond tea and chocolate, *Monsieur,* what sort of temptation had you in mind? If I didn't know better, I might believe you endeavored to tempt me into an indiscretion."

His eyes widened. I'd rendered him speechless, and I regretted being so vulgar. The feeling enveloped me like the sticky summer air, and I pushed past him to join the others.

He detained me with a hand on my arm, stopping me

with a simple touch. The others—I could not see them, but I could hear them chatting—were ignorant of our physical contact.

"There are a great many offerings with which I might endeavor to tempt you, *Mademoiselle*." His words were a sultry whisper, and he stepped closer. "Right now, I dare say, is not the time. But I will make time, if you like."

I closed my eyes against the feverish lurch of pleasure that sprang forth in my belly, powerless to move away. Even if I could have moved, I wouldn't, because then I would not have been able to savor the nearness of him. His scent—a mixture of coffee and paint and another note uniquely Édouard—beckoned me to lean closer, until the coarse texture of his beard brushed my forehead.

I pulled back, startled, reclaiming my personal space.

Édouard released me without another word and disappeared. I lingered for a moment, trying to regain my bearings.

When I rejoined the others, he was bent over a small spirit-stove where he'd busied himself heating the water for Maman's tea.

*Monsieur* Guillemet's deep voice resonated through the room. A flutter of ladies' laughter erupted. I noticed Fanny Claus watching me. She didn't smile, didn't blink. The way her morbid raisin eyes bore into me made me fidget. Had she sensed the exchange that took place between Édouard and me?

Nonsense. How could she?

Édouard banged around, opening and shutting cupboards, setting out tea tins, a kettle and cups. He seemed in no particular hurry to get the painting under way.

I was glad because I needed to gather myself.

I was not the type of woman to swoon, but it would've

been a lie if I claimed his sudden frankness had not affected me. His offer to *make time* was a stone plunged into deep water that left my emotions rippling from the impact.

Thank God, Fanny Claus turned her boring black gaze back to the conversation. I lifted my eyes to the vaulted, paned-glass ceiling to offer a silent prayer of thanks.

The glass ceilings made the studio appear larger and brighter than I'd imagined. Although, if pressed, I couldn't have described my initial mental picture of Manet's *atelier*.

I glanced around Édouard's space—at the makeshift balcony, complete with a piece of wrought iron, he'd assembled near the wall of windows. I supposed it was where he'd paint us. There was a dressing screen in the far right corner.

Leaning against the walls, in stacks five or six deep, were more canvases in various stages of finish. Other paintings hung here and there on the walls above a mélange of rolled cloth, clay pots, books, paint-stained rags, the accoutrements for a formal table setting, a copper kettle turned on its side and a silver candelabra.

Clutter in every nook and cranny—the sum of these parts equaled the man who whispered of temptation and forbidden promise, a man I longed to know much better.

I turned away from the untidy corner, as if the motion would erase my illicit thoughts, to a window covered by a large sheet of muslin tacked to the frame. Mid-morning light filtered through. The determined rays streamed in around the loose edges like the splayed ribs of an open fan. It reminded me of the fitful luminosity of the Tintoretto that so captivated Édouard the very first day I encountered him at the Louvre.

I walked to a worktable shoved into the far corner. The wooden surface was heaped with rolled canvases, discarded

drawings, dust-covered sketchbooks and volumes of litera-
ture.

I ran my finger over the dusty cover of Baudelaire's *Les
Fleurs Du Mal*. A number of years ago, the poetry caused
quite a furor, and some of the poems were banned after
he'd stood trial for obscenity. I'd never seen a copy of the
book.

I glanced over my shoulder and lifted the volume from
the table, thumbing through, pausing occasionally to read a
verse or register a sentiment.

I didn't understand why it was judged obscene. Based on
the brief passages I read, I did not understand. I glanced up
every now and again to assure myself Fanny Claus, or worse
yet, Maman, was not watching me.

Fanny's back was to me. Maman ignored me. But my
heart thudded at the thought of her discovering my perusal
of such a risqué book.

I tried to discern what all the fuss was about.

It didn't upset my sensibilities. Lightning did not strike
me dead for opening it. I did not faint or feel sickened, or
otherwise harmed.

But if men in higher places judged it obscene, what did it
say about my sensibilities that I saw nothing wrong in it?

And what, too, did my fascination with Édouard's work say
about me? Was I naive? I could see grounds for raised eyebrows:
He'd painted *nude* women out of context. It was no wonder
someone of weaker constitution might take offense.

Yet, it didn't offend me. I thought him brave and heroic
for being so modern, so willing to challenge the stodgy men
of the Academy.

If I could not discern what was improper in something
judged obscene, might there be something wrong with my
judgment?

I returned *Les Fleurs Du Mal* to its place and picked up a sketchbook. I flipped through roughs of still lifes, unfinished portraits and landscapes. But it was the full-length nude stretched out on a bed that gave me pause.

*Olympia.*

My breath caught.

A preliminary sketch? Even in its crude state its allure was undeniable. I stared in awe at the drawing for a moment and noticed something different about it. She was lying in a different position from the finished painting.

In the final version, her legs were outstretched and her left hand covered her sex, but in this rendition, her right knee was shamelessly bent and her left hand rested across her body.

I turned the book to view the sketch from a different angle, and I recalled the other day when Edma and I were in our studio. How we had dissolved into nonsense after Maman's severe disapproval of Édouard's visit. It was Edma's way to make folly out of a grave situation. While I obsessed over the unpleasant, she made light of it. That was just her way.

True to form, I'd sulked at my easel trying to work, trying to not dwell on Maman's foul mood, when Edma started making silly remarks, taking on the voices of the men who attended the soirée at the Manets' home on the Thursday prior. She tried to make me laugh, but failed miserably. I grew irritable because she broke my concentration.

She held a paintbrush under her nose. I guess it was supposed to be a mustache. She couldn't keep a straight face.

She deepened her voice into a slurred, faux baritone, imitating Stevens's drunken antics. "Just ask her, or must I do it for you, you poor, poor miserable man?"

I didn't know if it was the way her voice cracked during

her preposterous imitation of a drunken man that tickled me so, or how ridiculous she looked with that brush balanced between her nose and upper lip, but I succumbed to her giddy buffoonery and said, "You want misery? I shall give you misery." I grabbed the paintbrush from her and pretended to fence.

Edma clapped.

"*Mesdames et Messieurs,* I present to you the new Olympia."

I performed a dramatic, slow curtsy, waving my brush in the air.

Edma clapped louder, "Brava!"

The memory teased a smile to my lips.

"Do you like it?" Édouard's deep voice sounded behind me and pulled me back to the present. I snapped the sketchbook shut and returned it to its place on the worktable. But I did not turn around.

The silence between us was a silken cord that bound me to him, tying us together like lovers. All my senses melded until I imagined his breath against my neck and his hands in my hair, but then I realized it was just my blood rushing through my veins. I turned to face him, and he stood a respectable distance. "I hope you do not mind my looking. I was just . . ."

His expression, a look of sultry longing, of want and raw need, caught me so off-guard I could not speak.

"By all means, look until you have your fill." He picked up Baudelaire's book of poems and held it out to me. "Would you like to borrow it?"

I did not answer because the studio's front door banged open, and *Madame* Manet staggered through the threshold, lugging a large picnic basket with both hands.

"*Bonjour,* everyone!" she said.

Édouard handed me the book and rushed over to take the basket from her.

"Mother, what a surprise. I had no idea you were coming today."

I returned the book to the stack, knowing I could not bring it home. I couldn't imagine the scene it would cause in the carriage on the way home. Feeling more than a little indiscreet at having lost myself in Édouard's belongings and expecting Suzanne to trail in after *Madame* Manet, I moved away from the table to join the others.

"I brought your lunch." *Madame* Manet greeted Maman and the others. "I brought enough for an army. There is plenty for everyone."

Édouard closed the door.

No Suzanne.

Why did she not accompany *Madame* Manet? Why would she let her mother-in-law bear the burden of the long journey and transporting the food alone?

Édouard set down the basket and kissed his mother on the cheek. "How very kind of you to come all this way, Maman."

*Madame* Manet beamed and retreated to Maman's side. "*Madame* Morisot, I am most elated to see you." She hesitated, and I wondered if she'd mention the unfortunate events at the soirée, but she did not. Probably for the best, because I wasn't sure how Maman would respond.

Instead, she asked her son, "How is the painting progressing?"

"We have not begun. But I was just about to suggest we get to work." He looked at me. "Shall we?"

He dragged a chair to the balcony setting, and indicated for me to sit. Once I was in place, he lifted my left arm to rest on the makeshift railing. My body hummed at his touch. Yet, there was nothing personal in it, nothing inappropriate. It was all in the name of work.

He stepped back to look.

"*Mademoiselle,* if you please, tuck your skirt underneath you so we might see the left front legs of the chair. *Mademoiselle* Claus, would you be so kind as to help her fix her train so it flows nicely over the back?"

Fanny Claus obliged. To accomplish the task, I twisted my body so the chair back didn't obstruct the line of the dress.

When I sat, Édouard studied me for a moment, brows knit. I wondered if he was displeased with what he saw, with both of us dressed in white gowns?

He said nothing but, "This painting will take several days, possibly weeks. Are you prepared to wear the same dresses for the duration?"

I nodded. "Will they not get dirty, *Monsieur?*"

"Perhaps." He stroked his beard and turned to Maman and *Madame* La Rue. "*Mesdames,* would it be possible for the *Mesdemoiselles* to wear a different dress tomorrow and bring the white frocks with them? They can leave them here to change into each morning. If they wear them back and forth every day, I'm afraid they'll get soiled."

My eyes darted to the dressing screen, and my breath caught at the thought of undressing behind it. Then my gaze shifted to Maman to gauge her reaction.

*Madame* La Rue looked to *Madame* Manet, who seemed undaunted by the request. Maman stared at me with narrowed I-told-you-so eyes, as if the suggestion flew from my lips.

"As long as you are comfortable with the idea, *Madame* Manet," said Maman, "I suppose I am, too."

*Madame* La Rue agreed and the discussion ended. Fanny

Claus and I would be dressing partners, for there was no possible way we could navigate the buttons that ran the length of the back of our dresses.

"Angle your body to the right, but look off to the left," said Édouard.

I did as he instructed.

"No, too much. Back to the center. Just a bit. Yes, there. Good. Good. Hold that."

He turned to his worktable and came back with an armful of items, among them a red fan and a necklace. He handed me the fan, then walked around behind me and slid a slip of black velvet around my neck.

I only caught a glimpse, but I saw the ribbon held a heart-shaped medallion. I felt his hand working at my nape, and I wondered if the necklace belonged to Suzanne or whether it was just a prop he kept in the studio for such occasion.

After he finished tying, he walked around to the front. "Hold the fan in your left hand and bring it up so it rests on your right arm.

"Yes, that's it. Perfect! Hold that pose while I arrange the others."

In an instant he accomplished the task. He directed Fanny Claus to stand next to me, and placed *Monsieur* Guillemet in the middle, slightly behind us.

With my face angled away, it was hard to see the props he selected for them, but I got the idea from conversation.

"*Mademoiselle* Claus, let the umbrella fall across your body, anchoring it with your left arm. Bend your arms at the elbows like so." He demonstrated. "Act as if you are putting on the gloves."

His instructions for *Monsieur* Guillemet were as simple as, "Stand between the two ladies, please, with your arms like so."

Édouard bent both arms at the elbow, one higher than the other, as if Guillemet were walking mid-stride.

I believed he was ready to start, when he frowned and walked over to the worktable and rummaged around. He came back with the homeliest hat I'd ever seen—a close-fitting cap with a big, ugly, dried pompon of a flower pinned to it.

For a split second I feared he would pull it on my head as fast as he slipped on the necklace. Alas, it was Fanny Claus who won the honor. I heard Édouard rustling around next to me, but I dared not turn my head to look and lose the perfect angle he'd assigned me.

I smiled to myself and imagined how ridiculous Fanny's long, expressionless face must have looked in that unfashionable cap.

The ladies sat to the side chatting. They did not seem a distraction to Édouard during the morning when he was setting up, but as the day wore on, and he began to put charcoal to canvas, I saw him grow tense, occasionally glancing at them as if he wanted to hush them.

I heard *Monsieur* Guillemet fidgeting behind me.

"Antonin, please stop moving about. I am trying to capture your pose."

Guillemet groaned. "My friend, we've been here for hours, it seems. I believe I speak for everyone when I say we need a rest."

"Are you all right, *Mademoiselle* Berthe?"

His question startled me out of my trance. I sat straighter. I was growing tired of holding the same position, but I wouldn't complain. I knew what was expected of me before I'd agreed to the task. I suppose I forgot how exhausting it could be to sit in one position for hours.

"I'm fine, thank you."

"Bear with me for a few more moments . . ."

Édouard's "few more moments" stretched on like a meandering river.

I gazed at the fan until my eyes watered and my arm fell asleep. I wanted to shift, but I did not dare after Édouard reprimanded *Monsieur* Guillemet. Careful not to move, I glanced at Maman and tried to catch her eye. I wanted her to know I was concerned about her comfort after sitting for such a long time. Surely, her back hurt.

"*Mademoiselle* Berthe, your kindness to pose for me is taking you away from your own work," said Édouard. "I do appreciate your help. Are you entering the Salon this year?"

"It is only July, *Monsieur*. It's too early for me to decide."

"*Au contraire, Mademoiselle,* it is never too early to have a goal in mind."

"Perhaps it is a good thing I do not have a goal. For if I did, I should not be so content to sit in your studio and ponder it, when time in my studio would be the only action that would help me reach that said objective."

He nodded. "Very well then. Here's to not having a Salon aspiration in mind, so that I may freely monopolize your time."

I thought certain Édouard would suggest a break, but he seemed lost in his sketching, tossing the occasional annoyed glance when the ladies laughed a little louder than they should have or got carried away talking at the same time. They seemed to be having a grand time. I was glad because Maman looked less like she was burdened by the obligation to be here for me and very much as if she enjoyed the company of new friends.

"There, that should suffice for today." Édouard set down his charcoal stick and stepped back to view his work.

"We shall reconvene tomorrow for a longer session."

I was not sure if I wanted to see how he interpreted me. I could not say why, other than we seldom view ourselves as others see us. Another's personal interpretation seemed so intimate. I'd never thought of it that way before, and I was not sure I was prepared to know how Édouard viewed me.

The others moved about. The three elder ladies crowded around the easel.

Maman peered through her lorgnette and cocked her head to one side. From her pursed mouth and knitted brow, I could tell she was not sure what to make of Édouard's morning's work.

"Well, like all things, I guess this, too, will take time." She lowered her glasses and looked at *Madame* Manet. "Your son knows what he is doing."

*Madame* Manet did not seem to take offense. She smiled and nodded. "Please eat lunch before you go. I brought plenty for everyone."

"Thank you, but we cannot stay," said Maman. "We must get home."

I was not aware of any pressing matters, but I was relieved that Maman did not want to stay. It was enough for one day.

Édouard was unpacking the basket and setting the feast on one of the less crowded worktables. "What is it that pulls you away?"

"My son, Tiburce, arrives this afternoon." Maman looked at me and smiled. "And we are expecting a caller. A *gentleman* caller. Berthe will want time to get ready."

# Chapter Seven

> . . . *I've dreamt in my life dreams*
> *that have stayed with me ever*
> *after, and changed my ideas:*
> *they've gone through and*
> *through me, like wine through water,*
> *and altered the color of my mind.*
>
> —*Emily Brontë*

Intuition's a powerful tool. Generally, when I trusted my instincts, they did not steer me wrong. Edma confirmed as much the afternoon I returned from Édouard's studio. She pulled me out for a walk and we took the carriage to the *Quai du Louvre*. She claimed we should get out because she sensed the tension between Maman and me, and she knew how this stretch of the river Seine calmed me. Yet, I wondered at the timing of the outing, with Tiburce's homecoming and Adolphe's pending visit that afternoon—he was the mysterious gentleman Maman insinuated was calling on me. Sometimes I didn't understand that woman.

Intuition told me something was brewing with Edma as well.

Once we walked down the incline from the street to the waterfront—out of earshot of the driver—my sister bubbled over with excitement.

"Endeavored to get you out of the house to tell you this, because once you hear you will simply delight in what I have discovered."

My sister drew in a dramatic breath and made a show of steadying herself. "Are you ready for this?"

"Yes, do go on."

"Léon is Suzanne's son," she said. "I have been dying to tell you this all day."

I blinked. "No he's not. Léon is her brother. *Madame Manet*—"

Edma shook her head. "Wait. Just wait—Fantin and his sister stopped by today while you and Maman were out. One conversation led to another, and he happened to mention Léon's relationship to Suzanne. So that can only mean Manet is the father."

"Edma, it makes no sense. The boy is in his teens. Édouard married Suzanne only a few years ago. If he married her for the child, why would he wait so many years to do so?"

Edma shrugged. "Fantin said Manet and Suzanne's wedding was a big surprise to everyone. Not even his closest friends knew of his relationship with her. One day he went away, the next he came back married. Even Fantin does not understand. And Manet, he certainly doesn't parade his *beautiful bride* about town. Before we met Suzanne at the soirée, neither of us knew Manet was married even though we've known of Manet for years. Why does he keep his union so quiet? You see, the only explanation can be that Léon is their son. He married her out of obligation, *not* because he loved her."

Suzanne and Édouard's son? It did not make sense, but Edma seemed to have it all figured out.

"That's quite scandalous, indeed, Edma. But, the fact remains that even if Léon is their son—which I do not believe—and even if Édouard married her a dozen years after the fact, they are married, and even explaining away the marriage does not make Édouard more available to me."

In fact, the realization accomplished nothing but casting me out-of-sorts. I thought it best to change the subject. "The way Maman carried on this afternoon about gentleman callers, one would think there was going to be a wedding in our family's future."

Edma blushed a pretty shade of pink as we strolled along the *quai*. She did not comment, but her silence—and dreamy smile—gave me pause.

"Is there something you would like to tell me?" I asked.

She shrugged. Noncommittal.

"Has Adolphe—"

"Oh, no, no, no. He asked me nothing."

Something in her smile suggested more, something she was not telling me. With all the friction between Maman and me, days had passed since Edma and I had talked freely. I felt distant and disconnected from her. As we walked in silence, I reminded myself that if there was something more, she'd tell me in due time. She didn't keep secrets as I did.

"Maman made believe the gentleman caller was for you?" she asked.

I nodded.

"And you said nothing to the contrary?"

"Of course not. She is already furious with me. If I'd corrected her in the company of others, our mother's anger would have opened heaven and earth. Do not look at me as if I took the coward's way out."

"But why? Why would she do that, other than to thwart any improper intentions she feared might be fleeting through Édouard's mind?"

That familiar sensation of tight spirals swirled in my stomach—the same as when he'd teased me earlier about temptations and *making time*—"Fleeting would be the word of emphasis, Edma. If the man ever entertained a single thought about me, I'm sure it was in passing."

"You fancy him."

I laughed and a slow burn simmered on my neck. I opened my fan and started fanning. "I suppose Adolphe shall ask Papa for your hand all too soon. Possibly early fall? Perhaps even late summer?"

"Do not change the subject, Berthe. We are not talking about Adolphe. We were speaking of Édouard. From the looks of him at dinner Thursday night, I am confident *Monsieur* Manet fancies you, too. Surely he has entertained several intentions where you are concerned. But it is much too early to label his intent *completely* improper."

My pulse raced. I fanned faster and took deep breaths to steady myself.

"See there?" She released my arm.

I turned my head so she could not see my expression and quickened my pace.

"Please do not hide your feelings from me." She touched my sleeve. "Me of all people, Berthe. I will not judge you, because if not for Adolphe, I, too, would be drawn to the irresistible Manet charm. Although it would be for naught because it is evident he has eyes for only one lady. And that lady is you."

I gasped—more out of relief than shock—and glanced at my sister through the lace on my hat.

"Tell me your feelings. Tell me everything. I have never seen you this taken with a man."

I did not know what to say, much less what to make of the jumbled emotions knotted inside me. Was I that transparent? But Edma waited. I was sure she would have waited all day.

I could trust her to keep my secret, but I would not endeavor to impose such a burden on my sister. Instead, I weighed my words. "I've never seen such an expressive face as his . . . I think he has a decidedly charming temperament." We walked in silence for a moment until I mustered the courage to admit, "His tastes, his pursuits, all of his passions please me. I suppose if he were not married I would find him immensely attractive. Alas, it is hopeless, Edma. Suzanne has claimed him, and that is the end of it."

"When has unavailability ever precluded desire? Berthe, have you ever seen a more unsuitable pair in your entire life? No wonder the poor man vibrates with discontent—and, I dare say, longing—when he gazes at you."

I stopped. Squeezed my eyes shut against the warmth spreading through my body. A slow thaw melted the icy protection covering my heart.

"It is hopeless, Edma. If this is how I am perceived in his company, I am ruined. It could have negative repercussions for you, too."

"Do not worry about me. What is to be will be. For both of us."

How I envied my sister's confidence. I felt as if I were standing on a rooftop contemplating a leap. I could no more choose my feelings than I could choose to stay on the roof if a tile slipped and sent me crashing to the ground.

"What are your plans?" she asked.

"It is not as if I have a choice."

"*Au contraire,* sister dear. You are in complete control. For that, I envy you."

Her words floored me. I stopped and gaped at her. "I do not understand."

She laughed. "You know perfectly well what I'm saying, and you of all people should not feign shock. False astonishment does not become you. You have said yourself it is not fair men are afforded all of the pleasures and women carry all the burden. If a married man may take a mistress, what is wrong with an unmarried lady taking a *monsieur?* Have you never thought of taking a lover?"

Her words transcended the clatter of the carriages rattling by. I was too mortified by her suggestion to do anything but glance around at the passersby and pray no one heard her. I quickened my steps, but my sister kept pace.

The murky water slapped the *quai*'s stone embankment.

Once the shock dissipated, irritation set in. "Edma, keep your voice down. You know I cannot do as you have suggested."

"What? Why can you not take a lover? Will you not even say the word? *Lover.* Say it, Berthe."

"Shhhhh!" My skin tingled.

"Come now, Berthe. Do you never have certain . . . feelings?"

"Of course I have feelings, Edma. Do not be ridiculous."

"Berthe, I am speaking of feelings that can only be satisfied by a man's touch. You know what I mean. . . . Your soul is much too passionate to pretend you feel nothing. It would be a crime for you to live not exploring those passions because society branded it improper. That, my dear, would not be living."

Her words held many preposterous grains of truth. But my sister could spin romantic tales from high upon her comfortable pre-matrimonial perch. She was in love, and I was sure from her perspective, my taking a lover looked sinfully exciting. She did not have to live with the repercussions.

I did not respond, but stared straight ahead, hoping I was not as transparent as I felt. Knowing that by not responding I gave away the answer that had taken root in my heart.

"Berthe, your strength is not shameful. I admire you for not giving up on your art to bend to convention—God knows it is not the easy path. If I were stronger I might be so inclined to devote my future to art and . . ."

"And what? Lovers? Rather than taking a husband?"

She nodded, and we laughed.

I was at once happy, terrified, and buoyant and hopeless, hopeful, and overwhelmed by the new possibilities blossoming inside me. I'd never felt so alive. Well, not since the day I first laid eyes on Édouard Manet.

Edma threaded her arm through mine and gave me a little squeeze. We strolled along the Seine in silence.

The sun shone on Paris—its wide boulevards and shiny new construction glinted in the afternoon light as if she'd shed her dingy gray cocoon and donned a brilliant new coat—as if she'd prepared to take a lover. Every place I looked revealed something glittering and new. Yet I knew very well nothing had changed since the last time I'd walked this bank.

It was the same cobblestone embankment, the same plane trees with their deep green leaves and peeling bark, the same *Pont des Arts* connecting the right bank to the left.

Only this time, my eyes were wide open.

I tilted my head to take in the Louvre and other tall buildings rising over the water, standing watch over us. The breeze tickled my face, and the river lapped against the boats moored along the embankment, as if all things natural and man-made joined together to welcome me to this beautiful new world. I could not help but smile as I breathed in the sweet scent of Edma's perfume mingled with the odor of the waterfront.

For the first time in ages, I could see beauty in everything.

"Tomorrow is Maman's receiving day," Edma said. "I shall go with you to Édouard's to allow her to stay home. Perhaps that will quell her peevish temperament. With her absent, perhaps you will be able to relax. Would be a pity if he painted you like this." Edma grimaced. We laughed.

"Would be a pity for Maman and you to be sparring with each other during Tiburce's homecoming," she added. "If I go with you tomorrow, it will reduce the chance of quarrels between you. Just leave it to me. I shall arrange everything."

At home, an anxious-looking Amélie met us at the front door. "I have a most urgent message for you, *Mademoiselle* Berthe."

"What is it?" I asked.

*"Pardonnez-moi, Mademoiselle."* She looked over her shoulder as if to assure no one else was near. "Could we go outside to your studio? For . . . privacy." She whispered the last word.

Edma shot me an urgent look, and the three of us walked across the garden to the studio.

"Come in," I said.

Amélie closed the door, reached into her pocket and withdrew a small leather-bound book. *"Monsieur* Manet left this for *Mademoiselle* Berthe."

My heart leapt at the mention of his name, and my blood ran cold when I saw the book was the volume of *Les Fleurs Du Mal* I'd perused in his studio.

"He delivered it himself?" I asked, hopeful in spite of myself.

*"Oui.* He could not wait. He handed me the book and

asked me to give it to you. There is a note tucked inside the cover."

I opened the book and saw the crisp crème-colored linen paper sealed with red wax bearing the initial M.

"Does Maman know of his call?"

"No, *Mademoiselle*. Please forgive me for not informing *Madame*, but—"

"No apology necessary, Amélie. You made the right decision."

Relief spread over the girl's face. She nodded. "If there's nothing else, I shall return to my duties in the kitchen."

"*Merci*, Amélie."

Amélie left. I tore open the note and read it aloud.

*Dear Mademoiselle,*

*You left in such haste you forgot the book. I took the liberty of delivering it to you. Keep it as long as you desire. The sight of you is all the pleasure the morrow will afford me. Until then . . .*

*Yours faithfully,*
*E. Manet*

I folded the note and tucked it inside my paint box where Maman would not find it.

"Why would he bring it to you if he will see you tomorrow at the studio?"

I said nothing.

Edma laughed, victorious. "Unless he was hoping to intrude on your gentleman caller. Persistent. Obviously a man who knows what he wants. But his timing is bad."

She shook her head and *tsk, tsk, tsked* as she walked to the window. "Oh poor, poor Édouard. Cursed with a bad sense of timing. 'Tis the undoing of many a great lover."

*Lover.* The word upended my belly, causing my hand to fly to my stomach in self-defense.

"Edma, stop it. If Maman hears you, she will have a fit."

My sister toyed with an arrangement of yellow mums sitting on the window table. "You must admit persistence is a very attractive quality."

I could not deny it, but it didn't mean I would admit it. I'd confessed enough for one day. Instead, I stared at his book in my hands.

"What is the book?"

When I did not answer, she crossed the room and plucked it from my hands. She gasped and her eyes flew wide. "It is banned, is it not? Where did he get it?"

I shrugged. She paged through, pausing now and again to read snatches of verse.

> *How you would please me, night without your stars,*
> *Which speak a foreign dialect, that jars*
> *On one who seeks the void the black the bare . . .*
> *A dream, a form, a creature, late,*
> *Fallen from azure realms, and sped*
> *Into some Styx of mud and lead*
> *No eye from heaven can penetrate . . .*

"Oh Edma, who cares if it is banned? It's a beautiful collection of poetry. I do not need some moralizing windbag saving me from myself by dictating what is right and what is wrong."

She frowned. "Perhaps you should give it back to him? Return it tomorrow and tell him it does not interest you."

"I do not want to give it back."

Edma arched a brow. "If you are worried about giving

Maman reason to have a fit, this will set her off should she discover it."

"I don't see how you can suggest I take a lover one minute and the next become straight-laced and upright over a book. She will not discover it. And she will have no reason to know about it, if no one makes her the wiser."

Edma's mouth fell open, and she handed me the book.

"Do you believe me incapable of keeping a secret? Be assured you have my most discreet confidence."

"Of course I do not doubt you, Edma." She alone was the one constant in this world of shifting light and shadows in which I found myself captive.

Edma I could trust. Myself, now that was another matter.

I listened at the drawing room door as Edma approached Maman about accompanying me to Édouard's the next morning.

"It will free you to stay home with Tiburce and greet your guests."

As I suspected, Maman was none too pleased. "I should think you would care to stay home and spend time with your brother, too."

"Who will accompany Berthe?" Edma asked.

"Berthe is twenty-seven years old. She is not a child any more. Since she seems to think she knows what she is doing, I resign myself from this situation. Let her go alone, for all I care."

"Maman, you do not mean it."

No, she didn't. What she meant was I should stay at home, too.

"Edma, I am at my wits' end, and I do not know what else to do with her. I have spoken to your father about your sister's headstrong ways. He feels I should just let her be. She seems to value her painting above all else. It is to the point where I have started to question her mental faculties, but your father will not hear of it. If you are so inclined to accompany your sister, so be it."

With that, Maman washed her hands of the situation and grumbled about the hardship our absence would pose since she'd only have Amélie to rely on for service when her friends called. We usually served the tea and cakes while she entertained. Though she seemed to like *Madame* Manet well enough, it was obvious her sanctions against the sitting were for my punishment. She knew when she bid everyone *adieu* at the *atelier* that she would not see them tomorrow.

She was making me choose.

Maman or art.

I would not be tested.

Later, as Edma dressed in preparation for Adolphe's visit, I sat in the chair in our room transported by Édouard's book. It was the epitome of modernity. I read, spellbound, a poem entitled "Le Balcon":

> *Mother of Memories, mistress of my dreams,*
> *To whom I am in love and duty bound,*
> *You will recall, as red the firelight gleams,*
> *What fond embraces, what content we found,*
> *Mother of memories, mistress of my dreams . . .*

I sat up straight in my chair, not believing what I'd just read. A poem called "The Balcony" in a book hand-delivered by a man who was painting my portrait in a work of the same name.

*Mother of Memories, mistress of my dreams . . .*

"Perhaps I should take Madame Manet to visit Maman

tomorrow during her receiving time?" Edma held up a pretty deep blue gown, then one of white silk adorned with tiny pink flowers.

"Don't be ridiculous," I said, glancing up from the page. "Maman will never forgive you, if you leave me unattended."

"I suppose you're right. She might say she no longer cares, but she does."

Edma settled on the blue dress and started to change. "What shall I do the whole day? I will go mad if I must sit talking to Fanny Claus's chaperone all day. I'm sure I have nothing in common with her."

"Sitting is what chaperones do. And that is what you have agreed to do. *N'est-ce pas?*"

She brooded.

"May I read the book he loaned you?"

I snapped it shut and covered the slim volume with my hands as it lay in my lap.

"Do you really want to sit with *Madame* Manet and company and read *Les Fleurs Du Mal*? I'm sure Édouard has other books you may borrow." I tightened my grip on the book. "But not this one, Edma."

# Chapter Eight

*Compare with me, ye women, if you can*
*I prize thy love more than whole mines of gold*
*Or all the riches that the East doth hold.*
*My love is such that rivers cannot quench,*
*Nor ought but love from thee, give recompense.*
*—Anne Bradstreet, To My Dear and Loving Husband*

The next morning, I awoke with youthful vigor restored. My refreshment was not the benefit of a good night's rest, but culled from a deeper source. Something vital awakened inside me—a newfound awareness roused after a life of unconscious living.

I was full of clarity and felt as if I could conquer the world—or at least the indecision that plagued my world since meeting Édouard Manet.

Still in her dressing gown after I'd been ready for more than a half-hour, Edma was as lazy as the last days of summer. I was set on going alone if she did not hurry. With white dress in hand, I doubled the skirt over my arm so it would not drag the floor and tucked Édouard's book into the folds.

"Come on, we must leave now. What is taking you so long?"

"Berthe, it is not even half past eight. We do not have to be there until ten o'clock. What is your hurry?"

"I want to arrive before the others."

I stood in the foyer for another ten minutes before my

sister graced me with her presence. She looked fresh, if not a little harried, as I helped her with her bonnet. We called goodbye to Maman and were on the steps when our mother appeared at the door.

"Why on earth are you leaving now?"

"We want to get an early start so *Monsieur* Manet can set to work faster," I said.

"You have not eaten breakfast."

"No we have not," Edma grumbled.

In fear that Maman would detain us—or find some reason to keep us from going—I grabbed my sister by the elbow and started walking. "No sense in troubling Amélie. She has enough work this morning preparing for your guests today. Manet will give us tea or coffee when we arrive."

Outside the gate, I could no longer see Maman. I did not let go of Edma's arm until we were settled inside the carriage.

Once we were on our way, the cool morning air calmed me. I set my white dress, with the book tucked inside, on the seat beside me, settled back and relaxed a bit.

Edma's mood seemed to have not suffered from my pushing her to hurry. "I dare say, Maman must not be too concerned about us going," she said. "If not, do you think she would have been so agreeable?"

Agreeable? She was not agreeable. I suppose she was in better humor this morning than she was yesterday, when she scarcely said three words to me. But I could tell she was still none too pleased. "The source of her good mood, no doubt, was Adolphe calling on you last evening."

For the third time in the span of a week.

Edma blushed a pretty shade of pink at the mention of her beloved's name and chattered about him as the carriage rolled us closer to Édouard. I was happy to let my sister carry on about Adolphe's gestures and expressions, his small tokens of affection, how he used words like *we* and *us* when he spoke of the future and its exciting possibilities.

She leaned in and lowered her voice. "Yesterday, you asked if I was anticipating a proposal." She smiled as if she couldn't contain herself. "Don't be surprised if Adolphe asks Papa for my hand before fall sets in."

I'd known it was coming. Yet I couldn't bring myself to face the possibility of Edma leaving.

It was unspeakably selfish to wish my sister to stay with me—two old maids painting side-by-side in our studio. Alas, knowing she would move off with Adolphe wherever his career might beckon—he was a military man, after all—and knowing I would no longer have the privilege to see her every day, made me want to weep.

I swallowed the pang.

What would I do without Edma? We'd never been apart. We'd been happy for our elder sister, Yves, when she'd married. It suited her. She did not paint and had worked toward matrimony with the same determination that possessed Edma and me as we perfected a painting for the Salon.

When Yves left, marriage was a dim light on the horizon for us. Now it glared as menacing as a comet aligned to hit the earth. Edma was not merely my sister, but my best friend. The thought of living without her was almost unbearable.

Her eyes shone. "Tell me, what do you think of him, Berthe? Would you find him a suitable brother-in-law?"

Tears burned my eyes, and I looked out the window until I was sure I had them under control.

She sounded so happy.

"Edma, anyone who makes you happy, makes me happy."

She smiled, serene and confident, a woman bolstered by love's glow. We rode along in silence until she asked, "Are you nervous about seeing Manet?"

Her question made me flinch. I shook my head, hoping not to seem startled. "Nervous? Why on earth would I be nervous?"

Edma shrugged. "I supposed . . . Well, I just thought— Have you considered what we talked about yesterday?"

I held a finger to my lips. "Edma, be practical. You're caught up in the thrill of romance, but Adolphe is a single man. Édouard is not. Do not encourage me to long for that which I cannot have."

I slid my hand between the dress's silk layers to the book. Its solid form reassured me.

Edma smiled, but her eyes held a sweet sadness—as if she grieved for all the unrequited lovers who walked the earth. For a quick moment, I feared I saw my own emotions mirrored in her eyes. I looked away and sat back with the echo of my words ringing to the rhythm of the horse's hooves on the cobblestone streets. I did not feel quite as sure of myself as I did when I awoke.

"This painting of Édouard's—who else is posing with you?"

I told her of the stoic Fanny Claus and her friendship with Suzanne—"She doesn't like me at all." And of tall, funny *Monsieur* Guillemet, and how the idea for the painting swept Édouard off his feet.

Before I knew it, we'd arrived at Édouard's studio. We weren't the first visitors of the morning. Degas beat us to the *rue* Guyot. I was none too happy to see him, as I'd hoped to have a few moments alone with Édouard to discuss the book.

So much for that.

*Talk to him about it while he paints, said Olympia. You'll have plenty of time, and it's obvious he has no interest in anyone but you.*

*You can't bring it up in front of the others, said Propriety.*

*Why do you care what they think? said Olympia.*

Édouard answered the door with a warm greeting. "Bonjour, Mesdemoiselles."

He ushered us in and presented his guest.

"*Monsieur* Degas, how do you do." I tried to hide my annoyance at his presence.

"I've come to see what all the fuss is about," said Degas. "To judge for myself if all the commotion Manet has created over his new masterpiece is worthy of the uproar."

"Uproar?" I smiled at Édouard. "What is he talking about?"

Degas smirked and studied me—a lazy, appraisal raked from my face, down to the hem of my skirt.

"May I take the dress from you?" asked Édouard.

I tightened my grip on the book hidden beneath the fabric and shook my head. "Just tell me where to put it."

Édouard motioned for me to follow. Heels clicking on the marred wooden floor, I followed him behind the dressing screen.

"You may leave it here." He stood just inside the panel, much too close to me.

I pulled the book from the folds of the dress.

He smiled. "Did you read it?"

I nodded. Nerves made my arm twitch, and my elbow knocked into the screen. It swayed, but didn't fall—*Merci Dieu*. It reminded me that, although we were tucked out of sight, it was a flimsy screen—not a wall. Edma and Degas

93

could hear every word we exchanged.

I pressed the book into his hand, glancing up at him a moment before I draped my dress over the top of the screen.

My mind skittered back to yesterday—to his playful teasing, to Edma's urging—and my blood rushed with temptation that beckoned me to lean into him again.

The silence in the outer room roared.

*Now, do you understand why it is frowned upon for ladies to go out without a chaperone?* said Propriety. *Especially in the company of a handsome man who has a habit of invading one's personal space.*

A tender smile spread over his face—as if he knew Baudelaire, in his poems, said everything we might say to each other. As he slipped the book into his pocket, the notion pierced my defenses.

He rejoined the others, and I lingered behind the curtain to straighten my gown so it wouldn't wrinkle. The melody of Édouard's voice floated up and out on the air as I gathered myself.

When I ventured out from behind my cover, Édouard was telling Edma and Degas about his inspiration for the painting. "It was an omen. I was so overcome by the sensation that I decided I must recreate it. I had to make it my own."

"I am certain you will endeavor to do so." Degas wheezed a dry, brittle *hrumph.*

Arched brows framed the flat planes of his face, which stretched down to a diminutive bowed mouth set in a permanent scowl. His small round eyes pinned me to the spot where I stood.

"Show us the canvas, Manet," said Degas, his voice cool and colorless as a winter morning.

"Oh, yes, may we see it?" Edma urged.

Édouard stroked his beard. "It's not suitable for viewing. I have only invested a half-day's work in it and still have a long road ahead."

Degas badgered Édouard until he dragged out the easel and angled the canvas so we could view the sketch.

Degas drew closer, stroking his clean-shaven chin, making interested noises such as *hmmmmm* and *umm-hmmm*. His brows arched like tiny umbrellas opening over his small black eyes.

"*Oui,* Manet. *Très bien.* I am sure you plan to work very hard on this one." Degas looked at me, not the painting. "For she will prove a challenge. But challenge is what you live for, is it not?"

His insinuation made me bite my bottom lip. We all ignored him as we would disregard a naughty child who'd spoken out of line. I wondered if we did not acknowledge his gauche behavior, if perhaps he would stop?

But he did not.

"Manet is a master, no doubt," he said to me. "Do not let him monopolize your time. He *will*, if you afford him the opportunity."

I glanced at Édouard, who was frowning and staring at the canvas. "I have no idea what he is babbling on about. He is a cynic and a pessimist. Pay him no mind."

"Ah, true, my friend. I may be guilty of all charges, but you are *married*. I do not know which of us bears the greater burden."

Édouard smudged a line on the canvas with his thumb. Then picked up a piece of charcoal and began to draw. "My dear friend, Degas, you are carrying the weight of the world on your shoulders. Since you bear the load, the rest of us should have no worries." Édouard stepped back to assess his work. "Although I've often wondered if mankind might not be better off if you were to set down your burden for a night, and enjoy the company of a good woman. We would certainly find you more agreeable for it."

Degas snorted. "I have no time for fools of either sex. From what I gather, *Mademoiselle* Berthe, you are no fool. Heed my warning. Watch yourself around this philanderer."

Édouard laughed as if Degas had made a joke, then turned the canvas to the wall.

"Ah, but *Monsieur* Degas, I am not so naive as to fall prey to *petit* flattery," I said. "In fact, I was wondering whether *Monsieur* Manet's wife will honor us with her presence today? I should love to know her better."

It was a lie. I was sure Édouard and Edma knew it, but I did not care. I had no desire to know Suzanne better. But I had to put Degas, that insufferable little man, in his place. He had much audacity, insulting Édouard in his own studio and suggesting I might be so weak I could not take care of myself.

Degas looked down his pointed nose. "Will we see your lovely wife, Manet?"

Édouard busied himself readying his supplies. "I do not know, Degas. Please feel free to call on her in Boulogne and inquire after her schedule, if you wish."

Days turned into weeks. Weeks pushed close to a month and the sittings stretched on. *Madame* Manet found better things to do, and Edma grew tired of spending her days sitting in Édouard's *atelier*. After strict discussion with *Madame* Manet and *Madame* La Rue, Maman decided it was acceptable for me to go to the sittings alone with the understanding that *Madame* La Rue would be present.

After all, Fanny Claus and her chaperone would be ample supervision for a woman of *my age*. Maman did not say it in so many words, but the meaning was implied.

As was the meaning behind the sighs and cross demeanor of Fanny Claus and *Monsieur* Guillemet. Their restlessness grew more acute as each day dragged on. The vague hints of displeasure blossomed into bitter protests about the amount of time Édouard was monopolizing. But their complaints seemed to roll off him as a carriage wheel spun over a cobblestone boulevard.

I did not mind. Time with him in his studio was time well spent. Édouard and I talked and laughed and discovered so much about each other.

We discussed Baudelaire and whether he was depravity and vice or the poet of modern civilization.

Manet entertained me with stories of the times Baudelaire came to the Thursday night soirées.

"My mother did not know what to think of him at first," he said. "Later she longed for his company."

"To die so young. . . . How I wish I could have met him."

Édouard tilted his head to the right and peered at me around the canvas, his gray eyes moist with sadness. "He would have been captivated by you."

Fanny Claus snorted in the background, but Édouard and I ignored her.

He was charming and proper—not a hint of impropriety, much to my dismay. After all this talk of Baudelaire and indecency, I longed for a hint of something more, but he was the perfect gentleman.

How frustrating.

Still, I wouldn't have minded if the sessions stretched on indefinitely. The minutes that stood between us when we weren't together weighed heavy and endless. The days with him were far too short.

*Madame* Manet took temporary respite from her Thursday soirées since she, Suzanne and Léon were still in Boulogne. It was for the best. I wondered at Édouard's separation from his wife. Perhaps an artist's wife grew accustomed to the models and the long hours her husband spent away.

Suzanne had her spy in the watchful eye of little Fanny Claus, who, I was sure, provided Suzanne with detailed reports.

About forty days into the painting, while we were taking a short rest to stretch our limbs, Fanny Claus walked over to the canvas, as bold as you please. Édouard had turned it toward the wall, but she scooted the easel back as if he'd invited her to peek.

Her face fell. "I am finished, *Monsieur* Manet."

She yanked off her gloves and the ugly little hat and tossed them aside. "It is plain to see you have eyes for only one subject in this painting. You will do fine without me."

Édouard was making a pot of tea. He stopped and gaped at her.

"*Mademoiselle* Claus, I am sorry if I have offended you. But I must confess, I do not understand why you are angry. Each of you is important to this composition. Perhaps I have detained you too long. For that I apologize. If you feel you must go, by all means, please go."

She left.

Later, when I took a good look at the painting, Fanny Claus's words rang true. The exquisite detail in which he'd painted my image made the vague sketches of the others look even plainer, as if their only function was to mark space on the canvas.

Surely he'd go back and paint them in more detail. Looking at us for the past month, he had ample time to commit our features to memory. But if the truth be known, I was elated by the painstaking detail he'd spent on me.

To think there was once a time when we were strangers, when Édouard Manet was just a name on a magnificent painting. Then I found myself in his studio as a friend discussing art and God and politics and the world in which we lived. He considered my opinions and did not think less of my strong convictions.

Why had we not met before he married Suzanne?

# Chapter Nine

*In studious awe the poets brood*
*before my monumental pose*
*aped from the proudest pedestal,*
*and to bind these docile lovers fast*
*I freeze the world in a perfect mirror:*
*The timeless light of my wide eyes.*
                    —*Baudelaire, Beauty*

I arrived at his studio the next morning, alone, as I had for the previous two weeks. I was a little later than usual, but I was still the first to arrive.

"I feared you'd deserted me, too." Édouard looked anxious standing in the midst of his *atelier,* but did not seem the least bit bothered by the fact that we were alone, without the benefit of a chaperone.

I set down my handbag, unnerved and exhilarated by this realization. "Of course I would not desert you." My words sounded far more certain than I felt. "Aren't the others coming today? Did I not get a message that you cancelled the session?"

"They're finished." He shook his head. "I still have much work to accomplish before I will deem this painting complete. Alas, I suppose I have imposed on everyone long enough. You may leave, too, if you choose."

His words released me, but his eyes asked me to stay. Fanny Claus was cross yesterday, but I thought she'd return.

When I realized she and *Madame* La Rue weren't coming back, I should have left. If Édouard and I were discovered alone together, it would have been disastrous, even in its innocence. Still I heard myself say, "I did not come all this way to turn around and go home."

We stood shy and awkward for a moment. I feared I might come apart for how clumsy I felt.

Then he smiled. "I was hoping you'd say that. Here, come and sit for a moment." He patted the arm of the divan. "Let us have some tea before we get to work."

He moved to the kitchen to start the water, as he'd done every morning since he began the painting. I perched on the edge of the sofa and glanced around the studio, seeing it with new eyes—the dressing screen with my lone white dress draped over the top just as I left it. Fanny Claus's gown was gone. She must have sent for it.

My gaze trailed from the easel pushed into one corner to the rumpled covers on the unmade bed on the opposite side of the room.

"Did you sleep here last night?"

"I did. I worked on the painting well into the evening, and it made no sense to go home to an empty house, with Suzanne, Léon and Maman still in Boulogne."

It pained me to hear her name pass his lips. But something dangerous bubbled at the thought of her being so far away—they'd been apart for so long. Propriety warned, *Watch yourself. You should leave, if you know what's best.*

The memory of his whispered promises that first day in the studio—vows of temptation more sinful than rich chocolate—drowned Propriety's caveat. What, in addition to chocolate, did he have in mind today?

More importantly, was I ready to discover the answer?

I stood with a start. "I suppose I shall change." Cringing

at the tiny squeak that masqueraded as my voice, I retreated behind the dressing screen.

I closed my eyes, took a deep breath, and forced myself to consider the consequences of staying with him—alone. What if Degas or Stevens or any of the many who were prone to happen by dropped in? I needed only bid him *adieu* and walk out the door.

I reached back with both hands and began unfastening the tiny buttons on my dress.

I'd imagined being alone with Édouard, even longed for it in my most private fantasies, but never had I dreamt I'd find myself in the situation.

Emotion and longing merged and crested like waves propelled by wind. A strange funnel swirled in my belly. I possessed no more control over these feelings than I could control the sea flowing onto the shore.

As I worked the first button free, Édouard rattled the teakettle. With the next, he drew the water. With the third, he set the kettle to the fire.

Button by tiny button, I worked myself free, hitching up the fabric to conquer the hard-to-reach places, until the dress fell to the floor.

Édouard coughed and dragged the easel to the middle of the room. I hugged myself, closing my eyes and running my hands down my bare arms to quell a shiver.

Oh, how scandalous and free I felt standing like that. Terrified and liberated, undressed and alone with this man I desired. I touched the partition's cloth. The shield that hid my nakedness from Édouard's eyes wavered beneath my trembling hand. And the knot in the pit of my stomach unfurled.

I lifted the white dress off the rail. Édouard seemed to stop moving. The room was suspended in a reverent silence as I buried my face in the silky white fabric. It held the scent of Édouard's studio. I breathed in the aphrodisiac for a moment before slipping it over my head.

The organdy flounces fell over my body like a lover's hands urging me out from behind the screen. I looked out and saw Édouard setting up his supplies.

"Would you help me with the buttons, please?"

He set down his palette and wiped his hands on a rag. He did not say a word, but watched me as he tidied himself, as if he knew what I was asking of him.

As he moved toward me, I felt it—an almost indiscernible click as the magnet of him pulled at the pin of my heart and all of my feelings and longing for him snapped into place.

I gripped the edge of the partition, but he placed his hands on my shoulders and turned me so he could get to the buttons.

He brushed aside a wisp of my hair fallen from its place. His fingers trailed across the nape of my neck. I inhaled a short, sudden gasp, and a shiver shadowed the trail of his fingers. My head tilted in the direction of his hand, and my sleeve slipped from one shoulder.

For the span of a breath he did not touch me. I did not move. I let the fabric stay as it fell, exposing the top curve of my breast that lay like an over-ripe fruit atop the edge of my stiff corset.

His hands settled on my shoulders light as a whisper. One hand still, the thumb of his other traced the exposed skin—a soft, barely-there caress that gave me permission to pull away . . . or not.

I lowered my cheek and dusted the inside of his wrist with the murmur of a kiss.

"Do you remember that first dinner? I told you I would

tell you what thoughts provoked such a look on my face?"

"*Oui.*" He stroked my jaw line, my cheek, my bottom lip—tracing it with the gentle pad of his thumb.

"I wanted to touch you here." I kissed his wrist again. "I wanted to taste the delights of you and judge for myself if you were not the essence of manhood."

He moaned. His left hand made its way to the inside back of my dress and traced the vee of bare skin to my waist; then around to my corseted belly. His hand splayed the expanse of my stomach, to the underside of my breasts. He pulled me against him and his body responded.

He slid his right hand down my collarbone to the fleshy fullness at the top of my breast and pressed his lips to my neck. My breath quickened to short, silent gasps. As I arched back, his finger brushed my nipple. I nearly cried out. The sensations were so new. Places on my body never touched sang under his fingers.

I was petrified and mesmerized. It was everything I'd imagined. Edma was right. It would be a sin to live life not knowing such passion.

He turned me to face him, weaving his hands in my hair, exploring the hollow of my neck, trailing his tongue over my earlobe. I feared I would explode from desire, but he lowered his mouth to mine—I started at the feel of his beard—surprisingly coarse against my lips—a sharp contrast to the smooth wetness of his full, deep, ardent kisses. He moaned a low, throaty sound of satisfaction that was unexpectedly animal, and I melted deeper into his kiss, allowing myself to sink into his body. I savored his taste—coffee and a hint of peppermint—the hard feel of him and the safety of his arms. The rest of the world melted away.

My first kiss. How I'd longed for his kiss.

How many nights I'd dreamt of being in his arms.

Feeling his body pressed to mine, yearning for the lingering seconds he'd look into my eyes before his lips touched mine for the first time.

He pushed down my other sleeve and stepped back, allowing enough space between us so the dress slid down my body and pooled at my feet like a white cloud.

He eased me down onto the dress, behind the screen. His mouth never left mine as he explored delicate places never before touched.

Through the haze of ecstasy, I thought I heard a woman's voice in the far reaches of my consciousness.

He tore away from me, and got to his feet in what seemed like a single, fluid motion.

"*Bonjour,* Édouard! Are you here?" Suzanne called out mere seconds before her footfalls announced her presence inside the studio.

# Chapter Ten

*What's the earth*
*With all its art, verse, music worth*
*Compared with love, found, gained and kept?*
—*Robert Browning*

I stood trembling behind the screen afraid to move, afraid to breathe. All I could think was how symbolic this was of my life—wanting that which I could not have. Craving that which was forbidden. Yet I ignored common sense in search of the illusive. Something to fill the void that seemed to grow larger each day.

The dress I'd worn to his studio was draped over the screen. If I attempted to pull it down, she'd surely see it. So I stood stripped, ashamed, and horrified. Unable to move. Unable to dress myself. All Suzanne need do was walk behind the screen and she'd catch me in all my unchaperoned, undignified nakedness.

To think that this was my first experience with a man. Even if he wasn't just any man.

On the other side of the screen, Édouard muttered, "Perfect timing that you should arrive now. I was preparing to go out. Won't you join me?"

I hoped his face did not reflect the tightness in his voice, and I wondered if Suzanne was suspicious.

"Édouard, I've only just arrived. Might we sit a while so that I may rest from my journey?"

"Haven't you been sitting since you left Boulogne? I

would think more sitting should tire you further."

The hem of my white dress protruded beyond the confines of the partition. Did I dare pull it back and attempt to dress, or did I stand there in my underwear praying that Édouard would get her out and away from the building so that I might escape?

There was only one exit, and Édouard's wife blocked my passage to freedom. My heart pounded so hard it hurt.

"Aren't you expecting *Mademoiselle* Claus and the others? I should quite like to see her. That's one reason I came today."

"In that case your timing is quite bad. Yesterday, your friend *Mademoiselle* Claus quit the painting, leaving me quite in a lurch. Without her, there was no need to detain the others. So I am left to my own devices."

Quite convincing.

I wondered for a moment if Fanny Claus told Suzanne that she and her chaperone would no longer be in attendance. That perhaps Suzanne thought it in her best interest to appear in person to check on matters. But the logistics were impossible. If Fanny Claus had sent a note to Boulogne, not enough time had passed for Suzanne to receive it and travel.

No, it was coincidence. Or perhaps something even more unsettling—a wife's intuition.

All I could do was wait and hope that intuition did not alert her to question the blue gown thrown haphazardly over the screen and the white dress that had fallen to the floor.

"I thought I might find you here."

"Édouard. . . ." His voice seemed to echo in the Louvre gallery. It sent a jolt up my spine that made me sit

107

straighter. I flinched, ashamed at having uttered his given name. Too familiar. I was losing myself again.

Edma peeked out from behind her easel and smiled. "*Monsieur* Manet. What a pleasant surprise."

"*Bonjour, Mademoiselle,* I did not realize it was you hiding behind the canvas. How lovely to see you." A pregnant pause. "Both of you."

The *musée* felt vast and cold despite the untypical Thursday morning crowd. In addition to Edma and me, one other painter copied the Rubens. Maman sat on a bench across the gallery. She'd dozed off reading her book. In the short time Édouard had been there, a handful of onlookers strolled by, pausing to scrutinize our work. Looking from our easels to the masterpieces on the walls, they uttered inane comments as if we were deaf or too dumb to comprehend their criticism.

It would be hard to speak to him—in this public place—after all that happened yesterday, but we needed to talk. He knew, and he found me, sought me, rather than leave me in fits and knots over the outcome of Suzanne's surprise visit.

Edma watched us. Her eyes darted from Édouard to me. I'd not told her of yesterday's events. I'd not told her because it would not happen again. I was ashamed. Ashamed at having almost been discovered. Ashamed of the perverse thrill that coursed through me when I thought of his hands on me.

It was wrong.

I would not put myself in that position again. I thought Suzanne would never leave his studio, but after a bit of persistence Édouard persuaded her to go with him.

Édouard was quite a persistent man. Much to my dismay, and despite all that had transpired, I found his persistence very attractive.

"What brings you to the Louvre today, *Monsieur?*" Edma said. "Business or pleasure?" She giggled. I cringed. It was so out of character for her to act like a silly, smitten girl.

I gripped my paintbrush so hard my knuckles went white.

"My business is of a personal nature."

He spoke to her, but his gaze was fixed on me.

Edma set down her pallette. "I see. In that case, I shall get back to work and leave you to your *personal business.*" She stood. "In fact, I find I need a closer look at the folds in Marie de Médici's dress for this study. If you will excuse me."

"Certainly." He sounded as relieved as I was at having the chance to talk alone.

Behind Édouard's back, Edma made a face at me, then covered her eyes with her hands for a brief moment before wandering over to the paintings on the far wall.

"I had to see you," Édouard said. "Are you all right?"

I shrugged, still unable to process the myriad emotions coursing through me. I was at war with myself. *You are so foolish for longing for him as he stands before you,* said Propriety. *Even after you spent hours fretting, feeling dirty after almost being found out.*

*Yes, but underneath it all,* said Olympia, *despite everything that has happened, you hoped he would come today. And he did.*

It eased my melancholy as a piece of bread saves a starving man from dying of hunger.

I glanced at Maman, still asleep on the bench across the room. Yesterday morning after fleeing Édouard's studio, I'd apologized to her. I'd walked in, found her, and said, "This standoff has gone on far too long. I've been foolish. I want things to be as they've always been."

She forgave me.

But only after I told her my days of sitting for Édouard Manet were over.

She agreed this war between us had gotten out of hand and seemed relieved to call a truce. She said she held no grudge against the Manets. She was angry with me over my choices. The way I'd chosen to live my life.

I shuddered to think what damage our relationship would suffer if she knew the half of what I'd chosen.

"It will never happen again." I murmured the words, a little cooler than my initial reception of him, and resumed painting—the same Rubens I was working on that day I first met him.

*Sure,* taunted Olympia. *You won't let him walk away. You desire him too much.*

Propriety scolded, *After foolishly giving yourself over to him for his balcony painting, you've neglected your own work. You've renewed your focus on painting. If you are to be a painter, then paint. If you must give into the temptation to flirt, you should choose a more appropriate man. But you don't have time. As it stands, you'll not have work ready in time to enter the Salon. Perhaps next time you'll not behave like such a whore, squandering your time.*

"Berthe . . ." He stepped closer, holding his hat. "You fled in such haste yesterday. I wish you'd stayed. I came right back after Suzanne left."

My hands shook as I painted. "Do you know how close we came to being discovered? How could we have been so foolish?"

When I fled, I was so unnerved I didn't even button my gown. I'd simply wrapped my cloak around myself and fled, as fast as I could. When I got home, I went straight up to my room, removed the dress and put on my bed clothes, telling Maman and Edma I was not well.

The terrible part was that despite the near disaster, the feel of his kiss was still fresh on my lips. They tingled with desire even as he stood before me, even as I told him, "It will never happen again."

I set down my brush, but did not look at him. If I'd seen longing in his eyes, I would've crumbled.

If something wasn't profoundly wrong with me, it would've mattered that he was married. It should've stopped me from giving myself to him. We should've never arrived at the place where we were forced to hide our passion. Much less hoping against all hope that we'd not be discovered.

"It was not right for me to stay with you alone in your *atelier*. Your studio's an open door. Anyone can walk in. I should have left when I discovered *Mademoiselle* Claus was not returning." I pressed my hands to my face and caught Edma looking. She turned away when she saw me, pretending she wasn't watching us. "Your wife must have known."

"She doesn't know. She'll never know what happened between us."

I remembered his hands on my body, his lips on my neck, and I shuddered. "It should've never happened, and I would thank you to take your leave, *Monsieur*."

My voice, a hissing whisper, trembled, and I picked up my brush again.

He glanced at Maman, still sleeping, and I knew he was concerned about waking her. I was concerned, too. It was bad enough my sister witnessed this exchange. She'd ask questions. *Merci Dieu* no one else was close enough to hear.

"Berthe, please. I must see you again."

"To finish what you started?"

"It is not like that."

"Then how is it, *Monsieur* Manet?"

Footsteps sounded from the gallery entrance behind us. I glanced back to see Degas approaching.

We fell silent.

Wonderful. Just wonderful. The last person I wanted to see.

"Manet? It is you. I'm not surprised. Every time I see you now, you and *Mademoiselle* Morisot are together. *Hmmmmmph.* Is this your work, *Mademoiselle?*"

"Yes it is." The words were a warning, daring him to give me an opinion. I was in no mood to abide his biting sarcasm.

Degas stepped closer to the canvas, bent down to look. For the first time since making his acquaintance, a new expression passed over his jaded face. I could not label the look, but his features softened as he gazed at my painting.

"*Bien. Très bien.* This is excellent. Better than most men. Manet mentioned your talent, but I had no idea."

"See?" said Édouard. "Didn't I tell you?"

I scowled, feeling as if I'd been duped. Manet would have Degas come along and flatter me to soften my countenance in case I was in a bad humor after yesterday. I felt quite sickened at the possibility that he told *Monsieur* Degas about our rendezvous and near-mishap.

"Did *Monsieur* Manet ask you to meet him here today?" I asked.

Degas's sardonic glare eclipsed his former look of near-respect. "I beg your pardon, *Mademoiselle?*"

I glanced at Édouard, who stroked his beard. Then back to Degas. "Didn't he ask you to come?"

Degas no longer looked at me, but at my canvas.

"If you are asking if I told him of your remarkable ability to paint, the answer is yes," said Édouard. "But no, *Made-*

*moiselle,* I did not, as you imply, bribe him to come here today to remark as such. He calls talent as he sees it and admires it, as he should."

"*Monsieur* Manet is too excessive with his compliments."

"I think not," said Édouard.

Maman let out a snore that echoed in the gallery. She stirred, but did not awaken.

"Do you show in the Salon?" Degas asked.

"I have in the past. This year I will not have time to get anything ready." I did not look at Édouard, because the statement made me think of all the time I'd squandered in his studio. And how it ended with me standing before him with my dress down, my defenses low, and his hands holding my body to his.

"It is too bad for them, but it is not a tragedy for you. The Academy rules the establishment with too lofty a hand. The art world needs something more than the Salon. We need an outlet that does not bind us to play by their rules."

"What else is there besides the Salon?" Manet asked.

Degas rubbed his chin. "That is what some used to say about studying outside of *l'École des Beaux-Arts*. But you, Manet, can attest to the fact that some very fine artists have come from outside the hallowed halls of *l'École*."

Manet nodded.

"The same will soon be said about the Salon."

Manet chuckled. "What? Do you think you can change the face of Paris's art world?"

Degas looked as if he would spit. "Not the face of art, just the manner in which it is viewed. *Mademoiselle,* Manet, would you be interested in discussing this at greater length?"

Manet shook his head. "I venture enough trouble with the Academy without organizing against the system."

"You, Manet, are a coward. *Mademoiselle,* are you interested?"

"I would love to hear more."

If Degas knew how to smile, I suppose he would've done so at that moment. Instead, he lifted his umbrella brows and nodded.

"I shall organize a luncheon at my home and send word. Until then, *bonjour.*"

He walked away, leaving us alone.

"Will you go?" Édouard asked. "If you do, I too will attend."

"*Monsieur* Manet, *s'il vous plaît.*" Please. I stood up. "You do not understand. We cannot do this. I cannot—"

"No, Berthe, *s'il vous plaît.* It is you who does not understand. What happened between us yesterday was not something I smirk at. Nor do I think less of you because of it. I think you are a talented artist who also happens to be a beautiful woman. Even if we cannot enjoy a relationship of pleasure, I hope we can share a friendship of equals. That is, if you are capable of such. If not, if you think less of me after what happened yesterday, then I beg you consider how you would label me if the tables were turned. It is only fair. You are welcome at my home and my studio anytime. *Bonjour, Mademoiselle.*"

Three days later, Maman and I attended Degas's luncheon. Édouard and I stood face-to-face once more. I did not think he would come after the way we parted at the Louvre. But there he was, and I was happy, despite myself.

As promised, Degas rallied his friends from the Café Guerbois to discuss such matters, but they moved the meeting to his home so I could join them, as it would not be proper for a lady to waltz into a café. I didn't understand what they might discuss at the Guerbois that would so offend my feminine sensibilities. I thought that someday I'd have a mind to walk into a café just for the sake of doing so.

Or perhaps not. When I thought about it, it didn't hold much appeal. It was hard enough convincing Maman that luncheon with six gentlemen in a private home was appropriate. I wouldn't test her further with talk of venturing into a café.

So there we were, seven artists and one irritated Maman, gathered together to talk about the dire state of the Parisian art community and how we—a group of virtual unknowns, plus one well-established rebel—could change the world.

I was not hopeful.

Besides Édouard and Degas, I sat with Camille Pissarro, Frédéric Bazille and Auguste Renoir, each of whom I'd never met, and Claude Monet, whom I remembered thanks to an error in the press a couple of years ago when his surname was mistaken for Édouard's because *Manet* and *Monet* were so close in spelling.

"Manet was not at all flattered to have some youngster poaching off his ill-gotten fame," Degas said, as we sat around the table enjoying bowls of steaming potato-leek soup. "He was peeved when Monet's mundane seascapes garnered more attention at the Salon than his latest outrage."

Monet grumbled over the *mundane* label Degas slapped on his work, but then laughed with the others. Édouard rolled his eyes. I wondered if he'd taken offense at being called old when Monet was not ten years his junior.

"Now, look at the lot of you," Édouard said. "Resorting to my old diversionary tricks, hoping to beat the system at its own game. You do me proud."

"Yes, Manet, and we are so pleased you changed your

mind and decided to join us today," said Pissarro. "When Degas said you declined, I thought you'd mislaid your rebellious streak. But here you are. Perhaps there is hope for this world after all."

Édouard's glance slid to me.

My stomach spiraled.

*Hope?* Perhaps.

We chatted over lunch. I picked at my food because my stomach was a jumble of nerves at seeing Édouard again.

But he was pleasant enough and sat next to me and made an effort to engage me in conversation. I could not help but believe he was sincere about wanting to be my friend.

After the intimacy we'd shared, all I could dwell on was that he would not be my lover.

Now, I found reassurance in how he wished to be my friend. If he were going to brag about his conquest he would have done so already, and the men at the table would not be talking to me as a colleague.

What happened between us was our secret. That secret was a sacred bond between the two of us. It seemed more precious than the illicit rendezvous we might have arranged.

"The art they show at the Salon is produced by trained monkeys," Monet said, when Degas's housekeeper, Zoë, served the apple tarts. "Each one copies one another, afraid to try anything new."

"It's true," offered Renoir. "Even the critics attest there was better work at the *Salon des Refusés* than in the Salon. When was the last time you saw an original piece exhibited?"

Édouard cleared his throat. "The Salon of eighteen sixty-three, artwork entitled *Déjeuner sur l'Herbe*."

He smiled at me and leaned back in his chair, his hands splayed on his vest.

"The critics deemed you a disgrace to morality," said Degas. "But at least it was modern. Other than your work, there's been nothing noteworthy since Delacroix and Ingres. We need to take control. Do something different."

"Striving to be different seems so artificial." I regretted the comment as soon as the words were born.

"She makes a very good point," said Édouard. "You must remain true to your soul. If you scribble on canvas like a monkey merely with the intent to be different, you are no better than the monkeys who conform to the system."

"It boils down to a question of modernity." Bazille's voice was big for such a quiet man. "It is time we stop living in the past and strive to bring modern art into the modern world. We must move forward and leave the past behind."

# Chapter Eleven

## January 1869

*I want to share*
*your air inhaling what you*
*exhale I'd like to be that*
*close two of us breathing*
*each other as one*
  —*James Laughlin, I Want to Breathe*

Impulse drew me to Édouard's studio. I'd not seen him in two weeks, since that day at Degas's home. True to his word, he left contact up to me. A very real part of me felt empty without him. After seeing him almost every day for the better part of a month, I missed him.

I took a chance calling alone, unannounced. Tempting fate after what came to pass the last time we were alone. But I was stronger. We were friends. There was always the possibility he'd not be in or wouldn't be alone. I decided to risk it because I would not know peace until I saw him again. If he was in, it would be fate's way of telling me I was supposed to be there. If he wasn't there . . . I'd turn and go.

I pulled my coat collar closed and sank my hands deeper into my muff as the carriage rattled over the Boulevard Malesherbes. The Café Guerbois was not far from there. I was tempted to ask the coachman to drive by, but a few restless snow flurries fell through the carriage window, and I shivered against the cold. As curious as I was to catch a glimpse of this exclusive male enclave, it would wait for another day. Maman was ill. I'd taken the carriage into the city to fetch a remedy from the apothecary. There was no one to accompany me, so I went alone.

The shop was just around the corner from Édouard's studio, and I could not resist dropping in to see him. To show him I harbored no ill feelings after what transpired a fortnight ago.

Heat rose up my neck at the thought. Yet, when I got out of the carriage, I could see my breath.

Before I contemplated my actions and lost my nerve, I climbed the forty-eight steps to the *atelier* and stood at his door.

I knocked, shoved my chilled hand back into my muff, my confidence wavering. But the door flew open so fast I gasped and wondered if he was expecting someone else, or going out—But, oh . . . the look that swept over his face when he realized who knocked at his door.

"*Bonjour,*" I said. "Were you leaving? I can call another time."

He wore a white button-down shirt tucked into trousers. His shirtsleeves were rolled to his elbows, and there was a splotch of crimson paint on his forearm. I was surprised to see him in casual attire. But it suited him. He looked *magnifique.*

"Even if I had an appointment with Napoleon himself, I should not go now that you are here. Come in, *Mademoiselle.* Please, come in. Oh, it is wonderful to see you. Would you believe I was just this minute thinking of you?"

"You flatter me."

"The truth is you have not left my mind since I saw you at Degas's table, more beautiful than the roses of the centerpiece."

I smiled and tried not to let myself be swept away on the wings of his flattery. He bowed, swept his left hand to beckon me inside. I followed, feeling as if my fractured soul were healing.

His studio was chilly, and I shoved my hands deeper inside my muff. "Why did you not light a fire? You will catch cold. Maman is ill. That is why I am out today. To fetch her medicine."

He stood there, a dazed smile on his face. "I am sorry your mother is unwell. If you are too cold, I will set a fire."

"Oh, no, please don't go to the trouble."

"It is no trouble. Normally, I would already have the stove blazing, but I have just arrived."

I felt victorious remembering the little deal I'd made with the heavens. It was a good sign to find him here. I could have missed him. If I'd called yesterday or perhaps tomorrow, I might not have found him in. As he started the fire in the *poêle*, my eyes searched all the familiar spots in the room.

The balcony set was still standing, and I was glad. I wanted to believe he left it up on purpose. But then again, it was not so long ago that he was working on the painting. Since the last time I was here. My gaze latched onto the dressing screen, and my stomach lurched at the memory of what happened that day. I looked away.

"How is the *Balcony* painting coming? You must be finished by now?"

"Almost. Would you like to see it?"

I nodded.

As he lit the fire, he indicated a canvas on an easel toward the back of the studio.

I turned it around so I could view it. I couldn't see much of a difference in Fanny Claus and *Monsieur* Guillemet's images. They looked the same as the last time I saw the painting. However, my likeness was even more detailed.

That was what they deserved for walking out on Édouard. My blood tingled, thinking of the time he spent perfecting my image, and I couldn't help but wonder what he thought of as he painted me.

Heat warmed my cheeks.

And there I was. Back again.

I set my muff on the sofa and started to remove my hat, but another canvas caught my eye.

Turned upside down and propped against the wall, was a portrait of . . . I cocked my head. Suzanne and . . . ?

I squinted at it as I walked over and lifted the small piece—only about seventy centimeters across and not quite as high. It was indeed Suzanne, a ghastly reproduction of her in profile, sitting at the piano looking as broad as she was tall and every bit the triple-chinned, dumpy hausfrau.

Even more shocking was the figure painted behind her. I turned the picture upright so I could view it, and recognized Édouard, slumped on a divan looking lost, staring into space with the unmistakable look of bored discontent.

The painting was bizarre and made me very uncomfortable, as if I were walking into the midst of a feud.

"Degas's handiwork," Édouard said.

He looked none too pleased, and I couldn't tell whether he disliked the unflattering nature of the painting or if he thought me nosy for picking it up.

"The man has some gall," he murmured and slammed the stove door.

I wondered if it was Degas's attempt to paint from modern life rather than romanticizing art—as his compatriots preached—or if somehow, it was a commentary on the state of the Manet marriage.

I believed it was the latter. The canvas was a gift. Why else would Édouard react so violently?

It was on the tip of my tongue to comment on the former—opening a discussion of Degas and Monet's ambitions to show outside of the Salon—when Édouard snatched the painting from my hands. Like a madman, he threw it on the easel and took a paintbrush to it, smearing an ochre rectangle down the far right quarter of the canvas, blocking out the piano and Suzanne's face. He left half her body visible as well as the image of him lolling on the couch. He also took care to leave Degas's little red signature scrawled in the bottom right corner.

"There," he said after he'd finished. "That should teach him."

I was stunned into silence.

He removed a still-life painting of a bunch of asparagus from the wall and hung Degas's family portrait in its prominent place.

The scene disturbed me on a level that knocked me off balance. Or perhaps what bothered me was that I'd come tempting fate when I knew better.

"I should go."

I walked to the couch and collected my muff and started toward the door.

"Stay. Please?"

I hesitated. I'd never glimpsed this angry side of him. It frightened me so much I wasn't sure it was safe to stay.

He must have read my thoughts. "I'm sorry. Degas makes me so angry. Sometimes he oversteps the bounds of appropriateness."

The spell was broken, and any fanciful thoughts I might have entertained were trampled under his tirade. I stood, wearing my hat and coat, clinging to my muff, as he poured tea.

"Come sit. I know you don't have much time, you must get back to your sick Maman, but please indulge me for fifteen minutes."

I removed my hat and coat and sat upon the big red divan, my dress puffed around me like a giant white cloud. I twisted toward him so that we might finish our conversation.

"Stay just like that," he said, picking up his sketchbook. He drew a few quick marks then got up, rummaged through a drawer in the chest across from the bed and pulled out a red fan—the same one I held in *Le Balcon*. He handed it to me. Stepped back to look, then knelt and tugged the hem of my skirt up so my black slipper showed.

"What are you doing?" I pulled my foot back, but he grasped it, and returned it to its original place.

"Don't move," he said. "I want to paint you just like this."

"Édouard, I must get back—"

"I know. Allow me a few moments to capture you just like this."

I could not resist. So I made small talk while he sketched, determined to lighten the air between us.

"I've come with news. My sister, Edma, is engaged to be married."

He smiled. "Is she?"

"I believe you know the fellow. Adolphe Pontillon?"

"Pontillon? You're joking? He's an old navy comrade of mine."

"He proposed just last week. We expected it sooner, but his military unit shipped out for a month. Our house is all aflutter with wedding plans and the such."

"When is the special day?"

"In late February or early March. They have not chosen the date just yet. I suppose with Edma's wedding, she will not be part of the new modern movement. Degas and company must make do with one Morisot." I stiffened at having uttered Degas's name, hoped it wouldn't push Édouard back into his black mood.

"Why?"

"Edma will give up painting once she marries."

"Why would she do that? Why would she throw away such talent?"

I'd asked the same question myself numerous times, and I was thrilled to hear him echoing my sentiments.

"Are you saying you would have your wife be a painter?"

"My wife is not a painter." He arched his brows. "But if my wife painted, I would be her greatest source of inspiration or I would not be doing my duty as a husband."

*There's implied meaning in that statement,* said Olympia.

Propriety ignored her.

His gaze lingered on my face and his hand paused, charcoal on the sketchpad. "You look so . . . so beautiful . . . in your white dress and black ribbon, sitting there with your cheeks flushed pink. I want to remember you this way always."

*See! See there?* said Olympia.

My pulse pounded. I desired him so much it was torture, and for that brief moment he was mine. We two were the only beings in the world. I savored the moment and its lush sensuality.

"Have you painted much these weeks that I've not held you captive in my studio?"

"*Oui.* I am concentrating on my copy studies at the Louvre, as I will not have time to finish something for the Salon jury to consider."

"Nonsense, if you work fast, you could have a masterpiece together well in time for the jury."

I shook my head. "It is doubtful, with Edma's wedding dominating every waking moment."

He frowned. "Do not let others distract you."

I lifted my eyebrows at him.

He laughed. "I saw that look on your face. How inconsiderate of me, *Mademoiselle,* to monopolize your time when I am warning you against just the such. I understand that you have work to tend to and precious little time in which to do it. It is not often a woman enraptures me. When that happens, the whole world slips away."

*What did I tell you?* said Olympia.

A sensation like a whirlwind lifted the pit of my stomach and took flight inside me.

"I do not mind. If I did, I should not be sitting here right now."

He smiled.

"So your sister is getting married," he said. "And you?" His words were so vague, I did not understand the meaning.

"Pardon?"

"Do you have a bridegroom on the horizon?"

"*Moi?* Getting married? Of course not."

"I am delighted to hear that."

"Why are you delighted that I should not give myself to another, Édouard?"

He did not answer me. I was not comfortable with the direction the conversation was taking.

"I should leave."

"Not yet. Please?"

I could neither stay in hopes of a companionable visit

nor could I summon the will to rise and take my leave. So I sat silently counting the beats between his looking at me and the paper as he drew. Until his eyes lingered on me, straying from the rhythm.

"You realize they're all mad for you."

"Pardon?"

"Especially Degas. I could tell what was on his mind when he came to the studio to see *Le Balcon*. And when he delivered that painting." He nodded to the altered canvas on the wall. "Beware of him, Berthe."

*Interesting, that is what Degas said about him,* said Propriety.

"You are angry over Degas's painting, Édouard. It has nothing to do with my friendship with the man. Please do not pretend that it does."

"It should not have anything to do with you, but he has made it so. He painted that portrait of Suzanne and me because of you, so that I would remember my place."

"Well, perhaps you should. You are married. Degas and I are not. He is my friend. And even if he is a little gruff, he is as safe as a kitten."

Édouard slammed down the sketchbook.

"He is the world's worst misogynist, and even if he were enamored with you, he is incapable of properly expressing it, much less loving you the way you deserve to be loved."

His words were well-aimed arrows that pierced my vulnerable heart.

"Pray, tell me, Édouard, exactly how is it that I deserve to be loved?"

He took my hand and pulled me up from the chair so we stood face to face. I believed for a moment he would kiss me, but he did not. I was more disappointed than relieved. He'd awakened something in me that would no longer sleep, something that longed for *more* and would not be satisfied with just the occasional visit where we fell into each other's arms, fearing we'd be discovered.

"We cannot do this," I murmured. Yet, he did not back away, did not release me. "You will not have me, yet you do not want anyone else to have me. It is the worst of inhumane treatment, Édouard, because I *do* deserve to be loved."

# Chapter Twelve

*Everything that was no longer exists;*
*everything that is to be does not yet exist.*
                    —*Alfred de Musset*

*February 1869*

*Dearest Berthe,*

*I have never once in my life written to you. It is therefore not too surprising I was very sad when we were separated for the first time. I am beginning to recover a little, and I hope that my husband is not aware of the void I feel without you. He is very sweet. Full of attention and solicitude for me. Please be happy for me.*

                    *Yours Always,*
                    *Edma*

*My Dearest Edma,*

*If we go on this way, we shall no longer be good for anything. You cry on receiving my letters, and I did just the same thing this morning. Your letters are so affectionate, but so melancholy, but I repeat, this sort of thing is unhealthy. It is making us lose what remains of our youth. This is of no importance for me, but for you it is different.*

*This painting, this work that you mourn for, is the cause of much sorrow and many troubles. You know it as well as I do.*

*Come now, the life you have chosen is not bad. You have a serious attachment, and a man's heart utterly devoted to you. Do not curse your fate. Remember it is sad to be alone; despite anything, a woman has an immense need of affection. For her to withdraw into herself is to attempt the impossible.*

*Oh how I am lecturing you! I do not mean to. I am saying what I think to be true.*

*Affectionately,*
*Your sister Berthe*

*March 1869*

I tried to pretend Edma was away on holiday without me, but I did not succeed in fooling myself into a better mood.

I had not seen Édouard since that cold January day at his studio. He did not come after me with a plea of friendship, and I did not seek him out only to have him tell me we would never be. I didn't trust myself alone with him anymore. I wouldn't throw myself at a man who did not want me.

I had a million tasks to tend to, important work left undone, as I helped Edma prepare for her marriage to Adolphe.

After all the celebrations surrounding the wedding, I was in no mood for a soirée where I was expected to assist Maman in playing hostess.

Alas, Maman was in a festive mood, having succeeded in marrying off her second daughter. She seemed on a mission to create a matrimonial trio. I suppose she believed she stood a better chance of striking a match for me if she cast me in the company of eligible men. So she'd taken it upon herself to invite every unmarried man I'd ever mentioned, including Eugène Manet, which meant she'd also extended an invitation to Édouard, Suzanne and *Madame* Manet.

They all came.

As well as Degas, Pierre Puvis de Chavannes and Fantin (who was still nursing heartbreak over Edma's nuptials), among others, including several unmarried men who worked at the ministry with Papa.

At least Maman was playing fair—an equal number of interesting, creative fellows to offset the dull business-minded professionals whom I feared would bore me until I nodded off as they rattled on about government, industry and finance and other dry subjects, which held no interest for me.

Without my dear Edma, I scarcely knew what to do with myself and hid in the kitchen helping Amélie.

It was an informal affair. *Hors d'oeuvres* and drinks, which Amélie ran herself ragged to prepare. Small consolation, it was not a dinner party. Still, I wondered why Maman could not just leave it alone.

She walked into the kitchen, set two empty wine decanters on the table and started barking orders. "Amélie, we need more canapés and the carafes need to be refilled. Please be more vigilant so that they are not drained empty. It looks bad when my guests must ask for refreshment."

The poor girl shoved a tray into the oven, wiped the perspiration off her forehead with the back of her hand and started filling a plate with *hors d'oeuvres*.

"Berthe, why are you in the kitchen when we have guests in the drawing room?"

I poured a bottle of wine into the carafe. "Because I prefer Amélie's company to the thirty intimate friends you have invited over tonight. Maman, I am sick to death of parties after all we have just been through for Edma's marriage."

"This soirée is for your benefit," she said. "Please come with me and be sociable. Perhaps you, too, will find a husband. There are plenty of eligible men out there. Surely there's someone who suits you."

*If you only knew, Maman.* I swallowed the urge to voice my thoughts and said instead, "I am not looking for a husband. Marriage is not something I will enter into unless I am in love."

Amélie banged the oven door shut.

"It is far better to get married with compromises than to remain independent and in a position that is no position at all," Maman quipped. "Within a few years what is left of your charm will pale, and all too soon, you will have far fewer friends than you have now. Tonight, you have your choice of any man in the room. Choose wisely, Berthe."

In other words, the bloom was wilting on the vine. I should present myself to be picked while picking was desired.

When I did not respond, she said, "Go along. You have not greeted the Manets. Please do make an effort, Berthe."

As Maman and I entered the drawing room, my gaze connected with Édouard's. It was true. I'd not yet spoken to him. It was the mark of a terrible hostess.

A young man whom I did not know—perhaps someone from Papa's office—played a lively Mozart concerto on the piano. As I made my way over to greet the Manets, I glimpsed Degas and decided to talk to him instead. I suppose a good hostess would have made obligatory greetings and not tied herself to one guest. But *hostessing,* as with *wifeing,* was not my strong suit, and I did not have the energy or the inclination to make the rounds. I opted for a long visit with Degas, whom I'd discovered was always good for a dry laugh. He, of all people, would see the irony in Maman's pitiful attempt to marry me off to the first man who would have me.

I stole a glance at Édouard, who stood near the door talking to Fantin.

So Édouard believed Degas to be mad for me. How ridiculous. But how convenient.

*"Bonsoir, Monsieur."*

Degas stood. *"Bonsoir, Mademoiselle.* How nice to see you this evening. I trust you have been well?"

We talked about our work, Edma's wedding and the progress he and Monet had made arranging a show independent of the Salon.

"Our most difficult task seems to be finding a gallery to host such an event. We've had no luck."

"Now that my sister's wedding is over, I would be delighted to help."

"That would be very kind of you." He reached into his coat pocket and removed a slender, rectangular object I soon recognized was a fan. "Here, I've brought you a gift."

I opened it and realized it was not just an ordinary fan, but an exquisite, hand-painted creation done in watercolor and brown ink. It portrayed a group of Spanish dancers and musicians.

"Did you paint this?"

He nodded. "You see here, it depicts the poet Alfred de Musset." He leaned in closer and pointed to the figure. I felt Édouard watching us as we talked. "You know of Musset, yes?"

I nodded. "The writer. He enjoyed quite a passionate liaison with *Mademoiselle* George Sand."

*"Oui,* this is she." He pointed to a figure drawn opposite Musset.

Degas's gift gave me pause. Why a painting of Musset and Sand? If I let my mind wander, I could pick out all sorts of insinuations—commentary on my affinities? Such as in the family portrait he presented to Édouard. But how would Degas know of my affinities?

Perhaps the watercolor told a tale of Degas's own desires?

The possibility made me shudder. No, that was not the case.

"Have you spoken to *Monsieur* Manet and Suzanne?"

"I have not." Degas swelled like a big toad. "He is no friend of mine."

"What is the matter?"

"*Quelle horreur.* He is a vandal, an ingrate. I gave him a gift and he defaced it. I presented him with a family portrait I'd painted myself. I go to his *atelier* to find he has painted over it."

I did not dare confess I was present the day Édouard did so. I also did not dare question the underlying meaning implied in the portrait and the fan. *Oh, Degas, what kind of innuendo?* I tapped the fan against my palm.

"Watch out for him," Degas said. "Manet cannot be true. He has a fickle heart and cannot be trusted."

His intimation made me uncomfortable. I did not like being in this position.

"*Monsieur* Manet is a gentleman."

"Come now, *Mademoiselle,* open your eyes. His behavior is reprehensible and it is as clear as the crystal chandelier that hangs from your ceiling. He has designs on you and others, and they are not so well hidden as he might think."

Degas's words knocked the breath out of me, but I managed to gasp, "That is an abominable thing to say."

"*Bonsoir,* Degas, do I hear you taking my name in vain?"

Édouard appeared, smiling. I was relieved because he could defend himself if Degas continued to persecute him. I would not be responsible for the task.

Degas talked on as if he'd not heard Édouard approach. "You claim Manet is a gentleman? Since when did he decide to spin moral fiber?" He turned in mock surprise. "Ah, Manet, speak of the devil."

Degas was angry, and after the display of temper I'd witnessed in Édouard's studio, I feared he might provoke Édouard and the two might brawl. "*Monsieur,* your timing is impeccable. Do please sit down. We were indeed talking about you."

"Were you?" Édouard took my hand, raised it to his lips and met my gaze. "*Mademoiselle,* it is a pleasure. It has been far too long."

"*Monsieur.*"

He lowered my hand and tapped the fan. "This is beautiful. A present from an admirer?"

"An ardent admirer," Degas purred. "Hand-painted expressly with the *Demoiselle* in mind."

The tone of his voice sent a most unromantic shudder up my spine that made me turn away from Degas.

"How have you been?" I asked Édouard.

His gray eyes seemed a couple of shades darker. He glared at Degas, who wore an irksome little smirk.

"I have been very well, *merci.* Busy, but well."

"I'm sure you've been quite occupied," Degas said. "What, with the beautiful *Mademoiselle* Gonzalés in your studio every day. How goes the painting of her?"

Édouard tensed. "It progresses."

"A new commission?" I asked.

"No," said Degas. "A new student. A lovely young creature at that."

I went numb. "I thought you were too busy to take on students?"

Édouard shrugged. "True. For the most part."

"Unless they are young and vivacious and ethereally beautiful," said Degas.

"This is the first time I have accepted a student in my *atelier*," Édouard stuttered. I'd never seen him so unnerved. "Her father is Emmanuel Gonzalés, the novelist. He asked me to give her lessons as a favor."

"She's quite gifted." Degas wheezed a dry, throaty laugh. "Not to mention twenty years old and stunning. She has huge—" Degas gestured at chest level, but gasped as if he realized his inappropriateness and moved his hands up to encircle his eyes, "—big, *big* . . . brown eyes that have made Manet the fool. Oh, and such a haughty will. The world grovels at her feet. Right, Manet?"

Édouard did not smile. In fact, he looked as if he were exercising great restraint to not strike Degas.

My breath stopped.

Fat Suzanne sat at the piano. She played her Chopin, eyes closed, as if she hadn't a care in the world. I could not decide if she was blind or stupid, or if she'd become so comfortable in her cushy station that she'd resigned herself to not give a damn about her husband's antics.

Whatever the reason, I'd grown tired of Degas and Édouard's antics. They seemed to enjoy stabbing at each other, but neither realized or cared that each lancing blow glanced off the intended and impaled me.

Enough!

I was finished playing the fool.

*"Excusez-moi, Messieurs."*

I slipped out the terrace door and headed to my studio. So the ethereal *Mademoiselle* Gonzalés occupied Édouard.

He'd replaced me with someone new, someone young and beautiful and more exciting than I.

I had no claim on Édouard, but how was I supposed to feel when a few weeks earlier he'd paid court to me with charm and devotion? But he did not follow through. Shouldn't that have been enough to prove he was a philanderer as Degas warned?

And I was a fool for believing there was something more in his eyes.

The full meaning behind Degas's words—*Manet cannot be true. He has a fickle heart and cannot be trusted*—dawned hard and fast.

I felt like an idiot, as if I'd not been paying attention and had painted myself into a predicament that could only be solved by starting anew.

Very well then.

*Mademoiselle* Gonzalés could have Édouard. My best defense would be to keep my distance from him.

In my dark studio, the air was quiet and lighter. I did not light a lamp, but stood alone in the darkness. The glow from the house shone bright, and I walked over to the window to look out at the night.

In that solitary moment it became clear that I'd failed at everything that mattered. I'd failed Maman by my unwillingness to compromise—to get married and give up my *hobby,* as she called it, for the respectable life of a proper lady. I'd failed myself by forgoing the Salon and nurturing feelings for a man I could not have. Worse yet, since meeting him I could not seem to finish a painting. I was floundering.

If I was going to be unhappy, why not resign myself to an unhappiness that made Maman happy? Why not go select the first man on whom my gaze landed and let him be the one? Through the window, I saw the party happening amidst the golden glow of candlelight. People eating and drinking, laughing and talking.

A solitary figure standing off from the crowd caught my eye. Eugène Manet stood alone. The party buzzed around him, yet he seemed a pillar of silence, keeping to himself.

Tears welled in my eyes. I knew I could no more go in there and choose a husband at random than I could escape my hopeless life by jumping the garden wall and running away.

I would be better off telling Maman I suffered a headache and calling it a night. Although, she'd be furious with me for leaving her to tend to the guests alone.

I picked up a clean cotton rag Amélie had draped over my easel and wiped my eyes. I glanced at Edma's easel, empty and abandoned in its usual place, as if she'd return any moment. It made my insides ache.

But just as Edma chose her path, I, too, had chosen mine. I never traveled the easy route. I should have known that about myself by now.

A faint knock startled me out of my thoughts. Édouard pushed open the door and stepped inside.

"Ah, so this is where you disappeared. I—"

"*Monsieur,* please. There is no point."

"Degas painted a most inappropriate picture of my arrangement with *Mademoiselle* Gonzalés. I must—"

"It does not matter. It is your business to settle with your conscience and your wife."

"She is nothing to me."

I knew I shouldn't, but I couldn't help myself—"Who is nothing—Suzanne or Eva?"

When he didn't answer, I whirled around to face him. He stood so close my shoulder brushed his chest. He did not step back. The edge of the windowsill pressed against my bottom. Golden light from the party cast his eyes the color of a stormy sea.

I do not know why I did it, out of desire or out of sheer anger for the way he'd trifled with me, but I leaned in and pressed my mouth to his, fast and hard.

His hands slid around my waist, moved up my back, raked into my hair, and he deepened the kiss.

His taste once so foreign was familiar, a taste I craved. It melted my determination and dissolved my defiance.

I pulled away and pushed past him without looking back and fled into the garden, running headlong into Eugène Manet.

*"Excusez-moi, Mademoiselle."*

He grabbed me to cushion the impact and for a moment we stood in an awkward embrace. Tucked into the fold of Eugène's strong arms, I felt Édouard's kiss fresh on my lips, the coarseness of his beard prickling my face. I jerked away from Eugène, half expecting Édouard to come barreling out of my studio.

Of course he did not.

He was much too suave to make such a grave mistake and give himself away.

Eugène steadied me with a hand on my shoulder. I stepped back. In the dim half-light of night I could see that he was flushed from our contact.

"Are you all right, *Mademoiselle?*" he asked.

"Yes, *Monsieur* Manet, I am fine. Please forgive my clumsiness. I was not watching where I was going."

"No, *Mademoiselle,* the fault is all mine."

We stood in awkward silence. Until he said, "Such a wonderful party. It is quite nice to see you. I have often thought of paying you a call, but . . ."

His voice trailed off and he stared at the ground, not at me. I could not help but compare his shy reserve to Édouard's brash boldness. My heart filled with such sadness, for a moment I feared I might dissolve into despair.

But I would not give Édouard the satisfaction.

Instead, I focused on the differences between the brothers. Eugène was taller than Édouard, gentler and more sincere in manner. I suppose it would have been a crowded house if two dominant personalities commanded the spotlight.

He offered his arm. "Shall I escort you back to the party?"

I remembered the soirée at his mother's home, that night he escorted me to dinner. Oh, how different things were then. A pang of remorse gripped me.

If I could go back and relive the weeks in between, would I change the outcome?

I shivered against the cool night air.

What was the use of pondering such nonsense?

"I would like that very much, *Monsieur. Merci.*"

I took his arm, and we walked to the house in heavy silence back to the party.

# Chapter Thirteen

## April 1869

*There is no excellent beauty that hath*
*not some strangeness in the proportion.*
*—Francis Bacon*

*My Dear Edma,*

*I see from your letter that you are enjoying the sunshine as we are, and that you know how to make the most of it. Spring is lovely; it makes itself charming even in a little, restricted corner of the earth like the garden. The lilacs are in bloom. The chestnut trees are almost so. I was admiring them a little while ago. Papa listened to me, then put an end to my enthusiasm by immediately forecasting the end of all these splendors.*

*I am wondering what I should do with my summer. I should be glad to come to you on condition, first, that it will not inconvenience you, and second, that I shall find opportunity to work. My inaction is beginning to weigh upon me. I am eager to do something at least fairly good.*

*I understand that one does not readily accustom oneself to life in the country and to domesticity. For that, you must have something to look forward to. I know Adolphe would not appreciate my talking in this way. Men are inclined to believe that they fill one's life, but as for me, I think no matter how much affection a woman has for her husband, it is not easy for her to break with a life of work.*

*Affection is a very fine thing on condition that there is
something besides, with which to fill one's days. This is
something I see for you in motherhood. Do not grieve
about painting. It is not worth a single regret. There is one
worry you are rid of. For the past month I have not seen a
single painter.*

*The Salon opens soon. I considered writing Manet a
note to ask him for an admission card. Alas, I hesitate to
do so.*

*I often imagine myself in your little home and wonder
whether you are happy or sad. I suspect you are both. Am
I wrong?*

*Affectionately,*
*Your sister Berthe*

Édouard called, but I was not at home to receive him. I
believed the fates made it clear there was no hope for us.
We could not pretend to be merely friends, yet I could not
put him out of my mind. Even in light of Eva Gonzalés.

Maman and *Madame* Manet's friendship made it in-
creasingly difficult to avoid him. I knew I could not evade
him indefinitely. The situation was hopeless, and I gave way
to despair. Maman believed there was something wrong
with me and tried to persuade me to see a doctor to treat
my malaise.

My spirits lifted when Degas dropped by with word that
Édouard's painting of *Mademoiselle* Gonzalés was not progressing well. Degas said Manet could not seem to get the
girl's face right. After more than a month's work, Manet
grew quite frustrated.

I supposed it meant Édouard and Degas had mended
their rift over the altered family portrait. What did Degas's
news say about Édouard and Eva Gonzalés?

★ ★ ★ ★ ★

*May 1869*

Imagine my trepidation about attending the Salon after not submitting work to the Salon for the first time in six years. At one point, I even contemplated forgoing the event altogether. But Édouard sent Maman a note, inviting us to the opening to view my likeness in *Le Balcon*. Celebration to follow at the Manet home immediately afterward.

Maman was as excited about the unveiling as if it were her portrait.

"After all the time I spent waiting while he created it, a piece of me is attached to it."

She'd developed a case of amnesia about the turmoil surrounding it. Given Maman's disposition, it was much better to have her embrace the occasion than not.

It had been two months since I'd seen Édouard. He called several times. But I managed to avoid seeing him with hopes that time would quell my feelings for him.

Although I did not know if I was ready to face him, I accompanied Maman to the opening, as an obedient daughter should.

At the Salon, on our way to room "M," a painting at the top of the grand staircase snared my attention, a piece by my friend Pierre Puvis de Chavannes. I stopped to admire it.

"Berthe, *Monsieur* Puvis de Chavannes is such a charming fellow. I have no idea why you do not encourage that acquaintance." Maman lifted her quizzing glass and looked at the painting. "No talent for art, but he is handsome and wealthy. A good match for you."

I did not answer her. Puvis might have been wealthy and handsome, as she called him, but he was too old. And his aristocratic air made him seem as old as the throne. Come to think of it, he was nearly twenty years my senior. He was Maman's age. No wonder she found him attractive.

I was not in the mood to debate. Thank heavens Carols Duran and his wife approached, and diverted her attention.

Soon we made our way to room "M" and were standing before Édouard's *Le Balcon*. He was nowhere to be found.

Maman stood much too close, viewing the painting through the narrow lenses of her quizzing glass. "Well, it looks much the same as the last time I saw it. One would think he would've finished it."

"Maman." I glanced around in horror, hoping no one heard her. "If this is how he chose to submit it, then it is finished."

"I am entitled to an opinion, and mine is that I do not think it looks finished."

I stared at the work in amazement. It looked larger than life hanging on the wall, in a prime location. Édouard had painted me in splendorous detail. Fanny looked dowdy. *Monsieur* Guillemet looked stiff, and. . . . He'd added the ghost of a new figure to the painting. Hovering in the open terrace doorway was the phantom image of a boy with a serving tray.

"*Bonjour, Madame, Mademoiselle.*" Degas sidled up to me.

"*Bonjour, Monsieur* Degas, Berthe and I were just commenting on Manet's painting. Rather unfinished, do you not agree? Oh, there is *Madame* Arneau, I must speak to her. Babette! Yoo-hoo, Babette."

The woman waved.

"May I entrust Berthe to your good keeping, *Monsieur?*"

"Of course."

"*Merci*, please excuse me." Maman hurried off and was swallowed by the crowd.

Arms crossed, Degas contemplated *Le Balcon.* "The painting is most definitely finished. So much so the epithet *'femme fatale'* has been circulating among the inquisitive."

"Pardon?"

Degas regarded me with his bored, intolerant expression that always made me fear his next word would be, "Imbecile!"

"People have branded you a *femme fatale, Mademoiselle.*"

I did not know how to respond. I snapped my gaze from his face back to the painting.

"An alluring woman." Degas spat the words as if they left a bad taste in his mouth.

"I know the meaning of *femme fatale, Monsieur.* It is just, I am more strange-looking than . . . alluring."

Degas's demeanor softened. "One could never brand your beauty strange. You are quite lovely. Léon . . . now he looks strange."

I glanced around, expecting to see Suzanne's son nearby. Yet I could not pick him out of the crowd. Degas's attention remained fixed on the canvas, a scowl wrinkled his forehead. Then I realized—"Is that Léon in the background of the painting?"

Degas arched a brow at me. "Who else?"

I squinted at the image. "Oh, I see." Actually, I did not see, but I would not admit it to Degas. "It is interesting how *Monsieur* Manet painted him. He is barely there."

"Barely there." Degas smirked. "That is a very good way to say it. I suppose that is how the Manet household would like him to be. If not absent altogether."

His words made me uncomfortable, and I recalled Edma's revelation that Léon was Édouard's son. Although Degas could shed some insight, I did not want to appear to perpetuate gossip. I would have to be subtle.

"*Monsieur* Manet does not care for his own godson?"

"Godson? Ha! Who told you Léon was his godson?"

"*Madame* Manet."

He snorted. "Yes, I am sure that is what she would have you believe." He wheezed a dry, humorless laugh. "Léon is no more Manet's godson than you are Edma's godmother."

What? What on earth was he carrying on about? The way he baited me, as if I knew nothing, grew so tiresome.

"I am well aware that Léon is Manet's son, *Monsieur*. But the boy is what—about fourteen years of age? Why did Manet wait so long after Suzanne gave birth to marry her?"

Degas's mouth twisted into a perverse little smile.

"That, *Mademoiselle*, is what everyone wonders, since he did not give the child the Manet name."

One arm wrapped around his middle, he stroked his chin with his free hand. "Of course there is the question of which Manet is the father. To keep things simple, the family prefers to refer to Léon as Édouard's godson. It cuts down on the nasty gossip, you see?"

No, I did not see. He was talking in riddles again. When he did this, I'd learned I was in for a wild ride before I discovered where his dramatic innuendos led.

Degas studied me with a look of sadistic amusement. "Can you not figure it out, *Mademoiselle?* Think about it."

"*Monsieur* Degas, *s'il vous plaît*. What are you saying? Just tell me." My exasperation bled through into my words. For all his good qualities, the man was quite enigmatic, and I was in no mood for games.

But before Degas could respond, Édouard appeared like an apparition, materializing out of the crowd with his mother, Léon and a young woman I did not recognize tagging along behind.

Degas leaned in. "Although I still do not understand

what compelled him to marry his father's mistress. He could have acted as the boy's godfather without going to the extreme of tying himself to a woman he does not love."

His father's mistress? Unfathomable. Had they shared her? Passed her about as they would a communal flask?

When Édouard saw me, he bypassed several well-wishers and came to my side. "Is this the *Demoiselle* of the hour?" He bowed and kissed my hand. "Ah, it is good to see you. You have kept yourself hidden away far too long."

My mind raced back to that night in my studio, and heat spread across my chest and up my neck. I uttered a silent prayer that no one would notice how flustered I was. Much to my relief, Édouard was busy greeting Degas.

"*Madame* Manet." I nodded to his mother. "Léon." And the boy. Léon returned the greeting and wandered over to examine a wall of paintings. *Léon is no more Manet's godson than you are Edma's godmother.*

What on earth did that mean?

"Berthe, my dear, you look lovely," said *Madame* Manet. "Everyone has given positively glowing reviews of *Le Balcon*. You do Édouard proud." She offered the compliment, distracted by the hordes buzzing around us.

It felt strange to receive praise for a painting that I took no part in creating other than to sit and stare into space. I didn't care for the passive role.

"She is my good luck charm," Édouard said. "I've already entertained an offer for the painting, although it pains me to think of parting with it."

The young woman pushed her way to Édouard's side. "I'm sure you will heal when the price is right." She was quite beautiful, and something in the way she looked at him made me a little shaky.

Édouard smiled and nodded a *touché*.

"*Mademoiselle* Berthe Morisot, may I present *Mademoiselle* Eva Gonzalés."

Oh—

"*Enchanté,*" she said. "You are as charming in person as you appear in the painting."

So this was the infamous Eva Gonzalés. She was quite poised for one so young. I would've ventured to guess not more than twenty years of age, if that old. Even at my age, I did not possess half the confidence she radiated. How had Suzanne taken to Édouard's little ingénue?

A pang of envy surged through me at her arriving with Édouard.

"*Merci,*" I said. "I understand you are the subject of his work in progress?"

Her brilliant smile faltered, but reappeared in the blink of an eye. She turned a knowing gaze to Édouard. "I believe he has put me on hold for the moment."

"Oh, *Monsieur* Manet, why?" I exaggerated my concern. I knew Édouard was well aware.

"Let me say the painting is not progressing as I'd hoped."

Eva tilted a defiant chin and turned her charm on Degas. I was just as happy because Édouard offered his arm, and we strolled past a few paintings.

"Have you just arrived?" I asked.

"No, we have been here since the opening. I was searching for you."

My breath caught. And I braced myself against the charm that always managed to weave its way into my defenses. I fortified my wall of self-preservation by reminding myself that I was merely a fresh dalliance. The bright, shiny Eva Gonzalés's company seemed a bit tarnished these days. Oh, the wonders a brief absence could work on the heart.

"How are the master and pupil getting on?"

He groaned.

"I am about to go out of my head. She is a very demanding girl. Chatters incessantly. Sometimes I believe she doesn't even draw a breath. I went to Boulogne last week to escape her."

"Then why do you not turn her out? Tell her you have too much work to do. I seem to remember you telling me that was your reasoning for not taking students in the first place."

"If it were only that simple. The good news is that her papa returns next week, and we shall discuss the situation. The change will benefit both of us. I believe she grows tired of this old man's company."

I glanced at my likeness from across the room. Its intensity startled me, and I paused to let the pins-and-needles effect subside.

"You painted a figure into the background of *Le Balcon*."

He turned, followed my gaze, and held himself a bit straighter.

"Yes, do you like it?"

I nodded. "Very subtle. It's Léon, no?"

"*Oui*. I thought the background needed a touch."

"Suzanne's *brother* is a fine looking boy."

Édouard nodded and turned his back to the painting to view a small landscape.

"Why does Léon not live with his parents?"

"His father is no longer living, and it is best for him to stay with Suzanne. Did you see Fantin's etching?"

I shook my head.

Léon's father was dead? Oh, well. *Someone* was not telling the truth. I wondered who?

"I am not surprised," he said. "The picture is hung so

high, I think people will strain their necks trying to view it. Poor man, not very good placement."

"Where is your wife tonight, Édouard?"

"She stayed at home. She does not care for large crowds. I suppose she will view the Salon after the first rush fades."

We lingered in front of the paintings we liked and muttered comments such as "ghastly" and *"quelle horreur"* under our breaths about those we loathed. My mind was only half on the critique.

Léon's father was dead . . . hmmmm? "When did you meet Suzanne?"

"Oh, many years ago. It was after I returned home from Rio de Janeiro, while I was in the navy. She taught my brothers and me to play the piano in exchange for room and board."

"Hmmm, I thought your mother said she came to France at the urging of Franz Liszt?"

"She did, but she fell upon hard times." He stopped walking and leveled me with a knowing look. *"Mademoiselle,* affairs do not always happen according to plan."

I could certainly attest to that.

"Then she met my father, who took pity on her and took her in."

"And when did you marry?"

Édouard narrowed his eyes, shot me a quizzical look. "October, five years ago. Why the inquisition?"

I shrugged. So Léon would have been eight years old when Édouard and Suzanne married. Why did he wait so long?

"Do you love her?"

Édouard blinked. A muscle in his jaw worked.

*"Mademoiselle,* she is my wife."

"I know she is your wife, but do you love her, Édouard?"

I was speaking in Degas-ish riddles, and I wondered if Édouard could decipher the core of what I was asking.

He ran a hand through his hair. "Love takes many forms, dons many guises. In fact, there is much speculation about the handsome, dark woman in *Le Balcon*. Just stand back and you will hear them wonder. Several have speculated that Manet is besotted with this enchanting beauty. Is she Manet's love? 'Does he love her?' they ask."

My breath caught as I awaited his answer. But a hand came down on my shoulder. *No! Not now,* I wanted to yell.

"Berthe?" When I turned, Maman's brow was stern and heavy. "You monopolize *Monsieur* Manet's time. I am sure many are eager for his attention. Why don't we take a turn about the Salon and view the rest of the show?"

"Does he?" I asked Édouard, ignoring Maman.

"Without a doubt, *Mademoiselle*."

He bowed to my mother. "*Madame* Morisot, I should be delighted to take a turn about the Salon." He offered his arms to us. "Shall we?"

# Chapter Fourteen

*Let me not to the marriage of true minds*
*Admit impediments. Love is not love*
*Which alters when it alteration finds,*
*Or bends with the remover to remove,*
*O, no! It is an ever-fixed mark,*
*That looks on tempests and is never shaken;*
*—William Shakespeare, Love's Not Time's Fool*

Maman excused us from the Manets' after-Salon soirée, claiming a headache. In the carriage afterward, her anger flowed like spilled red paint.

"I see what is going on, Berthe." Maman frowned. "I am no idiot. Neither are the revelers spouting *femme fatale* and *lovers*. Lovers, Berthe? Is that what you wanted people to think as you paraded around the Salon with him?"

*You don't care what people think,* spouted Olympia.

*Don't you dare admit that to your Maman,* said Propriety. *You should be ashamed.*

Propriety won. I remained silent.

"I encourage you to go to Edma in Lorient until this nonsense blows over. The change of scenery will suit you, and I do hope time away will quash any improper notions you might harbor about encouraging *Monsieur* Manet's attention."

I didn't argue with her. Édouard's confession and the Salon speculation frightened me, and I needed time to put everything in perspective. Was he sincere? If so, what did I

151

want? My heart overflowed with hope and longing, and it clouded the good sense that warned me to tread in this realm with caution.

Going to Edma in Lorient was the best solution. I missed my sister and wanted to see her. Adolphe was away. It would suit us to have some time together. The fresh air and sunshine would clear my head. I was ready to paint, to be productive. Rather than brooding over not showing in the Salon—or worse yet, dwelling on my place in Édouard Manet's life—I was more determined than ever to occupy myself with a worthwhile endeavor.

Lorient was a wisp of a town. One might overlook it if not for the harbor. Compared to Paris, it seemed a lifeless place. Adolphe's naval duties brought him there. The giddy newlywed, Edma, followed without a second thought.

I stepped off the train—the lone passenger to disembark—and sensed the monster driving Edma's madness. All browns and grays, it was a pitiful place. Few trees and even fewer flowers. As I stood alone on the platform, inhaling the sharp, briny air, I wondered for a moment if I was the only person awake—or even breathing—in this awful place.

Edma rounded the corner of the depot, a blur of yellow dress and dark hair, her skirts kicking up in her haste.

"Berthe, you're here. Oh, you're here." Breathless, she embraced me as if the harder she held me, the more she'd regain of the life force drained from her over the two months she'd languished. "Your train is early. I wanted to be here when you arrived."

"I have only just turned up." I pulled back to look at her. "Oh, how I have missed you."

"And I you."

My eyes welled. I blinked to keep tears from spilling

onto my cheeks. As the train chugged away, it seemed to blow a tedious sigh at the sheer dullness of the place.

It was dry and warm for April. The sun had baked the dirt street into a pattern of desiccated cracks. The carriage rattled along the naked, dusty path through the center of town. The harbor's gray water sat as listless as a sheet of glass, reflecting Lorient's dull palette of non-colors from the anchored boats and the short, sandstone wall that snaked along the waterfront like a dead serpent. In the distance, the sea roared, low and discontented.

Edma's house was but a short walk from the station, but she'd hired a hack to collect my trunks and valise. When I left Paris, I was not sure how long I would stay, so I packed for the long-term. The length of my visit would depend on how long Adolphe was away and how much work I could accomplish. But the sight of my dear sister pleased me so, once the carriage arrived at the modest, white two-story house Edma called home, leaving was the furthest thing from my mind.

"Here we are." A hint of humility whitewashed her words. She hesitated at the front door and plucked a dead bloom off a riot of red geraniums planted in the window boxes and let the withering petals fall to the ground.

"I hope you will be comfortable here."

"Edma, with you, I should be comfortable in the wild. As long as we are together."

Her mouth curved, but the smile did not extend to her eyes. She opened the front door, and we stepped inside.

Pausing in the entryway, I blinked, coaxing my eyes to adjust to the darkness, eager for a first glimpse of my sister's new life—the faded, light blue paint adorning the vestibule; the scuffed wooden floor; and most curious of all, "Edma, there is not a single painting on your walls. Why not?"

She frowned and looked about, as if noticing the discrepancy for the first time.

"I will send for some of my canvases in due time, but I need to figure out what will best suit this place." She took my hat and gloves and set them on the wooden table in the entryway. "You might say the house and I are still getting acquainted."

She looked down as she spoke. Not only had she quit painting, it seemed she'd divorced herself from art.

The driver stood behind us with one of my trunks hoisted up on his shoulder.

"Where shall I deposit this, *Madame?*"

"Please take it upstairs," Edma said. "The first bed-chamber on the right."

"Edma, why didn't you tell me? I could have brought your canvases."

She threw her arms around my shoulders and sobbed. "Oh, Berthe, I am so unhappy. Adolphe is always away. If this is married life, I—"

She buried her face in my shoulder and wept.

I patted her back, "Hush now," took her by the shoulders and held her out so I could see her. "I am here now. You suffer from too much solitude, that's all. Everything will be fine."

She wiped her eyes. The tears welled and spilled. "I don't know what is wrong with me. I'm sorry. You are here, and all I can do is cry like a baby."

"I do not want to hear another word of it."

I put an arm around my sister's shoulder and walked her into the sitting room. The driver's footsteps descended the stairs and stopped at the front door. He cleared his throat before calling a hearty, *"Bonjour, Madame, Mademoiselle."*

Edma held both hands to her face and swiped at her

eyes. I grabbed my handbag and settled with the man while she pulled herself together.

By the time I finished, Edma recovered.

"I suppose you are hungry," she said. "I'll ask Dominique to fix your lunch."

"No, Edma. You know how travel always upsets my system. I'll take a cup of tea and that will be fine."

She smiled, seemed relieved. "I've no appetite. The sight of food nauseates me. So if you are hungry, do not hesitate to ask Dominique to prepare you something."

"Edma, do not make a fuss. I will be all right now that I am here with you. Everything will be all right. What I would like more than anything is for us to sit down and catch up."

The waterfront was the only place interesting enough to consider painting. I arranged Edma on the short sandstone wall. Her pink scarf and blue-green umbrella added color and softened the hard lines of the harbor, bringing a spark of life to the dreary scene.

"Put your right hand on the wall," I said. She complied and smiled. Her mood was lighter. Although she still refused to pick up a paintbrush.

"That is no longer my life," she said. "There is no sense in adding to my frustrations."

I started to argue with her as I sketched the scene in long, broad charcoal strokes, but she cut me off.

"All too soon I will have much more to keep me busy."

I squeezed a dab of cobalt blue onto my palette. The new metal tubes were so much more convenient for painting on location than the old-fashioned pigs' bladders in which we used to store paint.

"I thought Adolphe was not returning for three months."

I added some vermilion and a smear of lead white to the

array, mixing them together to match Edma's scarf.

"That is right. He'll ship out again less than a fortnight later. My future occupation is a bit farther coming. Still, I have much to prepare." She patted her belly. A weary smile tugged at the corners of her mouth.

"Do you mean—"

She nodded.

I set down my palette and ran to her. No wonder she was so melancholy about being alone.

"You're with child?"

I hugged her again and again.

"I am not certain, but all indications point that way."

"Why did you not tell me last night?"

"I made up my mind not to say anything until I was sure. I've not even told Adolphe or Maman, for that matter. I shouldn't have told you until I knew for certain." She put a hand on her belly. "But I know in my heart."

"And I should have been furious if you had not shared it with me."

We laughed. "Please do not mention it until I have told Maman. You know how she gets. It would be a disaster."

I hugged her again.

"I am going to be an aunt. Oh, I cannot believe it. *Tante* Berthe. I love the sound of it."

I picked up my charcoal and Edma resumed her pose. As I watched her sitting there, a beautiful pink rose amidst the lifeless gray backdrop of still water and empty boats, a bittersweet pang pulled at me. I glanced at Edma's belly. A child was growing inside my sister, just as Édouard's son had grown inside Suzanne.

A seed planted by love.

Tangled in the myriad of emotions that had surfaced since Édouard's confession, part of me ached for the child I never knew I wanted until he came into my life.

Looking at my sister, so full of life, it was quite clear she'd moved on with her life.

This was how I decided to paint her: with her back to the cold, ugly harshness of the world. A blossoming rose thriving in the prime of her life.

*My Dear Bijou,*

*Your father seemed to be deeply touched by the letter you wrote to him. He appears to have discovered in you unsuspected treasures of the heart, and unusual tenderness toward him.*

*In consequence, he often said he misses you. But I wonder why. You hardly ever talk to each other. You are never together. Does he miss you then, as one misses a piece of furniture or a pet bird? I am trying to convince him to the contrary, that it is much better not to see your poor little face bewildered and dissatisfied over a fate about which we can do nothing. It is a relief. This is what we have come to think, and we conclude that it is much better for you to be with Edma. That you two should remain together for a while.*

*I visited Manet, whom I found in greater ecstasies than ever in front of his model Gonzalés. He did not move from his stool. He asked how you were, but I suspect he has forgotten all about you for the time being. Mademoiselle Gonzales has won all of Manet's attention. She has all the virtues, all the talent, all the charms. She is an accomplished woman.*

*Last Wednesday there was nobody at the Stevens's except Monsieur Degas who sends his regards.*

*That is all for now,*

*Maman*

I crumpled Maman's letter. Wasn't she content with four hundred kilometers separating Édouard and me? Why was she still so afraid of what might happen that she found it necessary to rub my nose in the fact that he'd forgotten me in my absence? That Eva Gonzalés held him captive in her spell?

Yes, I was wise to come to Lorient, to get away from him and the magic spell he'd cast on me.

I stood at the window and gazed out at the harbor, at the lonely boats and the still, glassy water. I once read that water symbolized life. But here it seemed dead. Perhaps it was an omen? The death of dreams.

In Paris, the city breathed for you when you wished to give up. It gave you no choice but to live.

I thought perhaps I would succumb to Lorient's death-call and stay there with Edma forever.

After four full days of work on the canvas, the painting came to life. Edma, too, seemed excited by it. I enjoyed her company. The weather was exquisite, and she insisted on accompanying me every day to the harbor to pose.

"Berthe, this is almost as good as being in the company of our friends. I have so missed the Salon."

I did not tell Edma of Édouard's confession. I tried to put it out of my mind, but Edma wanted details of the Salon. She hung on every word, nourished by my recounting of the evening.

"Did I mention I spoke to Puvis on opening night?"

Edma shook her head. "You said you spent most of the evening with Édouard."

"Ah, yes, he was in such high spirits, quite excited by Paris's reception of *Le Balcon*. For about an hour he led Maman and me all over the place, when I ran headlong into

Puvis, who seemed very happy to see me.

"Puvis tried to persuade me to meet him at the Salon again the next day since he couldn't stay that evening. While I talked to Puvis, Maman talked to friends. I completely lost sight of Édouard. I was mortified. Puvis left; Maman was lost in the crowd; Édouard had wandered off. I did not think it proper to walk around alone. It was embarrassing. When I found Édouard, I reproached him for leaving me."

"You didn't," said Edma.

"I did."

"What did he say?"

"He was quite put out. He told me I could count on all his devotion, but nevertheless he would never risk playing the part of my nursemaid."

"You're joking?" Edma laughed, a great big guffaw, which tickled me. Oh, how I loved the sound of my sister's happiness. It warmed me like a summer day.

"Sounds to me as if *Monsieur* Manet was none too pleased to see Puvis," she said. "Did they speak?"

Her insinuation made me smile. I mixed cobalt blue, Naples yellow and emerald green to match the tone of her umbrella.

"They were cordial, exchanged polite words, but the next thing I realized, Édouard was gone."

Edma twirled her umbrella. "My, my, what a temper if he is not the center of attention. I must confess my infatuation with Manet has ended. Do not let him discourage you from forming an attachment to Puvis."

I glanced up at her, surprised. "Oh, it is not like that."

The conversation trailed off. Edma's expression grew wistful, tipping her face into the warm breeze.

"Berthe? Do you remember what I said to you that day

we walked along the *quai?*"

I nodded and deepened a shadow on the canvas. "About my taking a lover?"

Edma blushed and looked out to sea. "Marriage is quite . . . well, it is a lot different than what I imagined. I never meant to mislead you. Perhaps suggesting a relationship with Manet was not—"

"What makes you think I could be so easily misled? Forget that nonsense." I tried to ignore the way my stomach pitched at the mention of taking Édouard as my lover and focused on my canvas—the results of my four days of diligent labor. Never had I been so pleased with my work. Maybe it was the energy pent up during my months of idleness that culminated in this piece. But I felt as if I were home. "It feels sublime to be on track again. I would so much rather produce one good work than an entire Salon full of mediocre scribbling."

She looked as if she wanted to say more, but instead uttered, "Good, then shall we call it a day? My back hurts from sitting on this hard wall."

"Yes, let's go. We've been here a long time."

I felt guilty talking about my triumph in the face of Edma's artistic purgatory.

But why? She carried a child—the thought took me by surprise and sent little shivers down my spine. Maybe Edma was home, too? Was it so bad she didn't wish to pick up a brush again? Perhaps she'd consider adorning her walls with a few canvases. I would paint her something new before I returned to Paris. I considered leaving the one of her at the harbor, but I wanted to hang onto it and submit it to the Salon next year. It was one thing to be rejected, but it made me quite disgusted with myself to know I hadn't even tried this year.

Inaction—the worst of diseases.

I glanced at the painting as we walked up the dirt road. In a way it was symbolic—everything that was meant to be always worked out as it should. Edma had a baby on the way. I had my painting.

"Who is that?" Edma said.

"Who?"

I shaded my eyes and followed Edma's gaze up the road to the porch of her house and saw the figure of a man sitting on the front steps.

At first I could not see because the sun was in my eyes. At four o'clock, the light was on its downward grade in the western sky, silhouetting the visitor. Without trees, the unfiltered light played havoc on my vision, and I thought maybe Adolphe had returned home early.

I squinted and for the span of a beat, my heart stopped. *No, it couldn't be—*

"Édouard?" I whispered.

My blood tingled and my head swam. Surely, the light was playing tricks on my eyes.

"Oh. I do believe it is he." Edma slowed, but I quickened my pace as well as I could lugging a large canvas and easel. As I drew closer, Édouard stood and removed his hat.

"*Bonjour, Madame* Pontillon. And *Mademoiselle* . . . I am so happy to see you. I feared I'd missed you after coming all this way."

He stepped forward and relieved me of my easel. I was self-conscious of the work that had so thrilled me only moments ago. I angled it away so he could not see it.

"*Bonjour, Monsieur.*" Edma's words sounded quite formal. She set my paint box down on the step. "I hope you have not been waiting long. We have been out making the most of this beautiful day."

He smiled. "You look well, *Madame.* I have just arrived. *Mademoiselle,* I am happy to see you have been working. Please, may I see what you've created?"

He'd come.

I hesitated, gripping the edges of the canvas with both hands, careful not to smear the wet paint. The breeze lifted the scent of the oil and it reminded me of the last time I was in his studio. Why? It was the same pungent scent that surrounded me most every day of my life. But it personified him.

He reached out and with a careful hand turned the canvas toward him. He was quiet for a moment, then a slow smile spread over his face.

"This is a masterpiece."

I recalled a time Degas remarked at how Édouard admired the work of all of his friends, and once Maman warned me to beware of the difference between a man's personal compliment and his professional evaluation. Yet, my heart lifted like a leaf soaring on the breeze.

"You possess such talent," he said. "I stand in awe of you. I would be glad to have this in my personal collection. Name your price."

Edma regarded him silently.

I took a step backward, because it felt as if he were standing much too close. "*Monsieur,* your praise is excessive. I cannot sell this to you. The paint is not even dry." I stammered, and I hated myself for it.

"What brings you to Lorient, *Monsieur?*" Edma asked, as if sensing my agitation. Her bemused expression suggested a mere fraction of the feelings coursing through me.

"What brings me here? Why *Mademoiselle* Berthe, of course."

My skin tingled.

Edma made a disapproving noise. She stood there for an awkward moment as if she didn't know what to do. "Well, if you will excuse me, I shall check on dinner."

She did not invite him to stay. The door clicked shut behind her, but opened again. Edma stuck out her head out. "Please do come in—when you're ready."

She disappeared inside, leaving me alone with Édouard.

# Chapter Fifteen

*The stars and the rivers and the waves call you back.*
                    *—Pindar, Greek—Lament*

Light the color of amber glass reflected off the lone tree in
my sister's yard. As Édouard and I stood on Edma's porch,
the glow deepened into a rich shade of burnt umber where
the setting sun reached through the leaves to caress the
branches and trunk. Twilight always made me wistful—
melancholy even—homesick for places I'd never been, achy
for some *indefinable thing* I could never put my finger on.

Édouard offered his arm. "Shall we walk?"

"That would be lovely." I laced my arm through his, and
I felt akin to the light—I was all at once mellow and fluid
and warm.

That evening as I strolled with him, I found that *indefinable thing* for which I'd longed my entire life.

We walked in silence for a while before I asked him,
"Why did you come?"

"You disappeared from Paris. I thought you would write
to me. But I waited in vain. I resorted to sending Fantin to
your Maman to do a bit of detective work to discover your
whereabouts. Now, here I am."

He placed his hand atop mine in the crook of his arm.
He'd gone to such lengths to find me. If Maman's letter
were true, I wondered how he escaped enchanting Eva's
death grip.

"Maman wrote that you have been quite enraptured with

*Mademoiselle* Gonzalés. I did not write because it sounded as if you did not have a spare moment to read a letter."

Édouard narrowed his eyes. His brows knit into a bemused frown.

"That is not true. Would your sister mind if we were gone so long as to take a turn about the harbor?"

I shook my head. "There is no one within four hundred kilometers who will mind."

Again, we strolled in silence. I wondered what he'd told Suzanne of his trip to Lorient. If he told her. And how long he planned to stay. Did he intend to ask Edma for a room for the night? I was not certain she would be amenable to that request.

Question upon question swirled in my mind, but Maman's comments about Eva Gonzalés surfaced, pushing other queries to the side.

"Relations are going well with *Mademoiselle* Gonzalés?"

He shrugged. Then after a moment's hesitation, shook his head. "No. As I told you at the Salon, she is very young and demands constant attention." He wrinkled his brow as if the mere thought pained him. "I do not have the time or patience for her."

"Is that so? Maman wrote—Let's see, how did she put it? That she found you in greater ecstasies than ever in the presence of the captivating *Mademoiselle*."

"I do not mean to dispute your good Maman's word, but *au contraire*. When she visited my studio, I was working like a madman to finish the *Mademoiselle*'s portrait." He waved his hand in disgust. "I have done as much as I intend to do with it. Yesterday, I informed her papa that the arrangement is finished."

I tried not to smile. Tried to stroll along as if we were discussing the weather and other banalities. But I found myself enraptured by the strange pleasure of standing so close to him—in public, without fear of happening upon an acquaintance who would delight in telling the world of the scandal she'd witnessed.

His hand was still on mine, tucked in the crook of his arm. Those we passed regarded us as if we belonged together—man and wife out for a stroll on this beautiful, warm spring evening. We did not see many people, but those we passed smiled and tipped hats in gracious greeting. Édouard held himself in an erect manner that suggested he was proud to be seen with me.

I experienced the sensation of knowing what it was like to belong with him. Yes, it would be like that if we were married.

I stopped wondering why he'd come to Lorient, leaning in a little closer to breathe in the familiar smell of him—the lingering scent of peppermint, wool and man. For a few beautiful, timeless moments we were one, and I lost myself in the blissful illusion as we walked together toward the harbor.

The air smelled of a salty sweetness I'd not realized before. Mmmmmm . . . was that lavender in the air? A hint of rosemary? Looking again at the cracks in the road, I recalled the first day I set foot in Édouard's studio, when the air smelled fresh and the world felt new and full of possibilities.

Before we reached the water, he veered off the parched road past a row of identical white plaster houses to a grassy knoll I'd never noticed.

We stopped at the top of the hill beneath the shelter of a weeping willow tree.

Dust motes danced in the fading golden sunlight that filtered through the tree's flowing branches, highlighting the new green that mingled with patches of the lingering winter brown.

He sat on the grass and tugged me down next to him. My stomach pitched because I thought for an instant he might kiss me. Instead, he settled back on his elbows and gazed at me, through half-open eyes, his leg touching mine.

I arranged my skirt around me, more for the sake of diversion than appearance. When I glanced up, it was obvious that he liked what he saw, but the intensity with which he studied me made me uneasy, as if he were comparing me to every woman he'd ever beheld.

I did not mind holding myself up to contrast when the competition pertained to something within my control, but I'd always shied away from contests of a personal nature because the rejection that followed hit too close; it was too private. I could always fix a problem with a canvas, paint with different colors or in different venues, but I could not change the person I was.

And that was fine, for I'd never desired to be anyone else—especially when I was with him.

It was much easier to turn away before a suitor's interest faded. That way I never needed to watch the interest dim. It never became personal. They never came back. Never pursued or tried harder. It was for the best, for the relationships would have crumbled and fallen away in due time.

A flock of birds screeched as it flew by in formation.

But Édouard—he was steadfast and persistent. He kept following. No matter how fast I walked away, I would turn around, and he'd be there.

"I enjoy looking at you." His voice was a husky timbre. He shifted closer to me. "I enjoy being with you."

I was exhilarated and frightened all at once.

What would he do if I reached out and took what I

wanted, like a common whore? That was how Suzanne captured him—although it was hard to imagine her being so bold.

Édouard and I shared the same madness, the same visions, the same disgust for imposters who claimed to paint the truth. That was how we came together—in truth and beauty. Not by one snagging the other. Not by trapping him into a life together by virtue of a child.

"Why do you call Léon your godson when he is your son?"

Édouard sat up, but did not meet my eyes.

"He is not my son."

Annoyance bubbled inside me, threatening to burst into full-blown distaste.

"You do not have to pretend with me, Édouard. I know that is why you married Suzanne."

I reached up and turned his chin so he looked me in the eyes. He seemed to pale a shade.

"No, that is not why I married Suzanne."

"Why then?"

"It is complicated, and I do not want to spoil our time together by talking about it."

"Does it mean you love her?"

He covered his face with his hands and rubbed as if he could wipe away my question.

*If he won't answer, will you stay with him?* said Propriety. *You really shouldn't stay with a man who's not forthcoming.*

I got to my feet and started to walk away.

"Wait. Please, do not go."

I stopped, but didn't turn around. "You love Suzanne. I will not compromise myself."

I took a few more steps.

"That is not it. Please stay, and I shall tell you."

I returned to my seat beside him, leaving more distance than before. Once I was settled, Édouard sighed and looked at me as if he might shed a tear.

"I have never shared this with anyone outside my family." He plucked a blade of grass and smoothed it between his fingers, glanced up at me again. "Léon is my brother."

I gasped disbelieving. "I do not understand."

He swallowed, and his throat worked through the emotion.

"When I was in the navy, my father fell in love with a young woman . . ." He hesitated and picked at the grass again. "That young woman was Suzanne."

I held my breath. He stared at his hand and worried the piece of grass for a moment. Then he recaptured my gaze and held it.

"He was married to my mother. She gave him three sons. He would not leave her. So he brought Suzanne into our home to teach my brothers and me piano. My mother did not like it, but she would not go against her husband's decision. About eight years before my father died, Suzanne gave birth to a son. It was all very hush-hush. My father sent her back to Holland before she became heavy with the child. She returned with her baby brother. My mother was livid. She did not want Suzanne to return, did not want her in her home, but my father was heartsick without her.

"He even contemplated leaving to be with Suzanne, until my mother relented and agreed to Suzanne's return. It would have been a scandal had he divorced my mother or if he'd given the boy his name, so everyone played along that Léon was her brother."

He paused and drew in a ragged breath.

"Six years ago my father died. My mother had no tolerance for Suzanne and was ready to throw her and the boy out into the street.

"I could not talk sense into her. It was as if all the anger she'd harbored over all the years had broken loose.

"Suzanne and the boy had no place to go—no money, no friends. She's a good soul, Berthe. Even if I'd given her money, what kind of existence would she have been able to provide for the child?

"So I married her."

I sat in stunned silence, clenching a fistful of skirt. Then he reached out, and traced a finger along my cheek. "I was thirty-two years old. I thought I might as well save her from a horrible fate. Because I'd never been in love . . . Berthe, I'd never loved until now."

My breath came in shudders. His hand trailed from my cheek, down my neck, my shoulder, my arm, grazing my breast. The caressing sweep rested on my thigh.

"I love you, Berthe. I have since the first day I saw you. Sometimes I fear I might go crazy for wanting you."

I looked at his hand on my leg, at the broad fingers and short clean nails. Most painters had rough, dirty hands.

His were clean.

My throat was too tight. A fullness blossomed in my belly and left me breathless until tears came to my eyes, spilled out onto my cheeks.

Like me, he'd never loved. Until now.

I place my hand on his. He spread his fingers so mine fell alongside his. He closed his hand snug around mine and pulled my fingers into his palm, taking possession.

If a person asked me why I loved him, I would have asked why was the sky blue? Or why did honey taste sweet? My feelings for him were as organic as the willow tree above us, running deeper yet than its roots below us.

And he felt the same for me.

He leaned in and kissed me, full and gentle. His tongue parted my lips and thrust deep inside my mouth, a tender urgency that compelled me to melt into him. He tasted of passion and peppermint, just as I remembered.

He eased me back onto the grass, and I knew my life was about to change.

There was no turning back.

I'd never had a man's hands upon my body, until his.

I'd never known a lover. But I would now.

As we lay fully clothed with the sun setting over the western harbor, darkness set in, cloaking us in a veil of indigo night. His hard body moved atop mine, and I felt I would burst from sheer need if he did not take me.

When it came to it, he hesitated, pulling back, looking deep into my eyes.

"Are you sure, Berthe? My love."

My breath caught at the sound of my name passing his lips.

"I do not want you to do anything you do not—"

I pressed a finger to those lips. "Shhhh, I want nothing more."

I pulled him to me, and he answered with a groan that escaped his kiss. Then he shifted to the side and lifted the skirt of my red dress and my petticoats, exposing my bare legs. Somewhere along the way my shoes fell off, but I didn't recall when or where. I forgot them and lay in glorious half-nakedness watching him undo his trousers to free himself.

He stroked my abdomen down to my inner thighs, caressing my womanhood until the bleakness that tethered me for as long as I could remember released, and my spirit rose up inside me like a giant balloon and burst.

I cried out.

"You are so beautiful," he whispered before his mouth came down on mine and he entered me.

# Chapter Sixteen

*I love in you a something
That only I have discovered—
The you—which is beyond the
You of the world that is
admired by others*

—*Guy de Maupassant*

A full moon hung in the sky as Édouard walked me back to my sister's house. Lying with him under the weeping willow tree, watching twilight give way to a curtain of night as the moon climbed high, time seemed as irrelevant as the number of stars dotting the beautiful, indigo sky.

I could have been content to stay under that tree, naked in his arms, forever—talking, laughing, loving again and again. Alas, he pulled me to my feet, helped me into my dress, and we walked down the hill, warm in the cocoon of our new love.

My canvas and paint box were still on the porch. I moved the painting out of our way to give us room.

"Please come in," I said. "Edma will let you stay the night."

He shook his head. "I should not want to prevail upon your sister's kindness." He took my hands. "And I would not be content to sleep alone in a cold bed with you so nearby. I shall stay at the inn and take the train back to Paris tomorrow."

Knowing I could not go to the inn with him, a hundred

173

horrid questions flooded into my mind. Why must he leave? Would I see him tomorrow before he left? If not, when would I see him again?

*What's next, Édouard?*

Panic, cold and sharp, stabbed my insides, and I wondered how he could stand there so calm when I was coming undone.

He nodded toward my canvas of the harbor. "It is a masterpiece. Every time I see that painting, I shall remember this day."

"Oh, that sounds like goodbye." I hated myself for uttering the words. They sounded so depressed, so needy.

"No, Berthe, it is just the beginning." He pulled me to him and kissed me. I wanted him as fervently as I did the first time he took me. "You had best go inside. Your sister will be worried about where you got off to with me."

As he walked away, he stopped at the bottom of the steps and turned back to blow a kiss.

*What's next, Édouard?*

As I watched him disappear into the salty Lorient night, I knew I would risk everything to be with him. I was tempted to go after him, to share his bed, make love to him as the sun rose and blessed our union.

But I did not.

Instead, I stood for a moment in the cool darkness, my heart breaking into a thousand tiny pieces hinged together by the glue of a promise—that this was just the beginning.

The house was dark when I let myself inside. No sign of Edma. She was asleep. I was disappointed because I wanted to talk to her. I wanted to share with her every marvelous detail—the reason Édouard married Suzanne; that we'd loved; we were in love.

I was a woman in every sense of the word, and it was every bit as wonderful as I'd imagined. The only thing I needed was for Edma to encourage me that the future held bright possibilities—that Édouard would divorce Suzanne and marry me.

I listened at the top of the steps and heard only the quiet of the house—the occasional satisfied creak and groan of the old home settling in for the night. If she was with child, she needed her rest. I decided not to awaken her and took the painting and my supply box straight up to my room to retire for a restless night, dreaming of love and marriage and babies.

Yes, perhaps I would give Édouard a child. I lay my hand on my belly, tender with the memory of his fullness. My body ached, but it was a good ache, and I wished Édouard was holding me.

I drifted off to sleep thinking that if Édouard had planted his seed inside me tonight, my life would be complete.

When dawn roused the daylight, I dressed, fueled by the hope that Édouard would pay a breakfast call before he departed. I hurried downstairs to tell Edma everything.

She glared at me when I entered the sitting room.

"Where did you go last night?" she hissed. "I had dinner waiting for you, but you did not bother to come home."

I blinked at her tone.

"If you are speaking of yesterday evening, I was with Édouard. You knew that."

"And you know very well that is what concerns me. I was worried sick about you—you . . . you were gone for hours. It was dark. I was so worried something had happened to you."

Something did happen to me and it was wonderful and the only thing I wanted more than sharing it with my sister was for Édouard to be there with me when I did.

"Oh Edma, don't be ridiculous. Nothing bad happened. I was with him and—"

"What are the townspeople to think, Berthe? My sister cavorting about with a married man doing God knows what."

"I beg your pardon. The town's people do not know me and have no idea of Édouard's marital status. Since when does that matter to you? I seem to recall a conversation—a day when we strolled along the *quai*—in which you encouraged me to pursue him despite all scorn and impropriety. Were you not sincere?"

She looked as if I'd slapped her. Her mouth opened, then closed without an utterance. A feeling of dislike flickered through me. "That is what I tried to tell you yesterday at the harbor—"

"Answer me, Edma, why did you encourage me to seek my pleasure, if you were not sincere?"

Her face crumpled into a mask of astonished horror. "Is that what you did out there? Seek your pleasure?"

"I did." I spat the words and let them reverberate in the cold space between us.

Edma closed her eyes, and I thought for a moment she might faint. But when she opened her eyes, I saw the unmistakable glare of revulsion.

"How could you, Berthe? This may not be Paris, but I still must live here."

"Why the change of heart, Edma? Why did you encourage me to confess my feelings for him if you were only to sneer at me in disgust?" My voice rose to a scream, but I could not help it. This was not my sister sitting here. The woman resembled her, but that was where the likeness ended. My sister was warm and accepting and understanding. This imposter with her wedding ring and foul mood was someone I did not wish to know.

"Were you taunting me—because you thought I would not have the guts to find the same happiness you have with Adolphe? Perhaps you do not want me to know that happiness?"

Movement in the doorway caught my eye. Dominique cowered, looking in askance.

"Do not worry, Dominique," Edma said. "Everything is fine."

I waited for the maid to leave. "No, everything is not fine. I shall leave this morning on the train."

"Berthe—" Her words bounced off my back as I bounded out of the room.

If I hurried I could catch the eleven o'clock train to Paris. Édouard would be so surprised to see me.

I could not manage my trunks. So I stuffed as many of my things as possible into my valise, grabbed my canvas and set off on foot for the station.

Edma tried to stop me, but I kissed her and said, "It is best this way. I do not want to upset you in your delicate condition. I shall send for my belongings later."

She let me go. I hated to leave her that way, but I didn't want to be subjected to her judgment. I should have predicted this would happen. Edma was the good girl, the one who always did what was right, who always encouraged me to go where she dared not venture. And I always went because I was . . . Well, I was not the good girl.

On the short walk to the depot, I shoved aside my sadness of fighting with Edma and focused on all the things I wanted to say to Édouard. That I loved him; that what we shared yesterday was the most beautiful thing that had ever happened to me; that I never wanted us to be apart again.

My stomach fluttered with anticipation of his kiss and the look on his face when I arrived at the station. I expected to see him waiting for me on the platform.

But he was not there.

I was convinced he was finishing his breakfast and would appear. I purchased my ticket and sat on the bench—waiting.

The ticket master was talking to someone who never appeared on the platform. It wasn't Édouard's voice. I discerned that right away. A handbill lifted on the wind and blew down the tracks until it lodged in a clump of greenery. I glanced around every so often, sure I'd see him ascending the steps to the platform.

The sun rose higher in the clear blue sky. Until in the distance, the faint rumble of the train announced the eleventh hour.

Still no Édouard. My body grew tense with anxious agitation.

As the train screeched and coughed to a stop, I slipped inside the depot and approached the ticket counter.

"Excuse me, *Monsieur*. Is this the only train to Paris today?"

"It is the final train today, *Mademoiselle*. The other left at six o'clock this morning."

My blood ran cold.

"Did a gentleman board the train early this morning?"

"*Oui, Mademoiselle.*"

I heard the conductor call, "All aboard."

"*Merci, Monsieur.*"

He nodded. Heavy with sadness, I turned and boarded the train for Paris alone.

# Chapter Seventeen

*It is terrible to desire and not possess and terrible*
*to possess and not desire.*

—*W. B. Yeats*

I'd been back in Paris two days and had not heard from
Édouard. One moment I was convinced he was not aware of
my return. The next moment I was sure he regretted what
happened between us and avoided me.

I was torn—If he attempted to contact me in Lorient,
and received no reply, he might harbor the same doubts
about my feelings I was experiencing. I had no idea what
Edma would tell him, if anything, for I'd not heard from my
sister since I left. I had no idea if she remained furious with
me or, for that matter, what she planned to tell Maman of
my visit.

Upon returning, I informed my mother I left because I
was not able to accomplish enough work in Lorient to war-
rant an extended stay and there was not enough time to
write her of my departure. It was not a lie. Beyond painting
the Lorient harbor, my sole inspiration dwelled in Paris.
Except a certain weeping willow tree, which I intend to
paint someday. For now, I preferred preserving its memory
in my mind rather than committing it to canvas.

Maman accepted my explanation for coming home and
her mood was lighter than before I left for Lorient. I imagined her smug over revealing Édouard's rapt attention for
Eva Gonzalés. But neither of us acknowledged this was the

source of her improved disposition. I concentrated on how Édouard freed himself of the beautiful, young pest, and prohibited myself from dwelling on the possibility that somehow Eva managed to worm her way back into Édouard's life. Perhaps she was what detained him?

No.

I hung the harbor painting in my studio where I could view it and recall Édouard's words—*Every time I look at it, I shall remember this day.*

It helped to look at the painting. But sometimes it served as a reminder of how difficult matters had become since that day. I related to Edma's image of the lone figure sitting on the cold, stone wall, waiting . . . the longer I remained a prisoner of my solitude, the more difficult the situation became.

As I paced the confines of my studio, walking between my easel and the sad stand where Edma used to paint, I realized the source of my angst did not stem from missing Édouard. I was sad over the way Edma and I parted.

If I were to recover my sanity, I had to make amends with her. I did not mind being the first to reach out.

I wandered into the drawing room and found Maman reading. She glanced up from her book. *"Bonjour,* my dear *Bijou."*

It had been ages since she'd called me *Bijou.* "Bonjour, Maman. You seem in good spirits today."

She lowered her embroidery into her lap. "It is nice to have you at home. Until you left, I did not realize how quiet this house would become without my children."

It was a strange remark because I was not so talkative that my absence would have made a noticeable change in our home's atmosphere. I sat down at the desk and pulled out a sheet of stationery.

Maman watched my every move.

"To whom are you writing?"

"To Edma."

"You miss your sister." She smiled. "I guess that is to be expected. I am glad you had such a good visit that you cannot wait to correspond with her. Perhaps after you are satiated with work, you will go stay with her again?"

I nodded and pulled a pen from the desk drawer.

"I do quite like the painting of Edma at the harbor. That alone was worth your trip. If you refuse to concentrate on finding a husband, I am glad you are at least painting again."

I wished Maman would stop chattering. I had no desire to venture into the volatile terrain of potential mates. It turned my mind to all the plans Édouard and I would make. How long would it take Maman to recover after Édouard and I announced our plans?

Maman and Papa were getting old, and I did not relish disappointing them. But I clung to the hope that she would embrace Édouard as her son-in-law and view our union as if Édouard had not made the mistake of marrying Suzanne.

I put pen to paper, hoping Maman would realize I could not chat whilst I composed.

*My Dearest Edma,*

*Please do not be angry with me. I am sick over the manner in which we parted. Please find it in your heart to forgive me and to understand. I have never felt this way for anyone before.*

*Much love,*
*Berthe*

Committing the words to paper released some of my anxiety. Perhaps I should've written Édouard a note to tell him I'd returned. I slipped another sheet of paper from the desk.

"I learnt a valuable lesson while you were gone, *Bijou*." I glanced up to find Maman watching me over the top of her glasses.

"What was it, Maman?"

"I underestimated you, my dear. It is not your fault that the public misread the meaning of *Monsieur* Manet's *Le Balcon*. After observing him with *Mademoiselle* Gonzalés, I have no doubt you are innocent. He is a flirt who needs no encouragement when it comes to attractive, vulnerable young women. You did nothing to entice him. I was wrong to blame you."

A funnel of angst swirled in my belly. The sound of her voice grated on my nerves as she sat there so smug and sure that her assessment was the only correct answer.

I wanted to scream that she was wrong. That she knew nothing of Édouard's intentions. Nor of the situation. He was not a philanderer! He was not a flirt!

He loved me.

And I loved him.

"I think your sojourn to Lorient set him firmly in his place. I believe after seeing him that day in his studio—the way he fawned on that young girl right in front of his wife—he realizes his flattery will get him nowhere with you. Suzanne was shaken by his actions. *Madame* Manet had me touch Suzanne's hands, saying she was feverish. While the source of her fever was obvious."

Fear as intense as a living thing danced through me, and I believed for a moment I would succumb to my anguish right before her. I could not bear to be in the same room with Maman and her incessant prattle. I rose from the desk, Edma's letter and the clean sheet of paper in hand, and walked toward the door.

"Where are you going?"

"To prepare this letter to send."

"Leave it here, and I shall see that Amélie takes it for you."

She would read it.

I managed to murmur, "I am not quite finished with it. I shall give it to Amélie when I am done."

"Save the letter for after lunch. It is noon. We shall dine together."

"I am not hungry, Maman. I still have not recovered from my journey." The truth was I had no appetite for food. Meats and cheeses and breads would not satisfy the hunger that gnawed at me.

"Suit yourself."

I shut myself away in the studio and stared at the blank sheet of paper for a long while. If I sent a letter, there was the risk of it falling into hands other than his. I could not chance that risk. Besides, it would only delay matters.

After lunch, Maman would lie down for her afternoon nap. I would go to Édouard then. He would be at his studio, and we could talk. Everything would be fine.

It was not a small canvas, and it was quite cumbersome to transport it in the carriage. But I brought it to him. Until we could be together, Édouard had to have the painting to remind him of how much we needed each other. How good we were together.

It made perfect sense.

From the street below, I could see his studio windows were open. It was a good sign. He was there. Although, never once did I doubt he'd be anywhere else.

The air smelled of springtime, of greenery and the faint scent of flowers from an open-air market down the street. I relished the aroma of brioche baking in the patisserie across the boulevard. No wonder Édouard's windows were open on such a fine day.

The horses whinnied, and the driver steadied them before offering to carry the painting upstairs, but I refused his help, opting to climb the four flights to his *atelier* alone. I moved slowly, taking care not to lose my balance as I traversed the steep incline.

I paused outside his door in the dim, quiet hallway to catch my breath before I knocked. I did not hear a sound coming from his studio. If I did not have such a strong belief in us, I might have been concerned at how he would receive me, or worried about whether he was alone.

I drew in a deep, steadying breath before I rapped on the door. I stood there, my heart pounding beneath my bodice, and I feared I'd knocked too softly and he did not hear me. I was about to knock again when the door flung open.

Never had I witnessed such a look of surprise on his expressive face. I thought he would hug me, but instead, he placed a hand on my shoulder and leaned across me to look out into the hallway. "Are you alone?"

I nodded, unable to speak for the sheer joy of seeing him. Pulling me inside, he shut the door, and took the canvas from me, leaning it against the wall. He drew me into a tight embrace and smothered my mouth with his, hard and urgent.

Oh, how I'd craved his touch.

There was nothing gentle about his kiss, as when we were together beneath the willow tree in Lorient. This kiss was fueled by pure, burning need: the rough desire of a parched man who was able to drink his fill. I encouraged him to drink deeper. He held me so tight, I felt him grow hard against me. An ache throbbed in the vulnerable places he'd claimed when we were last together.

Any harbored doubts melted away with each caress, each muffled moan of satisfaction.

He looked at me, holding me against him. "Hello, my love. When did you get back? I thought you would be with your sister for some time."

"I returned two days ago. I could not stay in Lorient knowing you were here."

He pushed a wisp of hair behind my ear, setting my hat askew. He plucked it from my head, and the hatpin fell to the floor with a tiny ping-ping. We both bent to retrieve it and laughed at how we bumped into each other. In our stooped position, he kissed me again, lighter this time, a peck of delight that welcomed me home. And I knew I was right where I belonged.

As he scooped the pin off the wooden floor, I was renewed—by the sound of his laughter, the bristle of his beard on my cheeks, and the touch of his hands on my body.

It felt wonderful to be alive, and I regretted not coming to him the moment I returned to Paris.

There was something intimate in the way he stuck the pin in my hat—a task I'd performed hundreds of times before—yet something in the sight of his large hands performing such a mundane task thrilled me.

"What did you bring?" He set the hat on a stool and reached for my painting. I realized it was facing the wall.

"A gift for you."

He looked at the canvas and his eyes brightened. "Ahhhh, *oui*. The masterpiece. But you should not give this to me. You should save it for the Salon."

"That is a long time off. I shall borrow it back when the time comes. But in the meantime, I want you to have it."

He inspected it at eye level and shook his head; a look of appreciation washed over his handsome fame.

"It is much too good to be hidden away here. I shall take it home and hang it in a place of honor."

I liked that. It felt as if he were bringing me into his home.

I glanced around the familiar space of his studio and warmth filled me. Everything rested in its usual place: the books, the props, the rainbow of rich pigments, brushes stored in jars, the paint tubes—some covered in pigment powder, others brand new—the dressing screen along the wall, the unmade bed in the far corner. It seemed ages since I'd been there. Was something different?

Of course it was. I was different.

The last time I was here, Édouard and I were not lovers.

"What are you painting?"

He gestured with his head. "Have a look."

I pulled off my gloves, tugging one finger at a time, and walked around to view the canvas.

I stopped, stunned to find Suzanne's likeness staring back at me. Clad in a delicate white dress and seated on a white divan set in front of frilly, sheer white draperies, she looked almost . . . beautiful.

Shock knotted into a dull ache in the pit of my stomach. I glanced at Édouard for an explanation. He was busy cleaning his brushes, as if there was nothing extraordinary about him glamorizing his fat, homely . . . wife.

For a moment, I believed the smell of turpentine would overpower me. Only then did I realize I'd wadded my gloves into a tight little ball. I smoothed them out—anything to divert my gaze from Suzanne's triumphant visage.

"What do you think?" Édouard smiled, colleague conferring with colleague.

*Why is he painting her?* Olympia demanded. *Why now?*

*Because she is his wife,* Propriety said. *He's probably feeling guilty. It is about time he painted her.*

*It doesn't even resemble her,* said Olympia. *This woman in the painting is some idealized imposter.*

*Perhaps this is how he sees her.* Propriety reigned victorious.

"It's quite—white," was all I could muster.

He squinted at the canvas, shrugged. "I began this painting years ago, but I never finished it. I guess I felt I owed it to her after the monstrosity Degas presented. It offended her."

*That's* what was missing. My eyes darted to the vacant spot where Degas's painting hung after Édouard washed over Suzanne's image. It was gone. Now he was trying to make it up to her by portraying her in a falsely flattering manner.

"But Édouard, Degas's painting of Suzanne was true. It resembled her much more than this does."

His eyes darkened, and for a moment I feared he might defend her. I could not bear it. I would not hear it.

"Édouard, you have always painted what you see. Is this how you see her? Is this how you feel about her? If it is, then we have no business . . . You have no business—"

"Berthe, I care for you, but she is my wife."

His words bounced off my ears as a frantic tumult consumed me, blurring my vision and stripping away all semblance of steady ground.

"In Lorient you said you loved me." I turned to leave so he would not see my vulnerability. Tears streamed, and I dashed the back of my hand across my face, but they fell too fast for me to conceal.

I managed but a few steps toward the door, and he was there. "Please don't go."

"Why did you come to Lorient?" I murmured.

"Because—" He looked anguished, as if he were searching for the right words, and reached out and pulled me to him. He held me, and I cried into his chest as if by expelling all my angst I could vanquish the demons that kept us apart.

But I knew it would change nothing.

Not if he loved her.

I pulled away from him, reached for the door handle. "Just let me go. You should've never come to Lorient. I should've not come here today."

He held the door shut.

"Please, Berthe, do not leave. Lorient was not a mistake. We shall work this out. Somehow, we shall find a way."

*Dearest Berthe,*

*Of course I forgive you. I only hope you can find it in your heart to excuse my outburst that drove you away. I am so frequently out of sorts, I do not recognize myself.*

*I try to remind myself of the miracle growing inside me—that is the reason my body feels swollen and tender. Sometimes it seems nothing consoles me.*

*I am ashamed of myself for misleading you during our walk along the quai. What I spouted was a romantic notion, and I believe I was caught up in the fantasy. Alas, as I have discovered, marriage is a sacred institution with which one should not trifle. I know you understand, my dear. Please forgive my foolishness.*

*I should be cheered if you would agree to come for an-other visit soon. Please, my dear, do.*

*Affectionately,*
*Your Sister Edma*

# Chapter Eighteen

## July 1870

*Blow wind to where my loved one is,*
*Touch him and come and touch me soon,*
*I'll feel his gentle touch through you,*
*And meet his beauty in the moon.*
                                        —*Ramayana*

I was grateful for evening's darkness. It hid everything but the moon and stars that burned as if they were all that mattered. At night, when I was alone, I would look up and see the sliver of silver moon hanging crooked in the sky or pick out a pattern of diamond stars and know it was possible that Édouard was gazing at the same spectacle. It was as if I could draw a line from myself to the stars and down to him, wherever he might be. It connected us, and the night erased everything else of no consequence.

I was naive to believe life would fall into place once we were lovers, that the extraneous would fall away to what mattered—our love. It was not so simple. If anything, life became more complicated over the months since that day of new beginnings in Lorient.

Edma came home for her confinement. She delivered a beautiful baby girl, and named her Jeanne. With my sister there, I could not find time to steal away with Édouard. As much as I wanted to.

Even after she went home, I did not see her as often as I wished. It was hard to sit by and accept that.

Alas, I was not trying to fool myself into a false position. For I knew that attraction climbed a steep grade to the crest of seduction. What followed was but a fall—hard and fast— with a most unforgiving landing.

I bided my time and resisted the urge to push fate into action.

A star fell from the indigo sky.

I feared it was an omen and ran my hand across my belly. I had no appetite for food. I wished Edma were here so I could ask her about the signs of being with child. I could not write and ask her such delicate questions. Perhaps with her changed position on marriage and family, she would not be so forthcoming with answers. Far different from the girl who urged me to pursue my passions.

Perhaps my condition was simply malaise or nerves. Everything was so uncertain. I could do nothing but wait, drawing lines in the nighttime sky, streaks of hope that connected my beloved and me.

After dinner, I joined Maman and Papa in the sitting room. The room was ablaze with lamps. I squinted at the brightness as I entered. Papa was in one of his moods. "Do not call me unpatriotic. Anyone with common sense would support Adolphe Thiers."

Papa was ranting again. Something he'd been prone to since his years as a prefect under Thiers. Papa was still as loyal as his first days, rallying around the former prime minister.

Poor Maman bore the brunt of my father's evening tirade. With my book, I turned to seek refuge out of earshot.

"Garmont is an imbecile, I tell you. If he'd left well

enough alone, we would not be on the verge of war."

War? I turned back. The subject loomed on restless minds for the past two years, but it was just an idea—born of those who feared France being surrounded by hostile powers—not a real possibility. "Papa, what are you saying?"

"I'm saying that a grave diplomatic error will cause a war with Prussia. It's imminent." Papa wrung his hands. "France is ill prepared. It will be a disaster. But your Maman will not hear of it. She reproaches me, calls me a doomsayer. She calls me unpatriotic."

Papa could be difficult. This I knew, but something in his ashen face and knitted brow told me this was real.

*July 14, 1870*

Hundreds of Bonapartists marched along the boulevards. I shuttered the windows, but even that would not drown the shouts of *"Vive la guerre!"*

It seemed all of Paris was starved for war. All too soon France erupted in a flurry of activity, readying itself to fight the evil Prussian forces that had bullied our country for years.

The government recalled all naval officers. Edma's husband, Adolphe, shipped out of Cherbourg. Edma stayed behind to await his return. Alas, she wrote that she knew in her heart it would be a long while before she saw him again, but she took comfort in the fact that the navy was strong and well fortified.

I could only wonder where Édouard was, as I'd not seen him since word of this crisis shifted everyone into hysteria. I asked my brother, Tiburce, what he'd heard of our *friends,* but he had no news. If Édouard had rejoined the navy, I hoped I would see him again before he shipped out.

The navy was well fortified. I wish I could've said as

much for the army. My brother, Tiburce, enlisted rather than waiting for the government to commit him. His youthful fighting spirit landed him an assignment in the Rhine.

Despite the army's weakened state, Maman was quite pleased. "This is my idea of how men should behave in a time of peril."

Was forgetting everyone not connected to the war the way a man should behave? I realized it was a time of national crisis, and I should not be selfish. But I thought Édouard would care enough to inform me of his plans or at least inquire about my well-being.

I grew anxious with concern over my condition. I didn't know if I was with child, and I had not felt like myself. I contemplated taking the carriage to his studio, but with all the talk of fighting, Maman would not let me out of her sight. If I set foot outdoors, she insisted on accompanying me. I could not talk to Édouard with her in tow.

So I waited, sinking deeper into despair as each moment passed.

Maman and I tried so hard to keep our spirits afloat. But it was difficult to be jovial when a few weeks into the fighting we learned that Tiburce's brigade, under the command of Marshal Bazine, was hemmed in at Metz. With this news, we could not convince ourselves this nightmare would soon end, that the sound of cannon fire in the distance was not as grave as it seemed. That the rain that fell from the sky was not Paris crying for its own.

*September 3, 1870*

The Prussians took the emperor prisoner.

The situation took swift escalation toward crisis. Forced

to stay in Paris because of his position with the new regime, Papa implored Maman and me to go to Edma in Cherbourg, but Maman would not hear of it. "Wherever my husband is, I shall stay beside him. How can I leave when I have no idea what fates befall my son? He will not know where to find me when he is set free."

Papa's expression was such that I believed he wanted us to go without him. But all I could do was reassure my mother that everything would be fine.

I wished I believed it.

*Dear Edma,*

*I received your letter yesterday. I have made up my mind to stay in Paris, because neither father nor mother told me firmly to leave; they want me to leave in the way anyone here wants anything—weakly and by fits and starts. For my own part, I would much rather not leave them, not because I truly believe there is any real danger, but because my place is with them, and if by ill luck anything did happen, I should have eternal remorse. I will not presume to say that they take great pleasure in my presence; I feel very sad, and am completely silent. I have heard so much about the perils ahead that I have had nightmares for several nights in which I have lived through all the horrors of war. To tell the truth, I do not believe all these things. I feel perfectly calm, and I have the firm conviction that everything will come out better than expected. The house is dreary, empty, stripped bare; and as a finishing touch, father makes inexplicable and interminable removals. He seems to be very much occupied with the preservation of some old pieces of furniture of the First Empire. On the other hand he smiles pityingly when I tell him that the cabinet, the mirror and the console in the studio are not absolutely worthless. To avoid argument, I refrain from interfering in anything, and, to tell the truth, all this interests me very little. Since it is possible to work where you are, why don't you do so? I do not read the newspapers much anymore. The Prussian atrocities upset me, and I want to retain my composure.*

*I am stupefied by this silence. I wish I had news of you—though I dare not hope for an answer to this letter—and of poor Tiburce, from whom we have not heard. Perhaps you will hear from him before we do; there are moments when I think of him with a terrible tightening of my heart. I embrace you, my dear Edma . . . If you are cut off from Paris, do not worry on our account. Mother is better, and Father is in as good health as can be expected.*

*Adieu,*
*Berthe*

*September 4, 1870*

The rain passed, giving way to heat and sunshine. It was much too bright outside for the state of our country. It seemed at odds with national morale. We'd received word that hordes had stormed the *Hôtel de Ville* in support of a new republic. Looking out the window, I saw mass chaos in the streets. The quiet boulevards of our beloved Passy were awash in a sea of red and blue uniforms; men rushed about. I did not know what would become of us in the face of such bedlam.

Papa maintained the war was wrong. He feared for the safety of his children: Tiburce, Edma, baby Jeanne and Yves. Yet, my being underfoot irritated him. He seemed disgusted by my lack of appetite. "Soon there may be no food, and I shall remind you of how you turned up your nose at the offerings today."

"Would you be happier, Papa, if I went to stay with Edma?"

"Of course not. Then I would have you to worry about, too."

Staying was the choice I made. So I did my best to stay out of his way.

*September 6, 1870*

Edma agreed to take baby Jeanne and stay with Yves in Mirande, so neither would be by themselves.

In a letter informing us of her plans, she begged me to come with her. I wished she'd come to the *rue* Franklin, but since Yves would not leave her home to be ransacked, as she put it, there was no alternative but for Edma to go to Mirande to be with her.

I wandered into the studio. Picked up a paintbrush and tried to work. Instead, I ended up staring at the canvases on the walls. The ones I'd intended to send to Edma when it seemed we had all the time in the world.

I consoled myself that it was a good thing I did not send the paintings to her in Lorient. She cared even less for her house now that she had *bébé* Jeanne on whom to shower all her affections. The paintings would have made it difficult to pack up and leave for Yves's.

My sisters were alone together. Their husbands were off fighting. It made sense for them to be together. I served my duty here looking after Maman and Papa. I set down the brush without as much as having touched it to the paint. It rolled off the table onto the floor. I did not have the energy to bend down and retrieve it.

*September 8, 1870*

Nearly two months passed without word from Édouard.

I did not know where he was, nor what had become of him. I scarcely knew what to think, except that I was devastated. I did not know of his plans or if he was alive. I shifted between hopeless grief—sure of his death—to icy anger, certain he'd forgotten me in the face of this crisis.

To add to my anguish, after two cycles' absence, I received the sign that confirmed I was not with child. Having learned the truth, I shut myself in my room and cried.

Out of relief or disappointment? I was not sure.

After weeks of being so certain, it felt as if our child had been taken away.

Not knowing Édouard's fate, the thought of having his child held vast importance. If the worst were to befall us, at least I would've possessed a piece of him to carry forward once the tragedy of war was behind us.

I continued to pray for his safety. Alas, I could not help but lose faith that Édouard was alive after so long an absence.

*September 12, 1870*

Like a ghost standing in the foyer, Édouard came to call, dressed in the smart red and navy blue uniform of the National Guard. He cut a striking figure.

Emotion clouded my logic. Common sense should have rendered me ecstatic to find him alive, safe, calling on me. For an instant, I wanted to run to him and throw my arms around him, to rejoice in his safety. But the sight of him standing there—looking sharp in his clean, pressed uniform, angered me and I swallowed against the urge to shout at him.

I did not want his reasons or his excuses or even to know how he'd spent his time while I'd been sitting there like a captive, missing him, believing I was carrying his child. As the edges of my vision grew hazy, I turned away and walked out of the room. I wanted to be as far away from him as possible.

I shut myself inside the studio and sat down in front of my easel, although I did not feel like working. A few moments later the door swung open. Maman paused on the threshold, arms crossed.

"Berthe? What is the matter with you?"

"Nothing, Maman." I picked up a brush and pinned my eyes on my canvas—a painting of Edma at baby Jeanne's cradle. "I don't feel like company."

"Come out and be civil to our guest. Manet has taken precious time away from his civil duty to call on us. The least you could do is receive him."

"I do not feel like it right now. I want to work. The light is right, and I must take advantage of it."

She stood silent in the doorway for a moment—just long enough to make me hopeful that she'd go away. "Very well then, I shall invite him out here. I should think he would like to see what you are accomplishing while he is out fighting for you."

Fighting for me? Édouard was not exerting himself in any fashion for *me*. I suppressed a snort, but by that time Maman was gone.

I heard her voice in the garden, "Berthe would love for you to come to her studio to see her work."

Oh, Maman. No! I stood too fast and knocked over my chair. Hearing their footfalls, I righted my seat and sat down, thinking it best to look calm and busy.

In my peripheral vision I saw Maman usher him in. I squeezed a tube of azure onto my palette and realized I did not need the color. Too late. They lingered by the door.

"Come in," said Maman. "Look around. Please make yourself at home."

"Let me see what keeps you so busy," Édouard said and moved behind me. "Eugène sends his regards to both of you."

"How is the dear boy adjusting to war?"

"Not very well, I fear," said Édouard. "He is not political by nature and even less of a fighter."

Maman clucked at this comment. Édouard shrugged and smiled at me. I looked away.

"Four days ago, I sent Suzanne and the family to the safety of Oloron-Sainte-Marie in the Basses-Pyrenees."

So that was what kept him. Worry over Suzanne. I did not want to know the nice things he'd done for her, the ways he demonstrated his care. A reminder that she was his wife.

I could not stand his hovering behind me, his not commenting on the painting. I stood up and crossed to the divan and sat next to Maman.

"You are very quiet, *Mademoiselle*." He chose the chair across from me.

"I am thinking about how relieved *you* must be to know that your loved ones are safe."

He perched on the edge of the chair.

"I should like to see each person who is dear to me safe, *Mademoiselle*. Do you plan to evacuate?"

"Don't be ridiculous. Of course not."

He stroked his beard and closed his eyes. "Please get out while it is still possible. Pissarro, Sisley and Monet have escaped to London. Degas has transferred from the infantry to the artillery. Renoir has been posted to Bordeaux. I do not believe you are aware of the gravity of this situation."

"Papa has determined it is safe for us to stay. That is

what we shall do until he advises otherwise."

My words exploded like cannon fire, followed by a beat of strained silence. Even the canvases on the walls seemed to glare in astonishment.

Maman fidgeted. "What is taking Amélie so long with the tea?" She stood. "If you will excuse me, *Monsieur* Manet, I shall hurry her along. I know you do not have all day to wait."

She bustled out in a flurry of silk copper skirt, leaving the door open behind her.

"I hid many of my unsold canvases in the cellar of my studio," said Édouard. "Special canvases, such as *Le Balcon* and your painting of Edma in Lorient, I gave to Théodore Duret to store in his vault. I would not want anything to happen to them."

He crossed to the door and pulled it shut. "I have missed you, *mon amour*."

"How can you tell such falsehoods? If you missed me, you would not have stayed away."

"I am sorry, but in case you have not noticed, France is at war."

I glared at him, resenting his flippant tone. "Your presence has been too scarce for you to notice, but since I saw you last, I feared I was carrying your child."

The color drained from his face, and I took perverse pleasure in watching him struggle with the thought. I stood and walked to the window.

"Do not worry," I said over my shoulder, toying with the drape. "It is solved. You are free. We are not . . . I am not . . ." My voice broke and I took a deep breath to steady myself. "The sign that proves I am not with child presented itself. There is nothing to bind us. You can go if you wish."

"Berthe, how can you say that?" He stood. "Our hearts bind us."

I laughed at him. A cold, humorless sound that made me want to cry.

"We could not bring a bastard child into such an ugly world. And now I know it is all for the best."

He stood behind me now. The words that he did not know how to deliver hung between us unspoken. He put a hand on my belly. I saw moisture in his eyes, but he blinked. I was sure it was relief.

"I have contemplated the logistics of freeing myself from Suzanne, but do you realize the scandal that would mire our relationship, Berthe? I am not sure you are strong enough to endure it."

"*I* am not strong enough? That's rubbish. It's just an excuse—"

From the window, I saw Maman and Amélie wheeling the teacart across the garden path. Édouard pulled away from me and walked back to the divan.

I stayed by the window wishing for rain from the dark gray skies, to spout the emotion I could not release.

Papa had a new fixation: He was preoccupied with what would become of our precious furniture in what he thought was the *inevitable* event we were forced to move. He was convinced our home was safe as long as the Forts of Issy and Vanves stayed in French hands. Ever the doomsayer, he'd already started making arrangements to have our possessions stored in a safe place in the center of Paris.

He was obsessed. When I mentioned it, we fought. So I avoided talking to him. What I found interesting was how he'd not seemed to notice our lack of communication. Perhaps because Maman gave him so much grief.

"How can you spend every spare moment fretting over possessions?" said Maman. "If the situation is as grave as *Monsieur* Manet declares, you should be more concerned over the safety of your family; do not worry over the furniture."

He bristled.

"If you wish to leave, you and Berthe may go to Mirande with Yves and Edma. But I will go nowhere," he shouted. "I have worked too hard for the treasures that you enjoy in this home, and I will not see them destroyed. You are so busy nagging, you did not give me a chance to tell you that I have made arrangements with a friend, *Monsieur* Millet, for us to move into an apartment in the *rue* Argensen when the fighting worsens."

"Both of you stop it," I said. "Stop shouting this instant."

But Maman, with that determined look in her eye, ignored me.

"Manet has excited you," she said. "You should not listen to him and you know it. He is always prone to exaggerate."

"You will thank me should the bombs fall on the *rue* Franklin." Papa stormed out the door and Maman collapsed in a fit of tears. I consoled her. I was stronger now. Édouard vowed to call again within the next week. When Maman took away the teacart, he implored me to receive him again, assured me that his absence was not a reflection on his feelings for me. That spark of hope fortified me. With it, I could be strong enough for both Maman and me.

I used to dream of going abroad. I'd formed quite an attachment to the idea of visiting New York in the summer. Of venturing out into the countryside and setting up my easel alongside a stream shaded by tall sugar maples with the broad green leaves the size of a man's hand. I imagined taking off my shoes and wading up to my knees into the cool water. It would be like a baptism for the start of a new life.

The world on the other side of the Atlantic seemed magical, like the secret life on the opposite side of a mirror. You could see it and press your hand up against it, but figuring out how to access it was nearly impossible. When I was a child, I used to believe if you wished hard enough you would awaken one glorious day to find yourself there.

New York was where I dreamt Édouard and I would start over. There, we could be anyone we chose to be—newlyweds, the happy young couple embarking on a life together. Pioneers, exploring a brave new world. There would be no scandal. No Suzanne. No disapproving looks. No wagging tongues sharp with criticism.

Just Édouard and me and the life we painted—falling asleep in each other's arms and making love every morning as the sun rose. Perhaps there we would be successful in conceiving a child.

As all able-bodied men defended Paris, I shut myself away from the outside world and clung to that dream to keep my spirits alive. When Édouard called we would make plans, and he would see I was not so weak as to forfeit our life together.

The more I thought about it, the more perfect it seemed. The war was the ideal cover. Suzanne was away. My presence irritated Maman and Papa more and more each day—so much so that I'd come to believe they were better off without me. I could tell them I was going to stay with Edma. Édouard and I would take a train to the coast, board a ship, and sail away.

★ ★ ★ ★ ★

*September 19, 1870*

True to his word, Édouard called at the *rue* Franklin with his brother, Eugène.

Maman and I entertained them in my studio since it was the only place in the house with enough furniture to offer our guests a place to sit. The house stood empty since Papa moved most of our possessions to the apartment he'd secured for us in the center of Paris. We were to move at a moment's notice.

"The Prussians are so brutal. The atrocities they perpetrate defy logic." Édouard shook his head, leaned in and lowered his voice. "Word is they desecrated a convent and raped a young novice. *Mademoiselle,* promise me you will not venture out alone."

I had no stomach for horror stories. Eugène must have read as much in my expression. He scooted forward on his chair. His teacup clattered against his saucer. "Édouard, stop such morbid talk."

I'd never heard Eugène speak so boldly.

"Can't you see how you are scaring the poor woman?"

"I am fine, *Monsieur.* Thank you for your concern. Even so, I shall not venture out of doors. I do not think I could bear to see my beloved city in such turmoil. I have been distracting myself by reading and working. In fact, that reminds me. Édouard, could you assist me with a book in the library? It is on a ledge much too high for my reach. Could I trouble you to fetch it for me?"

"Certainly, *Mademoiselle.*"

"*Merci,* if you'll follow me, I shall show you which one."

I held my breath, waiting for Maman to question my request or for Eugène to offer his assistance, but the two commenced talking about the strength of the National Guard.

Édouard and I walked in silence to the sitting room, listening to the faint murmur of conversation streaming from the studio. I heard Eugène say, "With the speed in which the Prussian army advances, sometimes I fear I will not survive this terrible ordeal."

Once inside, Édouard followed me to the bookcases. I turned to him.

"I am so happy to see you today. I wanted to believe you would come, yet the last time it was almost—"

"Shhhh." He slipped his arms around me and covered my mouth with his. "Do not waste our time together on unhappiness." He pulled me closer. I wished we could stay in the cozy, shelf-lined haven of the library and not have to rejoin Maman and Eugène in the studio. The drawn velvet drapes and soothing burgundy leather blended with the warm brass and wood, transporting us worlds away from the fighting outside.

"I was thinking about what you said the other day." I rested my head on Édouard's chest, elated to be in his arms again. To know he was alive and well and still cared for me. "We would not have to endure scandal if we were not here to face it."

"Hmmmm—" He answered, his lips on my neck. My head tilted in automatic response, allowing him room to possess me.

"Édouard, listen to me." I planted my hands on his shoulders and made room between us, but he tried to close the gap, tried to reclaim my body. "I want us to go away. Tomorrow. I have it all planned."

He regarded me through hooded eyes, and I could not tell what he was thinking. So I continued before he stopped me or I changed my mind.

"Meet me at the *Gare Saint-Lazare* at ten o'clock. We

can catch the eleven o'clock train for the coast. By the day after, we will be on a boat sailing for America."

Édouard blinked, smoothed his beard. Sighed. "Berthe, we are at war. I—"

"*We* are not. *We* can be together if we leave tomorrow."

He didn't answer me. Only looked at me with rueful eyes that sent a mournful shudder through me.

"Édouard, please—"

"Berthe? *Monsieur* Manet?" Maman's voice grew closer. "While you're in there, will you please fetch me a book, too?"

"Tomorrow at ten?" I sealed the plan with a kiss.

He nodded and swept a kiss on my lips with his finger. "The *Gare Saint-Lazare*."

# Chapter Nineteen

*If all the world were mine to plunder*
*I'd be content with just one town,*
*And in that town, one house alone,*
*And in that house, one single room,*
*And in that room, one cot only,*
*For there, asleep, is the one I love.*
                    *—Ancient Sanskrit Poem*

After Édouard and Eugène left, I had much to do without making Maman the wiser. I'd not considered how I'd get out of the house alone without her noticing. I was contemplating how I would get to the station when Amélie brought me a letter from Puvis.

*Dear Mademoiselle,*
    *I am not able to pay you a call in person. So I write with high hopes that this letter finds you and your family well during this very sad time for our glorious country.*
    *I am serving in the National Guard, in and around Versailles. Leaders assure us the fight will worsen before it gets better. For many, we will soon see our last hours.*
    *At times like this, dear Mademoiselle, one is inclined to take stock of one's life and what is important. I decided if I were to die today, I shall pass in peace only if you know how fond I am of you. Your friendship has always been a bright spot in my life, and my only regret is that I did not pursue you more diligently in more carefree days.*

*As I fight, please know I am defending you. Please do*
*not hesitate to call on me if I may serve you in any way.*
                    *Your devoted servant,*
                    *Pierre Puvis de Chavannes*

Puvis's letter astounded me.

Flattered me.

Touched by such a tender declaration. I had no idea of
the depth of his feelings. He'd been a friend, appearing now
and again in my life, but never had he given me any indica-
tion that his feelings ran so deep. I was relieved he chose to
express his feelings in a note rather than conveying them in
person. When one was so candid, so forthright, he did not
deserve to have his hopes dashed with his tender words still
hanging in the air.

Oh, Puvis. Such a dear, sweet man. My heart was heavy
as I uttered a silent prayer that he would live to see the end
of the terrible war.

I took the letter to my bedchamber, tucked it beneath
the mattress and removed my valise from the closet to start
packing for my new life.

The only way I was able to leave unnoticed was to time
my departure between Papa's leaving for work and
Maman's coming down for breakfast.

It was good that I was getting an early start because I
had to walk to the train station—a good five kilometers.

I waited ten minutes after Papa closed the front door,
and left a note for Maman on the desk in the drawing room
saying I'd decided to visit my sisters. I would write her a
letter with the truth once Édouard and I arrived safely in
New York. I let myself out, hoping that Amélie would not
hear the creaking floorboards and come out to investigate.

Or that my heartbeat was not echoing in the foyer as loudly as it thumped in my ears.

My heart weighed heavy as I pulled the door closed for what I realized was the last time. It clicked shut, and I stepped onto the sun-dappled walk bathed in the gentle light of early morning. I would miss my Passy. Although it was not my birthplace, it was where my heart would always reside.

Doubt seeped in around the edges of my well-constructed plan. But Édouard would be there. There was no other option.

He would be there. We would board the train and be at the coast by mid-afternoon.

That was the only possible scenario.

The streets of Passy proper were a quiet contrast to the sound of cannon fire in the distance. A few people passed—businessmen in carriages on their way to work, mounted national guardsmen patrolling the area, a boy delivering newspapers. Strolling along the cobblestone street, I kept my head down for fear I might happen upon a neighbor or a friend of my parents.

I'd only gone a short distance when the valise grew heavy. I'd packed only a change of clothes, as I knew it would be a long walk. I switched the case to my left hand and adjusted the strings of my handbag to assure my money was secure. I carried only enough francs to pay for our train fare. Since Édouard and I did not have the time to discuss logistics, I brought enough to pay for both of us. With his duties, I didn't know if he would have the opportunity to get money. The rest of my francs were tucked away in a pouch I'd sewn inside the bodice of my dress.

The breeze blew the faint smell of smoke from a far-away fire, but it smelled like freedom. I focused on the fact that by this time tomorrow Édouard and I would be on a ship sailing for New York.

All was going well until I'd traveled about one kilometer down the Avenue Kléber and hit a roadblock.

"*Mademoiselle,* where are you going?" The armed soldier was young, but talked as if he were a father reprimanding a child. "Why are you out this morning by yourself?"

I tilted my chin. "I am going to the *Gare Saint-Lazare* to catch a train."

"I am sorry, *Mademoiselle,* no trains running today. The station is closed until further notice. I cannot allow you to pass."

I stepped closer and he lifted his gun. The action startled me. Though he was not pointing it at me, it was in the ready position. I was offended by the brash gesture.

"I beg your pardon, *Monsieur,* but I must get through. I am meeting my fiancé."

"He is an idiot to let a woman walk alone in the streets. It is not safe after last night's tragedy."

The word caused goose flesh to erupt on my arms. "What are you talking about?"

"Versailles fell to the Prussians last night. Paris is surrounded. I have strict orders that no one is to pass."

"But I must—" I contemplated turning away as if I were complying with his orders and then trying to find another way to the station.

"Bodier, escort the *Demoiselle* home."

The man named Bodier indicated for me to follow. I realized all was lost.

Mere words could not describe the paralyzing dread that expanded inside me. All that existed within me was bitter cold and utter helplessness. It was as if I'd let go of Édouard's hand and he'd drifted off into the heavens and

210

there was nothing I could do to stop him.

*Dearest Edma,*

*I am writing you because I do not know whether in another few days we shall still be able to correspond. Paris has changed still more. I think of life before this war, and it seems to me it is not the same city. I received a note from Puvis de Chavannes, who writes as if our last hour has come. Moreover, I see that the National Guard is very restive. Manet's brother told me very calmly that he does not expect to come out of this alive.*

*Papa pins all his hopes on the success of Monsieur Thiers's mission. Father continues to be in good health and is driving us all crazy.*

*Kisses for Bébé.*

*Adieu, dear. Do enjoy the peace of Mirande. It is better than the agitation here.*

*Berthe*

*Dear Berthe,*

*We feel just as indignant as Mother does when Gambetta is unjustly attacked. It was he who did most for the defense, and it is he who is mostly denounced today. He is unanimously attacked in the provinces and held responsible for France's defeat. In this world success is everything.*

*This reactionary Chamber does not inspire me with great confidence. Those who advocate caution and moderation do not seem to be the men of the hour. However that may be, the task is grave and difficult. We must wait to judge them.*

*There is talk in the newspaper of the German army entering Paris. Perhaps you are now witnessing that spec-*

*tacle. Nothing is to be spared us.*

*Affectionately,*
*Edma*

*Dear Edma,*

*You are right, my dear Edma, in believing that nothing will be spared us. The Prussians are to enter our arrondissement on Wednesday. Our area is explicitly mentioned among those to be occupied by them. This news was circulated in the afternoon; it was expected that they would arrive tonight; then the report was denied in the evening, but this only meant that the entry was being delayed. Our rue Franklin, usually so quiet, was animated; the Place de la Marie and the main streets are filled with noisy crowds. The National Guard was against surrendering its arms, and protested loudly. All this is very sad, and the terms are so severe that one cannot bear to think about them.*

*Each day brings us some new sorrow, some new humiliation. The French people are so frivolous that they will promptly forget these sad events, but I am brokenhearted.*

*If I happen to voice this opinion at home, Father throws up his hands and says that I am a madwoman.*

*There was a great commotion yesterday. The National Guard contingent at Belleville declared that they intended to fire their guns when the Prussians enter. I think we are at the beginning of an emotional period.*

*Do you know all of our acquaintances have come out of the war without a scratch, except for that poor Bazille, who was killed at Orléans. The brilliant painter Régnault was killed at Bezenval. The others have made a great fuss about nothing.*

*Affectionately,*
*Berthe*

The air was filled with so much acrid smoke I could barely breathe. The boom of cannon fire sounded so often I wondered why each explosion continued to startle me.

We felt the presence of the Prussian troops all around us. I wanted to stay in my bed with the shutters drawn. I dozed between cannon blasts, and in my fitful dreams, sometimes Édouard was there. We were boarding the train at the *Gare Saint-Lazare* or he was kissing me as we stood on the deck of a great ocean liner bound for New York. The cannon would sound. I would awaken in my dark room, remembering that two weeks had passed since Édouard and I were supposed to meet at the train station.

He did not respond to the note I sent him asking him to call. But I realized it was impossible with the Prussians closing in on us outside. Mail delivery was erratic. It was entirely possible he did not receive the letter.

For two weeks I took to my bed, waging a private war with the demons that invaded my peace of mind. Maman called in the doctor, *Monsieur* Dally. But all he did was leer at me. I feared he would insist on examining me for his own pleasure rather than trying to help me feel well again. It was impossible to recover under such circumstances.

"Berthe, wake up." Maman came into the room and threw open the shutters. "Get up. Get dressed. You have a visitor."

Squinting into the brightness, I sat up. My mind skittered from hope that it was Édouard, to fear that it was *Monsieur* Dally.

Maman went to the wardrobe and selected a dress.

"*Monsieur* Puvis de Chavannes has come to call."

I scooted to the side of the bed and tried to stand. But I swayed from the effort. "Tell him I am not up to company."

"Nonsense. It will serve you well. You have been brooding far too long. Get dressed. I shall tell him you will be down momentarily."

Puvis. Maman *must* have been worried about me to roust me to receive Puvis. Although, I didn't know why, her attitude toward him had cooled. It seemed one minute she sang his praises, encouraging me he'd make a good match. The next, the mere mention of his name set her in a bad humor.

Today he was back in her good graces—for what reason I could not discern. Perhaps she saw him as enticement for me to get out of bed and get dressed.

I threw an arm over my eyes, attempting to block out the light. I should have known it was not Édouard. Bitter disappointment collected in my throat until I thought I would gag on the repulsive taste.

I pulled up the covers and tried to go back to sleep, but moments later Maman was in my room again.

"Get up this instant. *Monsieur* Puvis has something remarkable to show you, but if you do not come down within the next few minutes you will miss it. Come, I shall help you into your dress. *Now,* Berthe."

"All right! Stop shouting at me."

The thought of listening to Maman nag about how lazy I'd become was incentive enough to get to my feet.

It seemed I'd barely stood when she'd encased me in a corset that had become too big for me.

"You've grown so thin," Maman murmured as she threw the dress over my head. A swipe of the brush. A few well-placed pins in my hair. Maman smiled and deemed me presentable for company.

She accompanied me to the drawing room. Was she afraid if she left me on my own I would go back to bed?

"Here she is." Maman sang my arrival as if I were a late guest to a party. Puvis stood.

"*Mademoiselle*, how wonderful to see you. I came as soon as I could, considering the circumstances that befall our beloved country. If you will forgive me for being so bold after having just arrived, I have something to show you. Will you and your Maman please accompany me to the window?"

Maman herded me to where Puvis had thrown back the sash. High up in the sky was a giant red balloon. The bright light hurt my eyes, and I blinked at the spectacle.

Maman gasped. "What in heaven's name?"

"That is our good friend Nadar. He is the head of the balloon corps. Thanks to him we shall be able to resume communication with the outside world. I saw him floating in the clouds as I made my way here today and could not wait to share it with you."

We stood at the window in reverent silence.

"Everyone used to laugh at Nadar and his fixation with balloons," said Puvis. "Now he laughs at the world as he floats high above the ranks. 'Tis a sign of hope, is it not?"

I blinked. It more resembled a strange dream—this vision high in the smoky sky was like a child's toy left out in the rain. This sight, coupled with Maman's warm reception of Puvis, was very strange, indeed.

Perhaps I was still asleep and this was another nonsensical dream?

I glanced up to the sky at the red balloon, and my eyes adjusted to the daylight. I tried to see Puvis's glimmer of hope. That perhaps it was a sign that the world would soon be right again.

Then I noticed Puvis gazing at me, and I remembered his written declaration of love. I backed away and sat on the sofa.

I did not want to hurt his feelings after he came so far. He was a good man, a steadfast friend. Alas, I did not have a single romantic feeling for him.

"*Mademoiselle,* you look exhausted. Are you all right?"

I nodded. "By showing me this, you have given me new hope that I might communicate with my loved ones who are so very far away."

Why had I said that? I hoped and prayed the mention of correspondence would not inspire him to broach the subject of his letter to me. Not in front of Maman.

"Will you stay for lunch?" Maman offered. "It will be simple fare—bread and soup."

I could hear the frost forming around the edges of my mother's words. As the polite hostess, of course she would ask him to stay for refreshment in this time of war. But since Puvis had served his purpose—rousted me back among the living—Maman's invitation was as much a notice that the visit was over as it was an offer to dine with us.

"*Merci, non.* I wanted to stop by and check on you, but I cannot stay."

Maman and I sat, but Puvis remained by the window.

"How is everything?" I asked.

He shrugged. Shook his head. "It is hard to say, *Mademoiselle.* Every day we hold off the Prussians is another day that prolongs the war." He shrugged again.

"And what of our friends? Several of them serve in the National Guard with you—Alfred Stevens and Édouard Manet? What do you hear of them?"

"I'm sorry, I have heard nothing. You received news of Bazille, of course? And Régnault? Both dead. It is so sad."

I nodded.

"I have heard nothing else. But I am sure no news means the rest are fine. I have not seen their names on the fatality list, and I check it daily."

I sighed and glanced out the window again, but the balloon was gone. It was all right. In fact, I believed it was a good thing.

*November 1870*

*Dear Edma,*

*I write to you every day, hoping that out of all these letters some will reach you. The victory of Friday has raised the morale of many. We have heard the cannon all morning, but so far it is impossible to know the outcome. We are very well situated for hearing the cannon, but badly for obtaining news.*

*Would you believe that I am becoming accustomed to its boom? It seems to me that I am now absolutely inured to war and can endure anything.*

*We saw Monsieur Millet, yesterday: the owner of the apartment in the center of the city. We have resolved to move into the little garde-meuble in the rue Argensen. We would be very safe—and protected by the National Guard.*

*I think often of your Adolphe. I wonder what is happening to his squadron. The total ignorance in which we live is very distressing.*

*I embrace all of you,*
*Berthe*

*January 7, 1871*

"Berthe! Berthe!" Maman shrieked from the opposite end of the apartment. My heart plummeted to the pit of my stomach, which in turn dropped to my feet. A thousand horrors flooded my mind as I rushed to her. When I reached her, she was sobbing and clutching a piece of paper to her breast.

"Maman? Maman, what is it?"

"It is a letter. It is Edma. Oh—" Her words gave way to wails and sobs. Icy fear gripped me. This was the first letter we'd received since the post resumed service. I did not want to know the bad news that caused her to weep.

No! Not Edma.

I wanted to place my hands over my ears and stay that way, shutting out all that was loud and ugly and hurtful, but my arms would not move, and I stood there like an idiot staring at her.

"Here." She held the white paper out to me with one hand and swiped at her falling tears with the other.

"*Here,* take it. Read it aloud." She waved the paper. The slack skin of her flabby arm jiggled with the effort. I shook my head, and took a step back. As long as I did not read the words, no harm had come to Edma. I realized, standing and looking at the paper in her hand, that it might well be my last moment of sanity.

Maman sighed—more of a huff than a sigh. "Oh, what is wrong with you? Do not stand there like a ninny, Berthe. Everyone is fine. I just wanted you to read the good news."

*Good* news? What? I did not understand. The way she was sobbing and carrying on, I thought—

Maman sniffed and looked at the letter again. "That's what she said. *Fine.* Everyone, big and small, is well and accounted for."

Maman laughed through her sobs. Relief rushed over me in waves, yet I could not cry. My legs, still numb with aborted shock, were weak. I had to sit down. I backed into the divan just in time and landed with a soft thud.

Maman peered at the letter through her lorgnette, relaying the news as she read. "Edma says everyone is in good health, that Adolphe is at sea and that Tiburce—Oh!" she gasped, closed her eyes, crossed herself and tilted her head up to the heavens, as if reciting a prayer.

"What, Maman, *please?*"

"She says Tiburce has escaped from Metz—and is now a lieutenant! Such joy!"

Her words pushed me to the edge of the cushion.

"He is fine, Berthe, and a lieutenant to boot."

"Maman, I cannot get beyond the fact that my brother is finally free to share your joy in his promotion. He was a prisoner of war."

"Really, Berthe, if one is to be a hero, one must suffer a few close calls. But my Tiburce, he is too wily to succumb and will pull through unscathed. I shall never doubt that for one minute. Don't you doubt him either. He has the brains to outsmart the enemy and that is how he will rise to the top."

A cannon exploded outside in the distance. The Prussians were encamped from the Faubourg Saint-Honoré to the Place de la Concorde. The French militia had cleared out, taking up station on the opposite side of the Seine, with a line of sentries guarding the bridges. And Maman was celebrating Tiburce's promotion as if he worked in a bank.

I wondered if she had a true grasp of what was happening beyond our walls.

*January 14, 1871*

When I awoke the morning of my thirtieth birthday, I did not know who dreaded this day more—Maman or me. Neither of us could celebrate because the day held only two realities: there was no end in sight for the war, and I was old and unmarried—a disappointment to my parents.

Provisions were scarce. We'd been living on stale and unappetizing biscuits for a fortnight. Sometimes my stomach fared better without food.

This morning, since it was my birthday, Maman made a fresh batch, and I felt obliged to try to eat. So I sat with her at the tiny breakfast table and picked at the crumbling pieces.

"You are getting too thin, Berthe," said Maman. "You have hollows in your cheeks. You are no longer young. So you must make the most of what you have. No man will find a malnourished waif attractive."

I was in no mood for an upbraiding.

"Puvis has been attentive these past few months," I said to spite her.

He had gathered a bouquet of wildflowers and brought them to me yesterday, because he was not sure he would be able to call today for my birthday.

"Pierre Puvis de Chavannes is a strange old man," said Maman. "I do not like him, despite his wealth and his art. I have decided he would not make a suitable husband for you."

"Why, Maman? Because he dotes on me? Because Puvis and I have much in common, unlike the fat, boring *Monsieur* Dally who would rather eat me for dinner than engage me in conversation? I seem to remember a time not too long ago when you encouraged me to pursue a relationship with *Monsieur* Puvis de Chavannes."

She tried to interject, but I was too furious to let her berate me anymore. "What galls me, Maman, is that even in the midst of a war you still pin the worth of my existence on how attractive men find me. I would laugh at you. Only today I do not possess any humor."

She sat, head bowed, staring at the half-eaten biscuit on her plate. I left the table and retired to my room.

She was right. I was old. Perhaps that was why Édouard had forsaken me. Why, when he could have his choice of beautiful young models, would he want me—tired, sad, old and broken?

*January 30, 1871*

Maman came to my room with a cup of tea. She'd given up cajoling me into eating. But I did appreciate the tea. Now that Paris had surrendered and agreed upon an armistice with Germany, perhaps life would resume. This above all was the easiest to swallow.

As she handed me the cup and saucer, she wore a strange smile—an expression I'd not seen in months.

"I have wonderful news, *Bijou*. Edma received word that Adolphe is at home in Cherbourg. She has decided to join him as soon as the trains are running again. When she does, she will come to Paris for a few days to visit us. Perhaps you would like to accompany her to Cherbourg?"

I sipped the hot tea and longed to spend time with my sister. Yet, staying in Paris was my only chance to see Édouard. The thought leapt into my mind unbidden and made me angry at myself. That I would even think of forsaking my sister after Édouard had deserted me. It was unfathomable. I realized he'd been fighting a war, but if Puvis found the wherewithal to make regular trips from Versailles, couldn't Édouard at least send me a note to reassure me of his safety? Unless it meant—

No! He could not be dead.

Tea splashed over the rim of my cup as I returned it to the saucer. Propriety sat next to Olympia, trying to talk sense into the brazen whore. *What a pitiful creature you have become, willing to put your life on hold for a man who obviously does not care. You must stop ripping out your heart and offering it to a man who does not want it.*

"That *is* wonderful news, Maman. A trip to Cherbourg would be lovely."

*February 10, 1871*

*Dear Edma,*

*If you knew how sad this poor Paris is! And how sad everything is! I have come out of this siege absolutely disgusted with my fellow men, even with close friends. Selfishness, indifference, prejudice—that is what one finds in nearly everyone.*

*I am eager to see you; it seems to me that we have so much to tell one another, so much to grieve about together. Father said he has written you a long letter. He is far from sharing Yves's opinions; I do not share them either, nevertheless I still manage to disagree with Father. We talk so little to each other that this does not make much difference. We are awaiting the results of the elections with the same impatience as you.*

*Adieu,*
*Berthe*

# Chapter Twenty

## March 1871

*I love you*
*The more in that I believe*
*You have liked me for my*
*Own sake and for nothing else.*
                                        —*John Keats*

The trains were running again. Edma sent us a letter saying
we could expect her within the week:

> *I wish I could be more specific as to an arrival time, but it*
> *will depend when I can secure passage. So many people*
> *are moving about after being confined for so long. Please*
> *do not worry about me. When I get to the station, I shall*
> *hire a carriage to bring me to you at the rue Argensen.*

We wanted to believe the worst was over, but by the time
we received her letter, we were in the midst of a new situation, which made us fear for Edma's safety.

The Prussians were preparing for their ceremonial victory
march through Paris toward the Champs-Elysées. When that
fated day arrived, all we could do was pray Edma had heard of
the news and did not arrive in the midst of it.

The Prussians marched in the deserted streets, while Parisians sequestered themselves inside, bolting their doors
and shuttering their windows against the ceremony. Those

monsters caused enough misery. We refused to acknowledge how they'd brought our nation—and every French cit-
izen—to its knees.

It was all over within two days.

We held our breath until our dear Edma and little
Jeanne arrived with Tiburce a week later.

Our parents were elated by the family reunion.

"Too bad Yves could not be here," said Papa. "But it
gives me comfort that she is safe at home with Théodore."

Once Maman picked up baby Jeanne, she did not set her
down again. That gave Edma a much-needed break and
time for us to talk.

"What do you hear from our friend Manet these days?"
There was a sparkle in her eyes that encouraged me to tell
her everything.

But I had nothing to say.

"Which Manet? We have seen Eugène more than his
brother."

Tiburce, Edma and I decided to go for a stroll along the
*quai*. But once we arrived, we discovered hordes of people
milling about the approach to the *Hôtel de Ville*. Some were
shrieking, others were shouting, still more were weeping.
They seemed to be overcome by some sort of madness.
Then we noticed that the *quai* and the two main streets
leading up to the *Hôtel de Ville* were barricaded and lined by
rows of armed National Guard, chasseurs and soldiers of
the line. A red flag flew on the hôtel tower. The military
cordoned off the area.

The sight made the hair on my arms stand on end. Edma
linked her arm through mine and scooted closer.

"Tiburce, what is happening?" she asked.

"I don't know."

He tucked us in an out-of-the-way spot on the grass near a chestnut tree, and said, "Stay here. I'll try to find out, but please do not move from here or I might not be able to find you again."

As Tiburce disappeared into the crowd, I scanned the faces of the guards dressed in red and blue uniforms, looking for Édouard, but I did not see him. In the midst of this frenzied scene, a familiar pang tugged at my heart. No matter what had passed between us, I hoped he was safe and unscathed.

Tiburce was only gone a few minutes when I saw Eugène Manet elbowing his way through the throngs.

My heart soared. "*Monsieur* Manet!" I waved.

His eyes brightened when he recognized us. He pushed his way over. I looked around to see if Édouard was with him.

"*Madame, Mademoiselle,* I am happy to see you, but what are you doing here? This is no place for ladies."

"We were out for a stroll with our brother, Tiburce," I said. "He has gone to inquire of the situation."

"It is not good," said Eugène. "There is unrest over the new government. Thiers has ordered the National Guard disarmed. The Guard is taking a stand by rolling out cannons. It is not safe and I fear the worst is not yet over. Many are unhappy that the siege ended in an armistice and not victory. I don't know if the brewing discontent will come to a peaceable end without more bloodshed. I would suggest that your brother escort you home at once. In the meantime, I shall stay with you until he returns."

Edma gasped.

"Please tell me this is not true. I am on my way home to my husband. I have not seen him in eight months. Will this madness never end?"

Eugène placed a gentle hand on her back.

"I wish I could assure you it would."

As each moment passed, Edma grew more anxious. She stood on tiptoes and scanned the crowd for Tiburce. She took a couple of steps out into the crowd, craning her neck in all directions.

Eugène and I stood in awkward silence.

"How is your brother?" My heart pounded so that each beat recalled a cannon blast.

A noisy bunch pushed between us, laughing and shouting, reeking of drink and unwashed bodies. Eugène stood closer to me to shield me from another loud bunch of ruffians.

"He was released from duty a week ago and has joined his family in the south-west. I am set to follow tomorrow."

With those words, my heart stopped.

If any hope of Édouard returning to me simmered within me, Eugène supplied the water to douse the remaining embers.

"I see." I felt as if my insides were hollow. I could not cry, which was a good thing standing here with his brother. I could not feel anything except numb dread spreading throughout my body. "Please give *Monsieur* Manet and his family my regards. Tell him I am much relieved to hear he has escaped the war unscathed."

Eugène nodded and stroked his beard.

"With trouble brewing, I wonder how long he will stay away. He harbors strong opinions about this regime, and I am sure he will want to help the cause."

*The cause.* Papa detested the cause. As far as he was concerned, they were a band of revolutionary zealots looking to reinvent trouble. How ironic that Édouard should be among them. I'd determined to take a wait-

and-see attitude before I branded myself for or against them, but I was beginning to believe I detested them as much as Papa did.

"And you, *Monsieur?*" I asked. "Will you change your plans with this shift in political climate?"

"I am not inclined to fight, *Mademoiselle.* If I were to change my plans, it would take an alluring enticement to tempt me to stay in Paris."

A man with an empty wine bottle in one hand and his arm around a toothless blonde in a dirty, low-cut dress tried to push between us, but Eugène shifted closer to me, forcing them to stumble around us.

The proximity of Eugène's body next to mine made me uncomfortable. He gazed down at me with a strange look on his face. I was doing my best to hold my hollow self together in the midst of the commotion, in the wake of his news about Édouard's departure. For lack of knowing what to do, I pulled away from him and turned to look for Edma, but she was no longer in my range of vision. I turned in a circle looking for her, bumping into people who were trying to pass.

"Where is Edma?" I cried. Nearby, a cannon blasted. I covered my ears. "Where is my sister?" The crowd shifted, surged forward. A burly man shoved past me. I fell backward. Eugène caught me. Righted me. His hands encircled my waist and held me until I was steady.

"I see her," he said. "She is over there with Tiburce." Through the crowd, I caught a glimpse of her, wringing her hands, talking to my brother, and I knew the situation was grave.

"I want to get to them so we can go home."

Eugène took hold of my hand and pulled me through the crowd. Someone groped me as we bumped from one dirty drunk to the next, inhaling vile, fetid odors the likes of which I'd never in my life experienced, but Eugène did not let go of my hand. In a matter of moments, he deposited me next to Tiburce and Edma.

"We must get the ladies away from this madness," Eugène said. "May I accompany you to the *rue* Argensen? I should very much like to pay my respects to your parents."

We took a different way home, thinking it would be safer to keep to the wide boulevards rather than the winding back streets.

But about halfway home, we encountered the most horrid smell. It was so strong that even covering our mouths and noses provided no relief.

A rotting corpse was propped in an open doorway holding a sign that said, "Death to Thiers." Edma screamed and fainted into Tiburce's arms.

I closed my eyes and buried my face in Eugène's shoulder.

He put an arm around me and held me close the rest of the way home.

*My Dearest Edma,*

*The day of your departure, after that sad walk on the boulevard that upset us so greatly, we had a visit from the fat Monsieur Dally. I was still disturbed. The doctor had been returning from the Place Vendôme, where he had been attending the wounded and helping to collect the dead. He told me their names, at least the names of those he knew; I was greatly worried, nervous, being troubled for fear of hearing bad news. The sad evening that the four of us spent together brought back the siege to me as if I had never come out of it. Life has been a terrible night-*

*mare for six months, and I am surprised that I am strong*
*enough to bear it.*

*Affectionately,*
*Berthe*

May 1871

The courts closed. Papa was free to go. He insisted on
moving us from the *rue* Argensen to Saint-Germain.

"How can we leave our son in the thick of battle?"
Maman insisted.

"Your staying in harm's way will do nothing to keep him
safe," Papa yelled. "If you wish to support him, you will go
to a safe place so he may remove you from his list of worries."

Maman looked as if he'd slapped her into reality. She
said nothing, only started packing what was left of her belongings to take to Saint-Germain.

Because of the new outbreak of fighting, I decided
against accompanying Edma to Cherbourg. It was a good
thing, too, now that we were to move again.

The day before we left, I received a letter from Puvis.

*Mademoiselle,*

*Please be so kind as to send me news of you and your*
*family to Versailles, poste restante. I have been here for*
*several days with my sister and brother-in-law, who is a*
*member of the Assembly.*

*No other place is more unlike Paris than this. That is*
*why I should have chosen it in any case, in order to escape*
*certain sights and certain contacts. I was happy to leave*
*my awful quarter, where informing against one's neighbor*
*is becoming a daily occurrence, and where one may at any*
*moment be forced to join the rabble under penalty of being*

*shot by the first escaped convict who wants the fun of doing it.*

*I hope that your parents will not think that the place can hold out forever, and that they will leave Paris to await the denouncement elsewhere. If Versailles were not overflowing with refugees, it would be the best place for you, but short of Versailles, there are Cernay, Saint-Cyr, Marly and many other places.*

*One is bathed in a feeling of grandeur in this admirable and magnificent setting, the sight of which is reassuring, since it recalls a beautiful and noble France, and one can forget for a moment how false and corrupt she is today. Once again, I repeat my prayers to you: please let me know what is happening to you. I assure you all my respectful devotion.*

*Pierre Puvis de Chavannes*

Saint-Germain was a haven compared to the war-torn Paris we left behind. But it didn't shelter us from news of the tragedy that further befell our beloved city.

"The *rue* Royal is deserted. The entire quarter is dismal and dreary," said Papa, who'd come in from his afternoon stroll. "All the shops are closed; people stand at the window watching the marchers move toward the Place Vendôme to seize the post of the National Guard."

Papa shook his head. Maman and I could do little but stare at his drawn face. "It is a bloody massacre. They were marching without arms. Twenty-five men killed."

He fell into a chair at the table and buried his face in his hands. None of us needed utter a word to know what each was thinking.

Tiburce was leading the unarmed front. My brother, who thrived on being in the thick of the fight, believed he was invincible.

All we could do was wait and pray he was right.

A few days later Tiburce dropped in for a moment to assure everyone of his well-being. He was safe and more exuberant than ever, looking handsome in his uniform adorned with a party ribbon in the buttonhole. Maman made such a fuss one would have thought Thiers himself had paid a call. But I, too, was relieved to see Tiburce looking so well.

"I am on Admiral Saisset's staff. We have taken over the Grand Hôtel. The greater part of the place is barricaded. The windows are covered with mattresses, and we have plenty of cannons and guns." He paused to sip his tea. He made me think of a little boy who'd come in for refreshment after spending the morning playing war with his friends. "During the first negotiations, I volunteered to relay communications to General Chiseret and Lullier. I am acquainted with them, so I was the natural choice to deliver the communiqué."

Maman sighed, "Ah, such a brave, brave boy."

Tiburce puffed. "I have known some tense moments." His eyes shifted to Papa, who looked very old as he slumped in his chair, a vacant expression of worry creasing his forehead.

"It is all in the posturing. For example, we publicize that our forces are two thousand strong. In reality, five hundred is a more accurate count." He laughed. "They're terrified of us. Never fear, reinforcements are on the way."

Papa frowned. The sound of the clock ticking in the background seemed distorted and loud. "This is an atrocity. You cannot fight with so few men. Please stay here and forget this foolishness. They will manage without you."

Maman snorted and threw her head back. "He has a commitment to Admiral Saisset. He cannot simply *forget* to follow through on his word."

Papa looked dejected. Maman indignant. Tiburce's expression did not waver. Ever the diplomat, he tried to mend the peace. "Father, I have men who rely on me for their orders. I am no longer on the front line. When we rally tomorrow at the Grand Hôtel, it shall go quickly. We shall be covered. Since they have used force, we shall pick up our arms."

He stood to leave.

Maman rose to hug her hero.

Papa turned his face to the window.

"You have done your duty," she said, holding her son's face in her hands. "Take good care, my boy."

I watched Tiburce walk out the door. I was proud of his zest. I envied his sense of purpose. It had been a hard time for everyone, but he'd not been passively subjecting himself to the whims of fate. I'd wasted the last year of my life fretting over situations rather than fighting to change them, and I was ashamed of myself.

My discontent grew beyond the disruption of war. It started with Édouard. I placed my happiness in his hands, gave him permission to mold my emotional well-being as he deemed fit. Look where it landed me. I was to blame for my own unhappiness.

It was up to me to make a life for myself.

I'd received another letter from Puvis. He asked me to call him Pierre. He was sweet, showering me with attention, where Édouard removed himself from my life.

Pierre wanted to see me, said he wanted to win Maman and Papa's approval. It overwhelmed me, but in him I'd found the affection of a fine man who understood my soul belonged to my work.

Tiburce found his purpose in his work. I should follow

his example. I wasn't equipped to go to battle on a national scale, but seeing Tiburce march off with such pride, I realized I could take possession of my life and trump the demons I'd battled for so long.

I could win my own war.

*My Dearest Edma,*

*The more I think about your life, the more favored it appears to be. I wish you would tell me whether it is possible to work in Cherbourg. This may seem an unfeeling question, but I hope you can put yourself in my position and understand that work is the sole purpose of my existence, and that infinitely prolonged idleness would be fatal to me from every point of view.*

*The countryside here is the prettiest in the world; there would be a lot of subject matter for someone who liked bare landscapes and had the necessary equipment for work. Neither of these conditions exists in my case, and I no longer want to work just for the sake of working.*

*I do not know whether I am indulging in illusions, but it seems that a painting like the one I gave Manet could perhaps sell, and that is all I care about.*

*Since you understand perfectly well what I mean, answer me on this point and now let us talk about more interesting things. Everyone is engrossed in this wretched business of politics. We can hear the cannon throughout the day; we can see the smoke on Mont Valérien from the terrace. From time to time we meet people who have got out of Paris. Their accounts are contradictory: according to some, people there are dying of starvation; according to others, the city is perfectly peaceful. The only thing certain is that everyone is fleeing from it, and this is sufficient proof that life there is not pleasant.*

*We are almost reassured about the fate of our house on the rue Franklin, but I see this morning that they tried to destroy the batteries of the Trocadéro from Mont Valérien; such an operation cannot be carried out without splattering the neighborhood, and we are philosophically awaiting the outcome.*

*Affectionately,*
*Berthe*

There was nothing for me in Saint-Germain.

Nothing to paint.

Nothing to anticipate.

If I were to quit dwelling in the past and move forward, I must move myself to a place where I was able to live. With a valise filled with painting supplies, I boarded the train to my sister's home in Cherbourg. Maman and Papa were quite safe in their little Saint-Germain sanctuary. I could go to my sister with a light heart.

As the engine pulled out of the station, I did not glance back at the old life I left behind. The war had demolished more than walls and monuments. I was a different person than I was a year ago, although I did not see how *anyone* could suffer through the terrible atrocities we'd lived through this year and emerge the same. It was impossible. I was broken, yet not irreparably damaged. It was as if I'd been taken apart and reconstructed anew. The old ways were less complicated in certain ways, but now. . . . Now I knew I would steer my ship wisely, as Maman was so fond of telling me.

I did not know if it was that I was happy to be in Edma's company again or if my relief stemmed from being out from under the web of Maman and Papa's tension. Even the air in Cherbourg seemed lighter. I found many pleasing vignettes to paint outside so I could enjoy the beautiful spring days. I'd begun a new life in this charming place, leaving behind my old unhappiness.

"Edma, turn your head to the left and look down at little Jeanne. This will make a beautiful painting."

My sister's morale about domestic life was improved from when I visited her in Lorient, where she led such a bleak existence. She had a baby now. Like our brother, she had discovered her purpose in life.

*Dear Mademoiselle,*

*Your letter brings me much pleasure, and I should like to prove this to you by my promptness in answering it. I wish, however, that it had been more detailed about several things, such as the welcome you received from your sister, who must have been happy to see you again, and also about the outcome of your journey. You know how much such things interest me, whether they pertain to your art or to your personal life—which I presume to be the case at the present, for one hardly paints while traveling in a railway carriage. You are enjoying fresh air in the company of your family who love you, you are seeing a place that is new to you and you are no longer hearing the stupid cannon. Meanwhile you are as well informed as we are of every important event and you are always in your own company. Why then should one be sorry for you? You ask me what is being talked about and what is happening in Versailles. Well, it's always the same things. The rue des Reservoirs has not become easier for Parisians to climb, and they mark time in their souls even more than on the street. As for me, I produce as much as I can, but these things remain in a latent state, so to speak—formless sketches or spots of color that I expect nevertheless to turn to account some day. It is cold, sharp, unpleasant. The shade frigid and the sun pitiless. Add to that some great dust squalls that blind you from time to time and an absolutely artificial existence, and you will know as much about Versailles as if you were living here.*

*Thiers upbraided the Chamber in very severe terms at yesterday's meeting, to the acute displeasure of the great majority, despite appearances to the contrary, and despite the vote of absolute confidence that followed his lashing.*

*Above all please write and tell me everything you are doing and thinking. It is more than likely that we shall soon return to Paris. You must come and see what is left of my poor studio.*

*Ah, those cannon balls—brutal things, aren't they? I often think of those very pleasant hours I spent last year in that big bazaar that has become a dressing station, filled today with every sort of disease. Not so long ago, it was full of strollers, paintings, sculptures, pastries, etc. The point is that time passed quickly there. All this is now strangely gone with the wind, and no sooner will the ruins be more or less restored than one will be oneself a ruin. If only Ivy would grow around old me the way it grows around the statues of Versailles.*

*And so you see you must tell me in great detail what is happening to you, whether you are working, whether you are succeeding—in other words, everything.*

> *Adieu, dear Mademoiselle.*
> *I remain forever your faithful servant,*
> *Pierre Puvis de Chavannes*

*June 1871*

Maman wrote that Tiburce arrived home. He gave additional details of the horrors of fighting, but did not confirm everything the newspapers had reported. She said Montmartre was captured, but the Place de la Concorde put up such a resistance that the shells rained all about our house. We'd not much hope that the *rue* Franklin would soon be cleared. There was a rumor that a neighbor's home was demolished, but only part of the wall was damaged and the furniture was still intact.

The Communards stole the linen, some pictures, a clock—all the things they could carry, and of course, they emptied the wine cellar, then scrawled disgusting epitaphs on every available surface.

I trembled to think what would happen. Maman said that once Paris was taken, *Monsieur* Thiers would resign, and without him there would be nothing to restrain the reactionaries. We would advance to full-fledged monarchy. New struggles with no respite. I was afraid that such would be our lot.

*May 25, 1871*

> *My Dear Bijou,*
>
> *Paris is on fire! This is beyond description. Throughout the day the wind kept blowing in charred papers; some of them were still legible. A vast column of smoke covers Paris, and at night a luminous red cloud, horrible to behold, made it all look like a volcanic eruption. There were continual explosions and detonations; we were spared nothing. They said the insurrection is crushed, but the shooting has not yet stopped. Hence this is not true. By ten o'clock, when we left the terrace, the fire seemed to have been put out, so that I hoped very much that everything had been grossly exaggerated, but the accounts in*

*the newspapers this morning left no room for doubt. Latest official dispatch: the insurrection is now driven back to a very small part of Paris, the Tuilleries is reduced to ashes, the Louvre survives, the part of the Finance Ministry building up from the rue de Rivoli is on fire, the Cour des Comptes is burned down, twelve thousand prisoners, Paris strewn with dead.*

*Maman*

*June 1871*

*Dear Berthe and Edma,*

*I saw the Hôtel de Ville the day after I returned to Paris. How frightful—the substantial building has been ripped open from one end to the other!*

*It was smoking in several places, and the firemen were still pouring water on it. It is a complete ruin. Your father would like all this debris to be preserved as a perpetual reminder of the horrors of popular revolution.*

*It's unbelievable, a nation thus destroying itself! Going down by boat, I saw the remains of the Cour des Comptes, of the Hôtel de la Legion d'Honneur, of the Orsay barracks, of a part of the Tuilleries. The poor Louvre has been nicked by projectiles, and there are few streets that do not bear traces of the struggle. I also noticed that half the rue Royale is demolished, and there are so many ruined houses, it is unbelievable—one rubs one's eyes wondering whether one is really awake.*

*Tiburce has met two Communards at this moment when they are all being shot—Manet and Degas. Even at this stage they are condemning the drastic measures to repress them. I think they are insane, don't you?*

*Maman*

★ ★ ★ ★ ★

*June 10, 1871*

*Dear Mademoiselle,*

*We returned to Paris several days ago, and the ladies asked me to send their regards to you and to Madame Pontillon.*

*What terrible events have befallen us this year. How shall we ever get back to normal? Each of us blames another, but we're all responsible for what has happened. We're all ruined; we shall have to work hard to glimpse life as it was before.*

*I happened upon your brother a few days ago. Yet I have not been able to visit your mother as I had hoped. Eugène went to see you at Saint-Germain, but you were out that day. I was pleased to hear your beautiful home in Passy escaped damage. I hope, Mademoiselle, you will not prolong your stay in Cherbourg as I would like very much to see you.*

*E. Manet*

# Chapter Twenty-One

## July 1871

*Many Waters cannot quench love,*
*Nor can the floods drown it.*
*—Song of Solomon 8:7*

If we began again, it would end. It was a pattern with Édouard and me. He sensed my pulling away, and courted me to close the distance. His charm whitewashed the ugly gray between us, over which he'd paint a new scene of budding possibilities that would never blossom.

I left his letters unanswered, which made him all the more attentive. He wrote nearly every day—twenty-eight letters since I'd been in Mirande. When I joined Edma at the breakfast table, I saw another of his attempts at correspondence lying beside my plate. I picked it up and held it for a moment, unopened. Seeing my name scrawled in his bold, familiar script, a dreaded sense of compression gripped my chest.

Why was it that he did not want me when he could have me, yet tried so desperately to win me the moment I resolved I was finished with him?

And I was finished with him.

It was as simple as that.

"What does Manet have to say today?" Edma asked, then bit into her brioche. Her gaze lingered on the letter.

I placed it on the table and sipped my coffee. "I don't

know. I have not opened it."

She looked up at me. "He has written you every day."

"He has."

She bit into her bread again. Chewed. I stared out the window at Marie, Edma's maid, who was hanging bed linens out to dry on a clothesline that ran parallel to the house.

"Is it about business? Perhaps he wants to introduce you to his dealer?"

"Perhaps." I took another sip of coffee. My stomach was too upset to consider a bite of food. "When Jeanne awakens, shall we go back to the meadow so I can work on the painting?"

"That's fine." She nudged the note with her finger. "But aren't you going to open it?"

The truth was I could not. Not sitting there with Edma. She would expect me to read it to her and how would I explain? If this letter was anything like the others he'd sent . . . declarations of love, remorse for having fallen out of my favor. The content was such that it would raise Edma's eyebrow.

Perhaps both of them.

"You're still involved with him."

She stated the words in a matter-of-fact manner, as one might have said, "The coffee is cold" or "It is raining outside." They caught me off-guard. I stared into my cup.

"He is my friend, yes. If that is what you imply?"

The word *friend* felt like a lie and my ire rose to a burning level. What kind of friend deserted another in such a dire time?

I was not good at deception, and I would've done myself a disservice to say too much.

"Then if he is merely a friend, why does he write to you

every day? Even Puvis, who has intentions, does not write to you every day."

"I do not write to Édouard." My words were a sharp knife slicing through the thick air.

"Exactly."

It was warm in the house. The table was next to a window with an eastern exposure that intensified the heat. As did Edma's inquisition. I picked up Édouard's letter and fanned myself.

"If he were your friend, as you claim," she said, "you would feel compelled to write to him on occasion. And you've not written him a single note." She reached out and touched my hand. "Oh, Berthe, what are you doing? Puvis is in love with you. Do not ruin this chance."

I pulled my hand away and tucked the letter into the folds of my skirt, out of her line of vision.

"Ruin what?"

"Your chance at marriage."

I picked up my cup again, resisting the urge to succumb to my anger.

"He has not proposed. Even if he does, Maman and Papa will never accept him. You know their feelings. They can't stomach him."

"Yes, but it is so obvious he is smitten with you."

I set down the cup with a thud. "Edma, since you married, you have become as bad as Maman when it comes to selling me to the highest bidder. The part that angers me the most is that you have never once asked me if I am in love with him."

She dabbed at the corners of her mouth with a serviette. "Which gentleman should I enquire after, Berthe? Manet or Puvis?"

I glared at her. At least she had the decency to avert her

eyes to her half-eaten roll.

"Oh never mind," she said. "It is obvious."

I spent the morning in my room. We did not go out to the meadow, but it was just as well. The time alone working on the canvas from memory softened my mood. Even in my rage, I had my wits about me enough to realize I did not want this visit to end on a sour note as in Lorient. I did not want to run home in a fit of temper as I did then. I did not want to say things to Edma I'd later regret. After all, her concern held grains of truth—Manet proved to be an unworthy candidate for my devotion.

Perhaps unworthy was too harsh a word. I would like to think he would have been much more reliable had circumstances been different. Alas, he was committed to Suzanne. Whether he married her out of love or pity, the woman's hold on him ran deeper than his feelings for me.

I held that point in the forefront of my mind.

I slipped my brush into a jar of turpentine. The red paint dispersed like blood in water. I picked up his unopened letter and deposited it in the trash. Édouard and his scattered whims were not part of my new plan.

I'd make a name for myself as an artist. That name would be my own, not that of a man I did not love; not that of a man I married for the sake of becoming someone's wife.

By noon Edma and I made amends, but it was too hot to paint in the meadow. We sat outside in the shade of the willow tree fanning ourselves while little Jeanne toddled about the poppies in the tall, wispy grass.

"Are you in love with Puvis?" Edma asked.

I sighed, but was not put off by the question. It hung between us like a curtain begging to be pulled back.

"I admire him and appreciate his steadfast friendship, but if *Monsieur* Puvis wants to ask for my hand in marriage, I fear I have given him the wrong impression. You are the one who has helped me realize this."

We sat for a few moments in companionable silence, but I felt my sister's disappointment, although she did not voice it.

The white sheets Marie had hung to dry that morning fluttered in the faint breeze. Edma and I tilted our chins up to catch the warm wind.

"Give it time," Edma said. "Emotions are still running high after the terrible year we have spent. The world is up-side down."

I nodded. "But when all is right again, I do not expect my feelings to have changed. Don't you suppose Puvis is so anxious to marry because he feels the need to attach himself to something stable, something normal and familiar, after the war? Every letter he's written talks about the war causing him to take stock of his life.

"I hesitate not so much because I fear he will change his mind after life resumes, but because . . . because I do not possess the feelings for him a woman should possess when contemplating marriage."

Edma nodded and traced a seam in the quilt we sat on.

"Maman and Papa would be glad to hear that." My sister seemed a bit deflated, but acted as if she were trying to come to terms with my revelation. "You know how they disapprove of him. So, you see, Maman is not willing to marry you off to just *anyone*." She smiled and imitated Maman's voice. "I will not settle on just *anyone* for you, *Bijou*. He must be respectable, a man of means—a busi-nessman or politician."

I made a face at Edma.

"Oh, Berthe, it is not that I am trying to marry you off." Jeanne toddled over and plopped down on the blanket next to her mother. "I simply want you to know the happiness I have found."

I squeezed her hand.

"But Edma, you are making a life with the man you love. It is not an arrangement born of middle-aged necessity."

She gazed at me, and I could see the wheels of her mind turning. For a moment I feared she would bring up Édouard again. "So it is not marriage that you are against?"

"Of course not."

She nodded as if she'd just fit another piece into a complicated puzzle. She started to speak again, but the rattle of a carriage in the distance distracted her. We shaded our eyes against the glare of the unrelenting sun to watch a driver coax horses to a stop in front of Edma's house.

Two handsome, well-dressed men disembarked.

"*Messieurs* Manet!" Edma called as she got to her feet.

My breath lodged in my throat. I wanted to run—far, far away—but instead, I sat there rooted to the earth like the chestnut tree I sat beneath.

"*Bonjour!*" Édouard threw his arms wide and laughed as if he'd just delivered the punch line to a magnificent joke.

Eugène doffed his hat and waved. It would be nice to visit with Eugène. I'd grown quite fond of him.

His brother, however, was another matter.

My sister met them halfway, but I stayed with Jeanne, who held out her little arms for me to pick her up. I obliged, grateful for the diversion.

As they drew closer, shock coursed through my body at how thin Édouard had become. His cheeks were hollow and his once-robust frame was but a spit of what it once was.

I drew baby Jeanne to me and buried my face in the

downy softness of her hair to avoid looking at him.

"What a lovely coincidence," said Edma. "Berthe and I were just talking about you."

"Berthe, why didn't you tell me the *Messieurs* Manet were coming today?" I detected a certain glint in Edma's eyes that warned of pure mischief.

We had settled in the living room. I leaned back into the chair and picked up the painted fan Degas gave me and fanned myself. "*Moi?* How was I supposed to know any better than you? The *Messieurs* Manet are popular gentlemen. I cannot keep up with their social schedules."

Édouard shifted, and I sensed a bit of discomfort beneath his affable exterior. He cleared his throat. "Did you not receive my letters, *Mademoiselle?* I sent word of our arrival, but it is possible the correspondence is late arriving. The mail is still unpredictable. I do beg your pardon for barging in unannounced. I hope we are not intruding."

He made no attempt to leave.

Something about his presumptuousness galled me, or perhaps what bothered me was the part of me that I'd taken care to bury deep inside was crawling to the surface because of his presence. I fidgeted.

No. No, that would not do at all.

"Come to think of it," I said, "a letter did arrive this morning. I have been so busy with my work that I've not had a moment to open it."

It gave me great pleasure to let Édouard know I was not hanging on his every word.

He raised a brow. "Perhaps work is what keeps you from answering my letters? When I didn't hear from you, I decided to pay a call to see for myself what occupied your thoughts."

A beat of bated silence painted the room with nervous tension. I vowed not to be the one who broke the quiet.

"Work occupies her thoughts, as does a certain *Monsieur* Puvis de Chavannes," said Edma, with a dreamy look on her face.

I darted a narrowed glance at her. What was she doing?

Édouard stiffened. Eugène's head snapped in my direction. All eyes were on me. Edma's dreaminess changed to a wicked smile. I was stunned for the first few seconds my sister commenced leading Édouard down the false path, but seeing how mention of Puvis's name got under Édouard's skin sparked tingles of excitement that skittered through me.

"I shall hint at a piece of news I am sure my sister won't mind me sharing," said Edma.

Eugène's gaze shifted to Edma, but Édouard stared at me.

"There could very well be an *announcement* soon. All I will say is that it has to do with a certain *addition* to the family." She giggled and covered her mouth. "Oh, but it is much too soon to talk about it. We have told no one." She winked. "I have already said far too much."

Edma stood and walked to the window. The *Messieurs* Manet slumped dumbfounded in their chairs. I wanted to laugh out loud. I wanted to leap up and hug my sister for getting even with Édouard on my behalf—even if I had no intention of marrying Puvis.

Oh, Edma, Edma, Edma, such a wicked girl.

It served Édouard right. And to think my sister did not even know the half of it.

Édouard's upper lip curled back. "What, you and Puvis? How? When did this happen?"

I wanted to say, "It happened while you were not paying

attention, Édouard." Instead, I covered my tracks. "*Monsieur,* nothing has happened. Edma should not have said what she did; there has not been an offer."

"But you expect one?" said Eugène.

Dead silence blanketed the room.

"Berthe, dear, may I prevail upon you for a favor?" Edma turned back to me from the window. "I know how you wish to visit with our guests, but would you be so good as to go outside and take the wash off the line? It is starting to cloud, and I am afraid we will get a shower. If you will be so kind, I shall make arrangements with Marie to start preparing dinner. *Messieurs,* you will stay to dinner with us, will you not? We shall not hear of sending you back to Paris with empty stomachs."

Édouard did not answer. As I passed him on my way to the door, I noticed he looked positively green as he stared at the wooden floor. I wondered if he'd heard Edma's invitation.

"*Merci,* we would love to stay," Eugène said. "In fact, I shall help *Mademoiselle* Berthe gather the wash."

Hand on the door, I glanced back at him.

"No, Eugène." Édouard's voice was a growl. "I shall help the *Demoiselle* outside. You stay here and assist *Madame* Pontillon."

Eugène did not protest. Why did he not stand up to his brother? Weak men were so unattractive. Guilt surged through me. Eugène was a decent fellow. This axiom should not apply to him. In the same vein that my soft spot for strong men who were bold enough to pursue that which they desired should not extend to Édouard.

They were the exceptions to the rules.

I did not wait for Édouard. I went outside and retrieved the basket on the grass near the clothesline and started yanking down the fresh linens.

"Your sister's right." He stood behind me. I did not turn to him. "See those clouds? It looks as if a storm is brewing."

A warm wind, a few degrees cooler than when Edma and I sat outside, caught the sheet. It billowed up around me. A strong arm reached over my head. I looked up and saw his arm silhouetted against the stormy sky. His hand toyed with the pin that held the sheet to the line, but he did not pluck it loose. "Are you going to marry Puvis?"

My shoulders sagged, and I wanted to turn around and scream at him. It was not Puvis I loved.

Was Édouard so blind he could not see the only feeling I possessed for Pierre was friendship? Then again Édouard had been absent for the past year. How could he gauge my feelings?

How could this be happening? How could I be so mis-guided and lacking in self-respect that I'd allow my walls to crumble with a single question?

As much as I hated myself for it, I knew all it would take was for Édouard to say the word. I'd leave with him, and never look back. But the suggestion would have to come from him. I'd laid out the plans once. They did not come to fruition, and he didn't even bother to contact me afterward.

No, I'd never suggest it again.

How could I be so weak as to even contemplate it?

I yanked a pin from the line, grabbed the corner of the sheet, moved down to the next and repeated the yanking and tugging process.

I tossed the sheet in the basket.

Discontent was a curse. I felt nothing for Puvis, the good man who tried in vain to woo me. Yet, I suffered as if my soul would die without Édouard, the one man I could not have.

"Do you love Puvis?" His voice was a coarse, rumbling growl, a low shout that bore into me, but I did not answer him.

With one strong tug, he turned me to face him. I stumbled and fell against him. We stood chest to chest as the breeze carried the scent of rain and fresh laundry and the white linens billowed around us.

His arms slid around me, and I felt his hot breath on my cheek.

I lay my head on his chest. "You deserted me," I whispered.

He kissed the top of my head. "Berthe, there was a war. I could not very well have gone off with you."

His words mocked me. I pushed away from him. Stumbled back a few steps. I needed room because standing so close to him clouded my senses. I wanted to curse Edma for starting this. Why did she do it? If not, most likely we would've had a polite visit. He would've gone back to Fat Suzanne. I would have carried on with my new life. But now, too many words were spoken, too many wounds reopened. What was one more—

"Then you had no intention of going away with me that day?"

He closed his eyes and took a deep breath. "My feelings for you remain unchanged."

He reached for my hand. I pulled away.

"I don't know what you want from me, Édouard. When I try to forget you, you reappear. When we get close, you push me away. I refuse to play this charade."

I remembered that first day in the Louvre, and my mind skipped back to an even earlier time when that unbidden attraction first lit the darkness. For a moment I longed to go back. But it was hopeless. I wished I did not know all I knew then, that so much had not passed between us.

"Édouard, we have been tormenting each other for three years. I cannot bear it another moment. Go away. Please let me be."

A raindrop fell onto my arm. I tried to move away from him to save the rest of the linen from the coming storm, but he grabbed my arm. The wind blew stronger. I jerked out of his grasp. A gust pulled a corner of one sheet loose from the line and the soft cotton whipped around my legs.

"Please, Berthe. Come back to Paris with me."

I grabbed the sheet—a fistful—to keep it from falling to the ground.

"Why, Édouard? What are you asking me?"

My pulse raced, and I tightened my grip on the fabric.

"I want to . . ."

His eyes were tender and frantic as he searched my face. I held my breath against his unspoken words.

"I want to paint you. I haven't been able to work since you've been away."

"What?"

So that was it? That's what it came down to. I yanked the other corner from the line and tossed the sheet into the basket.

"Find another model, Édouard. Any beautiful tramp will do. You do not need me."

"Yes I do."

His voice cracked. I turned and faced him, my hands on my hips.

"I do need you." His courage wavered. He looked away. "*Le Balcon* was so well received. Not like Olympia, not like the others."

"The others." I laughed. "There are the others and then there's me. Is that all I am to you? Instant respectability? Is that the face you're putting forth to the world now? Édouard Manet, painter of chaste decency?"

He gaped at me as if he could not comprehend what I was saying.

"What happened to the rebel who would risk anything if it were true?"

He did not answer me, and I found this weakness sickening. "I do not have the time or patience to play this game of chase anymore." I turned away and snatched down another sheet.

He walked around and stood in front of me, blocking me from finishing my task.

The rain fell harder, hitting my skin like pin pricks.

"Get out of my way."

I tried to push past him, but he grabbed me and pulled me to him, covering my mouth with his. There was nothing soft about his kiss. It was hard and hungry and desperate. The sheet, our erratic screen, fluttered up around us and back down again. All Edma and Eugène need do was look out the window and they would see us. But I didn't care. I couldn't help myself, I kissed him back as angry and punishing as he took me. Leaning into him. I grabbed handfuls of his jacket, pulling him to me. Then my hands fisted into his hair. I anchored myself to him, every centimeter of my body melting into his this one last time, because I knew when I let go it would be the end of us.

"Do not marry Puvis."

He pulled back just enough to let the desperate words take flight on his husky, breathless voice.

"Don't," was all I could manage.

"Do not marry him," he said again, his forehead pressed to mine, his lips a whisper away, "because I love you. I cannot bear to think of you with him."

# Chapter Twenty-Two

*Is the day better than the night?*
*Or is the night better than the day?*
*How can I tell?*
*But this I know is right:*
*Both are worth nothing*
*When my love's away.*

*—Amaru*

Days later, Édouard's words reverberated in my heart. I'd come to the conclusion that if he'd spit in my face it would've been easier to accept than his mocking declaration of love. For uttering those sacred words only because he could not bear to think of me with another was not love. He wanted to place me on a shelf, safe and away from the hands of other men, taking me down at his whim, and storing me away when I became an inconvenience.

He went back to Fat Suzanne.

I stayed in Mirande with Edma.

The relationship with Édouard was over. It was better that way.

Why had I not realized it would come to this before my love for him penetrated the cracks of my character, deepening them so they'd never close again? Now I paid the exorbitant price for my lack of self-control.

It was sad how relationships always ended. It was inevitable that one person found the other lacking and love ceased. That's why I would not prolong the inevitable.

I heard Edma and Marie bustling around downstairs and felt guilty for having taken to my bedchamber for the past few days. Edma was gentle with me, not asking too many questions. I was sure she saw the whole sordid episode through the window, like an opera staged in her yard. If she didn't see it, I was sure it was obvious that something was amiss when Édouard returned alone with the clothesbasket.

She didn't mention it when I returned that night. Long after Édouard and Eugène left. I was grateful for her prudence.

As I dressed, I heard footsteps outside my bedchamber door. Then a faint knock. It was Edma holding a breakfast tray.

She looked very pretty, smiling in the dim hallway. Like a patch of sunshine lighting the darkness. I couldn't help but smile, too.

"Oh, Edma, you needn't bother to bring food to me. I was just dressing to come downstairs and help you."

"It's no trouble." She set the tray on the small writing desk and turned back to me beaming.

"What?"

"I received a letter from Adolphe this morning. He's coming home in three days."

"That's wonderful. I know how much you've missed him."

She perched on the edge of the bed, and I could tell by the look on her face she wanted to talk.

"What I said to the *Messieurs* Manet about there likely being an addition to the family . . ."

I groaned because I was not at all prepared to discuss the day's events.

"What I said was true," she continued. "I can't believe I'm telling you—again—even before Adolphe knows, but the doctor just confirmed it and if I don't tell you I think I shall simply burst—"

"You mean?"

Edma nodded. "We are going to have another baby. A gift from Adolphe's last leave."

I hugged my sister, enjoying the rush of happiness surging through me. "So then, you did not lie to the Manet brothers."

She shrugged and shook her head. "Lie? Me? Never!"

"Well that's good. I was beginning to worry at how convincing you are in your falsehoods."

I winked at her, and we laughed together.

"Speaking of that, there is a letter on your tray from Puvis." She walked over to the desk, retrieved it and handed it to me.

I opened it.

*My Dear Mademoiselle,*

*Today I went to your home in Passy with the purpose of conveying a certain intention to your parents. A challenging feat, no doubt, given their feelings for me.*

*Alas, my future with you, my dear, is much too important to allow the matter of their feelings for me to keep us apart. Make no mistake, I shall win them over in due time.*

*I would have pursued this quest at once had I found them at home when I called. Alas, your brother, Tiburce, was the only one in residence. He assured me they would be gone for the better part of the day.*

*Upon hearing that news, I set out walking—all the way to the Bois de Boulogne. Where I stayed until the sky turned gray, opened and rained down upon me. I took the bad weather as a sign that the time was not right to speak to your parents. As I could not prevail upon them to receive me soaking wet, I went home, instead of walking back. Another day, my love. Another day.*

> *Until then, I remain yours faithfully,*
> *Pierre Puvis de Chavannes.*

Coward.

It was as if a strong wind snuffed a sputtering flame. He was nothing but a frightened little boy. This confirmed my instincts that life with Pierre Puvis de Chavannes, even if he was my only viable marriage prospect, would be a huge mistake.

I laughed the kind of humorless laugh one can't help when something they've suspected is proven, but I felt Edma's hand on my shoulder and it stifled the urge like a cork in a bottle.

"Is everything all right?"

"Yes. It's fine. Everything is fine." I folded the letter and stared at it for a moment, not sure what to do with it.

After Edma left, I tore it to shreds.

Edma did not want me to leave Mirande, but I couldn't stay with Adolphe coming home. They needed their privacy, their time together, after all this time apart. So much good to celebrate, what with France settling back into peace, and a new baby on the way. I would just be in the way. As much as I loved being with my sister, I was quite homesick for Paris.

I was ready to go home.

Maman was up to her old tricks again. This time she'd found an accomplice in *Madame* Manet. The two of them decided Eugène and I were like the remainders of two pairs of stockings, each with a missing mate. Alone we served no purpose, but together this mismatched pair could function—even if we weren't a perfect complement.

I couldn't imagine it. The idea was preposterous.

We shared no romantic interest. I shuddered to think of how he would act toward me if he'd witnessed the exchange between his brother and me at Edma's in Mirande.

He must have been as confounded as I was by our mothers' determination to pair us up. But if he was willing to come to dinner, perhaps he did not think less of me.

Perhaps he would act like a gentleman and forget the whole thing. If nothing else, maybe we'd have a good laugh at our mothers' presumption.

I moved from the washstand to my dressing table and dabbed Parma Violet perfume on my neck. I glanced in the mirror and thought of how good it was that everything was getting back to normal. It would be good to see Degas and Eugène. I'd missed them—Eugène and his gentle manners, Degas and his wry humor.

I brushed my hair.

Of course, Édouard might attend. He was invited, of course. I'd not heard from him since Mirande. Alas, our mothers had grown even closer. Édouard and I would have to come to terms with the change in our relationship eventually.

I was not yet prepared.

If he was angry about how things ended, there was always the chance he'd be otherwise engaged for the evening. I tried to ignore the thud of disappointment that gripped my chest, and counted my blessings: We were all well and able to come together after such a horrendous year.

Smoothing my low-cut, emerald moiré silk gown, I tried to focus on the positive. The dress was one of my favorites.

It was my first occasion to wear it since the war. It hung on my frame looser than I preferred, but it still made me feel good.

Yes, we were alive. I decided I would celebrate the fact that my family and friends had lived through hell to gather together again.

As I descended the last step, the doorknocker sounded. Amélie bobbed a curtsy and darted in front of me to greet the guests.

I heard Édouard's voice in the midst of the others. My heart squeezed, and I was annoyed at my reaction. As Amélie took hats and wraps, I ducked into the empty drawing room and arranged myself on the divan, trying to look unconcerned.

His words in Mirande taunted me. They ate my confidence as gangrene devoured a body. I knew cutting him from my life, as a surgeon's knife cut away a rotting limb, was the only measure by which my heart would heal.

If only it were that easy.

The party moved toward the drawing room, and I wondered how it would look to find me in here waiting. Perhaps it would have been better to make an entrance? Too late for that. I moved to the window, and that was where I stood when I heard Édouard's robust, *"Bonsoir, Mademoiselle."*

I turned.

He smiled and walked to me. He took my hand in his and lifted it to his lips. His eyes met mine the moment before his lips whispered over the back of my hand.

For all appearances, one would've never dreamt our last exchange was so volatile. I was flooded by a sense of relief that he'd come. It was as if I'd fallen backward into the plush safety of a big cottony cloud, but I caught myself before I allowed my good sense to slip through and seep away into the stratosphere of his eyes.

The reality touchstone was Suzanne, who glared at us from across the room. She was a contrast in size standing next to the others, for it seemed as everyone else had wasted away during the war, somehow she'd managed to increase in girth. I was astounded that Fat Suzanne was bigger than ever.

Édouard straightened and followed my gaze to his wife. He let loose of my hand, and I stepped away from him to greet her, *Madame* Manet and Eugène. Much to my relief, Maman floated into the room and took charge.

"*Bonsoir!* Do come in. Make yourselves at home. I am so very happy you could come."

I felt Édouard's gaze on me, and I was tempted to slip back into places I swore I'd never again traverse.

"Come, Berthe," Maman's voice trilled. "Sit next to Eugène."

She motioned him to sit on the loveseat. He obeyed. She motioned me next to him.

So it began. I would not embarrass the poor man by protesting. So I complied, giving Eugène a smile of resignation. In return, he looked a bit sheepish, but not at all disagreeable to our proximity, not at all as if he'd witnessed me kissing and fighting with his brother.

Maman directed Édouard and Suzanne to sit across from Eugène and me. As they settled on the dark blue flowered chintz divan, Maman gasped and stared at Suzanne as if seeing her for the first time that evening. "Oh my, Suzanne! Don't you look . . ." Maman raised her quizzing glass and raked her gaze down Suzanne's rotund figure. "Well, from the looks of you, you've come out of the siege with all the weight we've shed. You're quite healthy, aren't you?"

Pink washed over Suzanne's chubby face. Her lips bunched into a thin pucker, but she did not respond.

"We were of the good fortune to have plenty during the war," said Édouard. He looked thin and drawn. More malnourished than when I saw him last in Mirande. Perhaps it was just the contrast of his thin frame next to his obese wife. "If we'd been near, we would've shared with you."

It was a pathetic attempt to justify her overindulgence during a time of crisis. I wondered if she'd eaten his share of the food. An absurd image flashed in my mind—Suzanne sitting up and begging as Édouard fed her prime morsels from his plate. Even after all these years, I didn't understand what she possessed that held him captive. They were so opposite. She was so contrary to everything he stood for.

Since I'd learned the truth about Léon's paternity, I'd often wondered what tale their lack of parenthood told on the intimacy of their relationship.

How could he desire such a body? Maybe he didn't.

As seldom as Adolphe was at home, he and Edma managed to conceive twice. I realized not every woman was quite so fertile as Edma. But after being married for as many years as Suzanne and Édouard. . . .

"Superb weather we are having tonight," said Eugène. He'd angled his body toward me—one leg crossed over the other, his hands laced over his kneecap tight as a metal brace. Although, he was not sitting inappropriately close, I had the urge to scoot away from him.

"The days are cooling off," he added.

I nodded, not in the mood to discuss the weather. Suzanne and Édouard looked at us in awkward silence, until Édouard said, "*Mademoiselle*, tell me what you are working on. Your mother said you have redoubled your efforts to make a name for yourself as a painter."

I felt a pang for Eugène, who was so outmatched by his older brother. So I directed my words to Eugène, hoping to draw him into the conversation.

"In Mirande, I completed several small landscapes of Edma and Jeanne. I'm talking to several dealers about representing me."

"Perhaps an introduction to my representatives would be in order?"

My gaze flickered back to Édouard.

"If that would help you?" His smile made me wonder if the offer was genuine or if it was a power play to steal my attention from his brother.

"If you are sincere, an introduction would be very much appreciated."

His eyes flashed. He arched a brow. "I shall set it up."

Degas arrived and the party shifted into higher gear. I could see that he was in rare form the moment he walked into the room and wedged himself between Eugène and me on the loveseat.

"I'm sure you don't object, do you, Manet? I've missed the pleasure of this fine woman's company for far too long. We have much to discuss."

If Eugène minded, he did not voice his opinion. I smiled at Degas's sheer gall, at how he slid right into the space he desired for himself. For a moment I let my imagination take flight and considered life as Degas's wife. . . . Until he opened his mouth, and I realized the two of us could be great friends, but as lovers we would tear each other apart.

Lovers. . . .

Édouard's presence tugged at me. My gaze drifted to him. Maman perched on the other side of him, haranguing about something. Before I looked away, his gaze snared mine and the faintest smile tugged at the corners of his lips.

He'd grown so thin over this hard year. He looked utterly human, sitting there all gaunt and hollow. An angel fallen to earth.

"So what is this I hear about Puvis courting you?" Degas's words pulled me back. His curled upper lip left no margin to ponder his opinion of the matter. "What is the nature of your relationship?"

He drummed his fingers on the back of the loveseat while I tried to formulate words for that which I could not explain. I shrugged and threw up my hands. "He's been a good friend to me during a very difficult time. Unlike *others,* whom I shall not name."

I avoided looking at Édouard.

Degas stroked his thin mustache and lowered his voice. "Yes, and didn't I warn you that you could not count on Manet when it mattered? You didn't believe me. Perhaps you will listen to me now when I warn you away from Puvis."

I rolled my eyes. "I beg you watch what you say about *Monsieur* Puvis de Chavannes. He's my good friend—"

"No, *Mademoiselle,* I beg you listen to me. It is my duty to make you aware of the scandalous relationship your *good friend,* Puvis, has been carrying on with Princess Marie Cantacuzène. Are you aware of his relations with her? They've been carrying on for the past fifteen years."

The pit of my stomach dropped to my knees. "I cannot change what happened in *Monsieur* Puvis's life before we grew close." I shifted in my seat and glanced around to see who might have heard Degas's rubbish and to give myself time to process the implications. But all, including Eugène, seated next to Degas, seemed to be engrossed in other conversation.

Was he saying Pierre was involved with another woman

while courting me? Well, if so, it no longer mattered. Pierre would always be a good friend to me. He was there when I needed him. But our relationship was over, and I would not hold his past against him.

"You know nothing of this, do you?" Degas's nostrils flared as if he smelled something foul. "Um-hmm. I figured as much. Allow me to enlighten you. Princess Marie Cantacuzène is the estranged wife of the Prince of Romania, but they are still quite married and Puvis is still quite involved with her. What makes it even more baffling is the princess is your father's age, if she's a day old." Degas examined his nails in that bored manner he'd perfected. I wanted to slap him.

"Do not look at me like that," he said. "I haven't manufactured this for my own amusement."

I ran a hand over the loveseat's blue velvet, and a weight settled on my shoulders as everything fell into place: Puvis had never tried to kiss me; this explained his hesitation to ask Maman and Papa for my hand, and their irrational distaste for him—Maman and Papa knew about his relationship with the princess. Yet they didn't bother to tell me. . . .

It didn't matter. I'd known deep down we'd never marry. It was a diversion. An illusion. A mirage that disintegrated as we drew closer. It didn't matter, but why did it hurt?

I could've speculated all night and still the riddle of Puvis would have remained unsolved.

The air grew close and stale. With so many chattering people in the room and Degas sitting so near, it was impossible to breathe. If I sat there another moment, I feared I might scream. "Please excuse me."

Degas nodded. *"Naturellement."*

My shoes sounded too loud on the parquet floor. I could

hear the tread over the din of conversation as I walked to the window at the other end of the room.

I twisted the knob until my knuckles turned white and wondered if there was anything in this world that was real, that turned out as it originally seemed.

My hand slipped off the knob and smacked against the wooden casement. My reflection stared back at me, and I tried to process the odd emotions brewing. An ache pulsed inside me in the chasm that should have contained my heart; a melancholy discontent bubbled up from the depths of me, the bittersweet calm that finally the Puvis chapter of my life was closed.

It was almost a relief having discovered his Romanian princess.

I leaned my forehead against the cool glass. A white moth performed loops outside the window. I heard the hopeless thud as it threw itself against the pane. The little creature didn't know it was not always better on the other side.

I reached up and gave the knob one last grinding crank. It turned. The bar-latch gave. I stumbled backward, into someone standing behind me.

Édouard.

His hands fell to my waist. I pulled away.

"I came to assist you with the window. You were struggling."

It was not so much what he said, but how he looked at me as he spoke. He was so thin, so intense, a shadow of the carefree dandy who used to own the city. My heart ached because the man I loved was still very much intact.

"Thank you, but I've managed quite well on my own."

"*Oui,* I can see that."

I turned back to the window. The warm night air washed

over me. The moth flew in and rested on the windowsill. Having gained access, I wondered if it was hurt from throwing itself against the glass. So intent on gaining access where it shouldn't trespass.

"I couldn't help but overhear what Degas said to you. He has no manners. I'm sorry he revealed Puvis's secret to you in that manner."

I wondered who else might have overheard. Who else knew of this affair when I knew nothing of it?

"I suppose you think I'm a bad judge of character," I said, not quite sure how I expected him to respond. I couldn't see his face because he stood behind me, but I could imagine his expression, see him crossing his arms and stroking his beard as he frowned.

"*Au contraire, Mademoiselle.* You're quite astute. Save for the misconception that you believe I do not care for you."

He shifted behind me. I could see his face reflected in the angled glass. A gentle face, and my heart clenched.

"Do you care, Édouard?" I whispered.

"I love you. I wish you would stop punishing me long enough to believe me."

A chestnut tree danced in the garden breeze and a slip of pale moonlight peeked through the branches. Édouard stepped closer. Ran a finger along my arm. I could not speak as each caress stitched closed the chasm around my heart.

"Berthe," he whispered. "I have not been able to eat, or sleep, or paint without you. I need you. Come to me tomorrow?"

A bell rang in the background. As if from another dimension, Amélie announce dinner was served.

Édouard joined the others in their pilgrimage to the dining room. I lingered a moment, as solitary as *Victorie de*

*Samothrace,* and stared at the sliver of moon that lit the black abyss of night.

Ravaged by war, we were all different now. We'd seen things no human should see, lived through death and destruction, the end of life as we'd known it. Over the bloody year of war, the Prussians and Communards had killed our innocence.

Nothing would ever be the same.

If I garnered one thing from the war, it was a reverence for life's fragile and fleeting nature. One must live for the day because we were not guaranteed a tomorrow.

The white moth fluttered on the windowsill. In my mind I saw a cliff high above the Aegean sea where *Victorie* unfurled her wings in celebration.

As I tilted my face to capture Zephyr's warm breeze blowing in from the west, the white moth took flight into the darkness.

# Chapter Twenty-Three

## May 1873

*Love does not consist
in gazing at each other,
but in looking outward
in the same direction.*
*—Antoine de Saint Exupéry*

Édouard was as bold as the blue violets he sent the next morning. An unsigned note accompanied the flowers.

It read: *I care.*

Blue violets. I buried my nose in the flowers and tried not to think about the symbolic meaning—love. It was not coincidence. What man but Édouard would be schooled on the significance of flowers?

I set them on the dressing table where I could see them as I attended to my toilette.

I chose my low-cut black dress from the armoire—the pretty one with the lace around the décolletage and the black ribbon that tied at the waist. I hung it on the door and sat down at my vanity to brush my hair.

It was by sheer luck that Papa was at work and Maman was asleep when the flowers arrived. Amélie received them and delivered them to my bedchamber with a knowing sparkle in her eyes.

I picked up the small nosegay, twirled it in my fingers, sniffed it. The petals tickled my nose, but it was his audacity that made me smile and the truth in his words that took away my breath.

I would go to him.

I could no more stay away than the Seine could keep from flowing downstream.

Perhaps it was my destiny to be the other woman. It seemed my lot. Should I have married Puvis, I would've been the respectable wife. Yet the Romanian princess would always possess his heart.

Suzanne was Édouard's wife. Yet she was not the woman of his heart. Either way, I was the other woman.

Perhaps it was not such a terrible position to be in?

Édouard's old studio on the *rue* Guyot was destroyed during the Commune. His new studio took up the entire second floor of number four *rue* de Saint-Pétersbourg, two blocks from his home at number forty-nine. Suzanne could walk down if she dared. Or cared. I found it hard to believe she would expend that much energy.

Inside his *atelier,* my eye was drawn to *Le Balcon* hung against the far wall. Next to it hung my painting of Edma at the Lorient harbor. My hand fluttered to my lips, and I swallowed against the emotion bubbling in my throat. Perhaps I hadn't been so absent from his life for all the time we'd been apart. *Merci Dieu,* he had the foresight to entrust the paintings to Théodore Duret or all would have been lost.

His new studio was a beautiful place: spacious and elegant, with high ceilings and walls of tall windows.

Rubbing the stem of the violet nosegay between my thumb and fingers, I stood near the door and looked around the cavernous space in wonder. Not as much natural light as the *rue* Guyot with its windowed roof, but the light was quite nice. The space would be cooler in the summer.

I walked to the center of the room, turned in a slow circle memorizing every detail, picking out the old familiar pieces, learning their places in the new environment. The big, red, buttoned divan; his easel; the stool; the table with paint tubes and brushes; jars of pigment in jeweled colors; the books; the props; the rolls of fabric and paper.

The dressing screen.

The bed.

It was all there, like old friends welcoming me home. Yet everything was different.

This studio was twice the size of the other. Everything had its place. Nothing was haphazardly tossed or strewn. Even the bed was made. *Rue* Guyot had the air of a rogue artist's *atelier*. But this place—This place had the feel of a master.

"It used to be an old fencing school," he said.

The floor trembled like the hand of God shook the building. I braced a hand against his easel and feared for a moment that the earth would open and swallow us whole.

"The *Gare Saint-Lazare*," he said over the rumble. "The trains coming and going make the place shake all day long." He smiled. "Keeps me awake."

My gaze darted to the bed. The blanket was pulled taut. The pillows were fluffed. It looked as if it were never mussed. A sharp contrast to the rumpled mess that stood in the corner of the *atelier* on *rue* Guyot. As often as I'd been to his studio I'd never been in that bed.

I released my grip on the easel and only then did it dawn on me that it was empty of canvas. That his pallette hung on a hook and the brushes looked dusty.

"The place is lovely, Édouard. Please show me what you have been working on."

His face went blank. He crossed his arms over his chest, tucking his fingers in his armpits.

"I have not yet begun to work."

"You're joking? It's been several months now. You should see the canvases I have completed. I should have taken you out to the studio last night . . ." As I spoke, I looked for hints of new work and realized the only canvases I saw were old.

I looked at him askance. He shook his head, shifted from one foot to the other, extracted a hand to rub his eyes and muttered, "I told you, I have done nothing since we returned to Paris."

"Édouard?"

He looked at me, his eyes dark and forlorn. A helpless child of a man.

I don't know who moved first, he or I, but we stood together now, inches apart. He cupped my face in his hands and held me like that, rubbing a thumb over my lips, then two over my cheekbones. He slid his hands back and laced his fingers in my hair. A pin fell to the floor and my hair fell free. He ran his fingers through the curls, slid his hands down my shoulders, over my breasts.

He pulled me to him, and I could feel his hardness as we stood together, like two parched travelers preparing to drink from the well of life.

I leaned into him, aching for the feel of his body against mine, and kissed him. Soft. Tentative. I'd reached the fork in the road. If I embarked in the direction my body burned to travel, there was no turning back.

I knew where I must go. It had been a long journey to this point, but every step I'd taken led me to this very spot.

"I will make what is between us right." His whispered

promise was rough as gravel. "I will make you happy. You'll see—"

"Shhhhh." I drowned his words with a deep kiss. At that moment, I loved him so much it was painful.

There was only one way to ease my ache.

I took his hand and led him to the bed.

"Let's go away." Édouard kissed the top of my head.

I snuggled into his chest, molding my body to his side. He pulled me closer. "I want to stay here. With you. Just like this." I snuggled into him, relishing the scent of our union. *Mon Dieu,* I loved the smell of him. I ducked my head under the blanket and planted a kiss on his belly.

He sighed. "This is nice, but I want to go somewhere we can be like this every day, every night." With one finger, he tilted my chin up to him. His eyes were bright. I was glad to see the energy shining in him again.

"Let's go," he urged. "Right now. I'm serious."

He pushed himself up. The blanket slid down my naked back.

I ran my fingers through the hair on his chest. "Édouard, we can't. Not right now. Not like this."

"Of course not. We'll put our clothes on first."

He arched a brow at me, grinned and pushed himself to a sitting position.

He was serious.

I fell onto my back.

A funnel swirled in my stomach as I contemplated the logistics of what he suggested. All the work I'd started, the dealers I'd interested. I rested my arm across my forehead. My other hand grasped the covers to my breast. If we left, we'd be forced to start over professionally.

*You're afraid to go because he hasn't proven reliable in the past, has he? said Propriety. What do you expect, falling in love with a married man? If you run away with him, he will end up leaving you for someone else.*

Be reasonable, said Olympia. It's not as if the relationship has had a chance to grow under normal circumstances. You've been through a war. Give the man a chance to prove his worth.

"Papa has not been well. I can't go off and leave him now."

I heard him rustling around and sat up to watch him dress. Wrapped in the blanket, I drew my knees to my chest.

"I thought it was what you wanted," he said.

"I did. I do. But everything is so different now. When I wanted to leave, everything seemed so hopeless. But now we've both come so far. We can't give that up."

He finished buckling his trousers, and stood there—shirtless, his hair rumpled and his eyes looking deep into me. I desired him all over again. I wanted to cry for the astonishing depth of my love for him.

"Édouard." I motioned for him to sit on the bed. He obliged, and I laced my fingers through his, brought his hand to my lips and kissed him. "There is nothing I want more than this. But we can't go now. We need to be here. For Papa. For our futures. Together. We must both draw on the resources we have built in Paris to build a new life for ourselves. A life together."

He shook his head. "It will never work here, Berthe." He drew his hand away, and braced stiff arms on the bed. "We will both be ruined."

"Since when have you been concerned about that?" I caressed his bare back. "Édouard, I am not afraid to face the music here. You can withstand it, too. You have before and come out stronger on the other side. Stand tall. Let us be who we are in the place where we belong."

A train rumbled past and shook the room. I got out of bed, aware of his eyes on me, quiet and contemplative. I pulled my black dress over my head. Not bothering with my corset, I tied the black ribbon at the waist, then pinned my hair away from my face, leaving the back to fall free about my shoulders.

I sat down next to him on the bed again, leaning back on my elbows.

"You look like an angel sitting there like that," he said.

He went to the chest of drawers and pulled out a slip of black velvet ribbon and tied it around my neck, forming a little bow, and tucked the bouquet of violets in the bodice of my dress. He backed away until he reached his easel where he touched his brush to the paint, touched paint to canvas.

With each brushstroke, a picture of our new life together emerged.

*LE FIGARO—by ANSEL RACINE—May 25, 1873*
*"Manet's New Olympia?"*

*In this year's Salon, Édouard Manet has returned to his favorite subject, Mademoiselle Berthe Morisot. Speculation on the exact nature of the relationship between Monsieur Manet and his sultry Demoiselle is the talk of Paris. Given his Salon entry, Repose, his sensual portrait of her sprawled, seductive and inviting, on a red divan, one cannot help but wonder. Her black shoe is a sharp contrast, peeking out from beneath the virginal white froth of gown. Alas, it is the way she holds her red fan in her right hand, with her elegant left hand placed so boldly on the seat next to her. Her come-hither expression seems to beckon the viewer to sit next to her for an intimate tête-à-tête.*

*Given Monsieur Manet's well-known propensity to paint what he sees, one cannot help but speculate that Mademoiselle Morisot's smoldering glance is meant for him and him alone. One wonders what his wife might have to say about that? Especially since Manet has painted Mademoiselle Morisot more than any other subject—including his wife.*

I suggested to Édouard it might not be prudent to enter *Repose* in the Salon. Not until he was ready to reveal our relationship. But he would not hear of it. He insisted it would show in good contrast to his painting *Le Bon Bock*. He painted *Repose* before the war, and while I was quite fond of it, it was an extremely intimate painting, so telling. He captured everything I felt that day, as Racine pointed out.

Édouard borrowed it back from Durand Ruel, who bought it for twenty-five hundred francs just after the war. Édouard didn't want to part with it, but after living through such a grave year, he did what he had to do to survive.

I didn't mind the furor. We'd seen each other every day for more than six months. I was surprised no one was the wiser to the depth of our passion for each other.

I almost wished we'd been discovered. Édouard was still reticent about starting a new life in Paris. Because of Papa's condition and the plans I was forming with Degas and Monet, I could not leave. We'd come to a standoff, and did not talk about it.

I would not push Édouard, but I wouldn't leave. We'd settled into a routine of quiet resignation—loving passionately, working furiously.

"You should have seen Maman this morning," I said to Édouard as he painted. "She was furious over the *Le Figaro* article."

He made a soft sound of amusement.

"She said, 'I hope you're happy! It seems you are intent on ruining not only yourself, but your entire family as well.' She slammed her quizzing glass onto the table on top of the newspaper. I am surprised the glass did not shatter."

I glanced over Édouard's shoulder at the canvas. It was the portrait of me in the black dress reclining on the bed.

"I wonder what Racine will make of this one?" I remembered the tender way he'd tucked the blue violets into the bodice of my gown and it made me desire him all over again. "This is far more seductive than *Repose*, don't you agree?"

Édouard grunted, and I got the feeling he was not completely present.

"It's been a while since I've seen Maman in such a temper, but this will seem a picnic once we announce our plans."

He said nothing.

"Édouard?"

"Yes, my love. Your mother was upset?"

He was lost in his own world. I knew better than to expect much from him when he retreated. It would just end in an argument.

I walked to the window and looked out. I considered going home to my own work. God knew I had plenty to do. I'd promised Degas I would inquire about gallery space for the show we were planning separate from the Salon, but I hadn't the time.

I'd spent so much time with Édouard and devoted what little time that remained to my studio. Alas, I was beginning to question my distribution of effort, because my entry in the Salon had been such a grave disappointment.

My showing in the Salon had gotten me nowhere. My one small painting, the canvas of Edma and Jeanne in the field, hung on the wall unnoticed like rainwater collected in an abandoned pot. It was far worse to go unnoticed than to receive even the cutting criticism Édouard had endured.

Perhaps devoting more time to Monet and Degas's independent endeavor would be a better investment?

I turned from the window to watch Édouard at his easel. I envied the attention he'd harvested, and tried not to begrudge him that once again my image was the source of speculation.

Not my art. Not my talent. My person. The fact that I was an available woman and he was a married man. That he lavished so much attention on me and painted me *sprawled, seductive and inviting, on the red divan.*

If they only knew.

I walked over to the wall where a lone canvas sat on an easel. It was not there yesterday. I scooted it back and turned it to have a look. The painting was of a bedraggled woman and a child set against a backdrop of a wrought iron fence. Steam billowed in the background—a train yard. The *Gare Saint-Lazare.* The child, captured from the back, was smartly attired with a big blue bow on the back of her crisp white dress. The woman wore an unfashionable bonnet and plain blue dress. She sat beside the child reading a book, a sleeping puppy in her lap.

Her face was familiar, yet out of context. I could not place her, although I was certain I knew this woman's penetrating stare and long red hair that hung loose about her shoulders.

"Édouard, who is this?"

He threw a distracted glance over his shoulder, tensed as he turned around to face me.

"Be careful. The paint's not yet dry."

Irritation burned in the pit of my stomach. "I can see that. Who is she? She is familiar."

He stood for a moment staring first at the canvas, then at me. He turned back to his easel.

"It's Victorine Meurent."

Victorine? Victorine Meur—I gasped. *Mon Dieu*. My heart stopped. *Olympia*.

"She is back?"

"Ummm-hmmm . . ."

I didn't like that. I didn't like that at all, especially when I noticed the red fan nestled in her lap behind the puppy. *My fan*. The fan I'd held in so many of the portraits Édouard painted of me. Tears stung my eyes. I grabbed my cloak and left.

I was descending the steps when Édouard threw open the door and called after me.

"Berthe, where are you going?"

"Home."

I reached the first landing and did not look back. Édouard married Suzanne after Victorine left. I did not have to be a scholar to understand what his *Olympia* meant to him. Now she was back, and he'd painted her with *my* fan—

"Stop, will you? What is the matter?" I heard his footfalls on the steps behind me. "One minute I am painting and the next minute you are storming out. Come back inside and talk to me."

His voice was more irritated than tender. I held my breath to keep from sobbing. But I let him catch up with me, take my hand and lead me back upstairs. All the while I wanted to shout, "We can't go on keeping our relationship a secret."

Propriety scolded. *Do you know what this relationship will do to your father once word gets out? It will destroy him.*

My heart constricted at the thought. If I harbored one regret, one reason for not pushing Édouard into action, it was Papa. At best, I feared he would not live to see the new year.

But with Victorine back in Paris, Édouard and I could not go on like this.

He closed the door and picked up a rag to wipe his hands. Victorine's haggard face stared out at me. Propriety's voice screamed in my head, *He has no intention to marry you. Distance yourself from Édouard Manet once and for all. For your own good.*

He followed my gaze to Victorine's portrait. "Is that what's upset you so?"

"She's holding my fan."

"What?" Surprise washed over his face. I felt foolish and cast my gaze down at my hands. A streak of red paint marked the center of my palm. From Édouard, when he brought me back inside.

"Never mind. Édouard, I have thought long and hard about our situation. It is time. You must either move out with me now or this is the end. We will stay in Paris, for you know as well as I do I cannot leave with Papa in such a delicate condition."

"Do you believe staying here and dragging both of our good names through the Parisian mud will heal him?"

"This is where we belong. This is who we are."

He opened his mouth to speak, but no sound came out. Then wiped his fingers with the rag. He knew as well as I knew that we could not go another day living like this.

Another train rumbled by. I thought of the cloud of smoke in the portrait of Victorine and the child. Black panic swept through me. She'd been in his studio.

*Olympia who lay bare for the love of a man.* We were not so dissimilar, she and I.

The train passed, and the room was so still Édouard's sigh seemed the only sound for miles.

"I shall tell Suzanne tonight."

# Chapter Twenty-Four

## January 1874

*Love is strong as death*
*Jealousy is cruel as the grave*
                    —*Song of Solomon 8:6*

I awoke early and dragged my easel outside so that I might
occupy myself while I waited for Édouard to call. We did
not make formal arrangements, yet I was sure he would
come after he told Suzanne.

Yes, he would come so we might tell Maman together.

I loved to paint in the garden beneath the chestnut tree
outside my studio. Despite the chilly morning, it was the
best place for me to bide my time. The soft autumn light
and gentle breeze comforted me as I painted and planned
what we would say to Maman. I wanted to speak to her before we told Papa. To give her a chance to get used to it.
She would take it hard at first, but she was strong. She
would come to terms with the idea once she realized she
had no choice.

"*Madame, non! S'il vous plaît,* you may not go into the
garden unannounced!" Amélie's cry shattered the quiet a
spilt second before the gate slammed open, banging against
the ivy-covered stone wall.

I turned and saw Suzanne Manet standing with her
hands on her considerable hips. She was dressed in a plain
black coat, unbuttoned to reveal a plain gray frock. A small

black hat that looked too small for her large face balanced between coiled braids—one on each side of her head. Amélie skidded to a stop alongside her.

My heart raced. Édouard told her. I finished painting a highlight in the foreground before I set down my brush.

"*Mademoiselle,* I beg your pardon, I told her to wait—"

"It is all right, Amélie. That will be all."

The wind rustled the leaves and carried with it the scent of fresh baking bread and smoke from the puffing chimneys.

At least Suzanne had the good grace to wait until the girl disappeared inside before she tore into me.

"I will not give up Édouard without a fight. He is the only thing Léon and I have. If we lose him, we are destitute."

Her voice was a low growl, incongruent with the mealy-mouthed blind wife to whom I'd become accustomed. I preferred her silent because it made me think she knew her place.

I pulled my coat collar closed, picked up my brush and rolled it between my thumb and fingers. The yellow paint contrasted with the dark brown bristles and made me think of jonquils blooming in the early spring.

"Léon is Édouard's brother," I said. "We will see that you and the boy are well provided for."

She took a step toward me. I set down my brush, put my hands on my hips to match her stance.

"You don't seem to understand, *Mademoiselle.* I love him. He loves me."

"He married you out of pity. He told me so."

"Did he tell you he enjoys making love to me? He was in my bed just the other night. Did he tell you about the others? There are others, you understand. Don't think you are special. Victorine Meurent is back. *She* was special to him." Suzanne laughed a dry sound like crunching leaves.

"Get out of my garden." I picked up my brush and turned back to my easel.

She closed the distance between us. At this close range, I could see her gelatinous chin quiver with anger. Her eyes were narrow slits, and she shook a pudgy finger in my face. I pushed it aside, and she drew back a shaking fist as if she would strike me. When I did not move out of her way, she grimaced and lowered her hand.

"I will leave, but only after I say what I have come to say." She spat the word, spittle stringing and flying from her lips. I wondered if Maman would come out to see what was the matter. "If you do not leave my husband alone, I will ruin you. If you think Racine's insidious article in *Le Figaro* was bad—"

"I did not think it bad at all. Racine has a keen eye and spoke the truth about what he observed."

Suzanne bristled like a cat arching her back. "Leave him alone!" She gritted her yellow teeth. "Leave him alone or I shall make you so miserable you will wish you never met me."

She shoved over my easel. The canvas landed face down in the brown grass. I shook my head and gave her a pitying smile.

"Your threats do not scare me, Suzanne. You cannot ruin me. You are nothing, and even less without Édouard."

"Heed my warning, *Mademoiselle*. I will make both your lives miserable."

She turned and stormed out of the garden, leaving the garden gate open behind her.

Overcome by blinding hysteria, I set out on foot for Édouard's studio. Halfway there the wind blew my hat from my head. A man hopped off a carriage, caught it and pre-sented it to me with a flourish.

I scarcely remembered going inside to get my hat and coat before I left, but I did, I realized as I took it from him, swiping at my tears with my free hand.

"Are you in trouble, *Mademoiselle?*" he asked. "You're crying. May I assist you?"

*"Merci, non, Monsieur."*

I turned and fled, hat in hand.

I have no idea how long it took me to walk the distance from Passy to Édouard's studio. Time seemed to stand still. When I arrived, the sun was high in the October sky so I knew it was mid-day. Hours had passed.

I did not knock, but threw open the door, half-expecting, half-dreading I would find him with Victorine or Suzanne. Or both.

Édouard was alone. He turned to me wide-eyed.

"Berthe, what's—"

"Do you still go to her bed, Édouard?"

He rubbed his hand over his beard in a gesture that cov-ered his mouth.

"Answer me! Do you still go to Suzanne's bed? Do you do all the things to her you do to me?"

My screams scalded my throat, and my body was shaking so hard I felt as if I had no control over myself.

"What are you talking about? You're not making sense."

"Suzanne! I am talking about Suzanne. She came to me this morning and said . . ."

He took me in his arms, and I melted into him, sobbing against his chest.

"Of course she would say that." He kissed the top of my head. "She is upset. I told her I was leaving her. It stands to reason she'd brandish anything to hurt you."

"Answer my question." My words floated out between sobs. "Do you make love to her?"

"Shhhh . . . What kind of question is that?"

"An important question, Édouard. She said it happened just the other day. She said there were others, too. Is it true?"

I could hear his heart beat through his white shirt as I lay my head upon his chest.

"Berthe, don't do this."

I pushed away from him so I could see his face.

"Answer me!"

The way he looked at me, he needed not reply.

I knew.

I clenched my fists and started flailing, hitting him. My vision was blurred by tears. My fists knocked into his paint table. It crashed to the floor. His palette skidded. Paint tubes and brushes scattered at our feet.

He grabbed me with both hands and crushed me tight against him, until I collapsed in sobbing hysterics.

He held me that way until I calmed down. He walked me to the red divan, settled me on a cushion and handed me his handkerchief, sitting next to me with one arm draped over my shoulder.

I dabbed my eyes. "You might have at least warned me she was coming."

He shrugged. "I did not know. She locked herself in her bedchamber after we talked."

"Have you told your mother yet?" I asked.

He shook his head.

"Suzanne will ruin us, you realize."

"She can only cause damage if we afford her that power. I do not care what she does or who she tells. Racine told all of Paris as much in his article."

Elbows on his thighs, he leaned forward and pressed his face into his palms.

"We are courting scandal, Berthe." His words were muffled. "We will face dire social consequences. I cannot do this to you. I will not be the cause of your ruin."

I touched his hair. "I do not care."

"You will." He looked up, anguish in his sad eyes. "You will grow to hate me—"

"Édouard, this is the same speech you have given me over and over again. I am tired of it. I should have called your bluff and gone with you that day you wanted to take me away. Either we make a new start, here in Paris, today, or it is over. For good."

He bowed his head again and let his face fall into his hands.

"Berthe, be kind." I heard the choke of emotion. "Consider my position. I have a responsibility to protect my family name."

"Is that more important to you than I? Than us being together?"

"It is equally important."

My breath escaped in a heavy gasp. I started to stand up but he held my arm, so I fell back onto the divan.

"Please listen to me. I have something very important for you to consider."

His throat worked and a muscle in his jaw twitched. I could tell by his expression that I would not like what he had to say. A knot of dread tightened in my belly.

I wanted to stay there, silent, just as we were, because somehow I knew after his next words nothing would be the same.

My stomach seized and I feared I would vomit, but I could not move. I could not breathe. I wished at that moment Hermes, the god of people who lived by their wits, would swoop down in his golden, winged sandals, and carry me off . . . somewhere, anywhere but there.

"Please, Berthe, please understand. The only reason I would ask this of you is because I love you too much to lose you. If we open Pandora's box, it will be the end of us. You will never show at the Salon again—"

"I do not wish to show at the Salon." I don't know where the voice came from. It did not even sound like my own.

"My love. . . ." He reached out, traced a finger down my cheek, "We have been clinging to fantasies. You will grow discontented with me all too soon and end up hating me for ruining your life."

"It is Victorine, isn't it?"

He groaned. "*Mon Dieu,* no. There is no one else."

I was shaking again. I stood. Tears streamed from my eyes, blurred my vision. Hysterical screams crept up the back of my throat. "You are just looking for a way out."

He did not deny the allegation.

The seasons changed before I saw him again.

When the snow fell, I went to his studio. Strictly for professional purposes. A quest far more important than the personal worries or reservations I harbored about seeing him.

I did not want to surprise him, so I sent a note to advise him of my intent to call. He was hasty to reply. He said he would be happy to receive me.

I went alone.

I considered asking Maman to accompany me, but decided against it, realizing if she went, *Madame* Manet would feel obliged to greet her. Perhaps Eugène and Suzanne would come, too. Suzanne would gloat, no doubt.

Édouard and I wouldn't be able to talk business. There would be far too much commotion with everyone chatting. Alas, it was a good decision to go by myself.

We'd had no soirées. Nor had the Manets. A cooling-off period, as Maman called it. Distance designed to quell the speculation over the debut of *Repose*.

No one talked about it now. We were quite civilized, despite ripples that lingered like a bad aftertaste on the palates of those too decent to make a face. In fact, everyone in my inner circle acted quite lovely. Cordial and smiling, as if all were right in the world.

It rather reminded me of the story, "The Emperor's New Clothes." If everyone pretended Berthe and Édouard were not in love, then surely they would not be.

It made me ill. I believed it more closely resembled a sore thumb. Painful when bumped and so often in the way I scarcely thought of much else.

So I slipped out of the house that day, murmuring excuses about art business, to which Maman rolled her eyes before returning her attention to the morning edition of *Le Figaro*. The carriage ride gave me time to gather myself, to coax free the knot drawn tight in my belly.

I'd come with a purpose. This was my mantra, and I repeated it over and over as the carriage rolled to a stop at number four *rue* de Saint-Pétersbourg.

When his studio door swung open, Édouard stood on the other side. The knot in my stomach tightened. He smiled, stepped back to afford me room to enter. *"Bonjour, Mademoiselle."*

*Mademoiselle.* A cordial greeting. The brand he would bestow upon his colleagues or an acquaintance, perhaps. An icy draft extinguished the warmth kindled at the thought of seeing him again after so long. Warmth I hadn't realized glowed until snuffed out. I stood cold and awkward, not quite sure what to do, cursing Degas for having put me up to this task. But this was not personal. I'd come with a purpose and I was wise not to forget myself.

I stepped inside, dwarfed by the immensity of the place, although the studio looked the same as the last time. Neat. Almost too tidy, in fact. The capped jars of pigment lined up in a perfect row on the table in front of the window. The light shining through made them look like great cylindrical jewels—ruby red, emerald green, sapphire blue. They seemed untouched. No signs of stray color dusted the table. Everything was in its place. The bedcovers pulled taut as if never used.

The only sign that Édouard had worked was the canvas on the easel. But I did not see any new work lining the walls. It had been nearly three months. If he'd not been working, he would not be happy.

He stood at a safe distance; neither of us seemed to know where to begin.

I was tempted to peek at the canvas, but I didn't dare. It was a different size than the painting of Victorine at the train station. Where was that one? My gaze skimmed the room, but I did not locate it. He would have given it to his dealers. Of course.

Had he painted another portrait of her?

"Would you like to see?" He pointed at the canvas.

*"Oui, s'il vous plaît."*

He turned the easel around. It was a painting of *me*. Or at least a woman who looked like me. I stared dumfounded at the black-clad image of the woman with heartbroken eyes.

"It is not right." Édouard's voice cracked. "And I cannot seem to fix it."

I could not speak. I didn't know how to respond to a remark that seemed so full of innuendo. Or perhaps it wasn't. Perhaps from the start, I'd read too much into Édouard's intentions.

"I understand you came to talk to me about business, *Mademoiselle*." His voice penetrated my thoughts. "But could I trouble you for an hour of your time to work on the face? To . . . make it right?"

My stomach spiraled, and I hated myself for it. Because I would not put myself through it again. I'd come with a purpose.

"Of course, Édouard, as long as you dispense with the formalities. I would be most unhappy if I thought we were no longer friends after all we've shared."

He exhaled a heavy breath that seemed to lift a great weight from his brow.

"While I paint, you can tell me what you have come to say."

"No, I think I shall wait until I have your undivided attention."

He nodded. "You make me curious. I shall work in haste."

"Please *Monsieur,* take your time. It will keep."

His brows lifted, and he smiled. "Quite curious, indeed."

He dragged a high stool over for me to sit on, and I felt better because he seemed more himself. There seemed to be a dramatic drop in atmospheric pressure in the room. I could breathe again.

So he painted, and we talked—about everything and nothing. Talking and laughing, and it was so obvious we belonged together it was painful. It felt so good to have broken through the awkward standoff. I knew that even if we could not be together in the true sense of the word, I could not be without him.

Nor he without me, whether he knew it or not.

He looked up. His gaze lingered. There was a moment of bated silence. I could tell he wanted to say something.

"What, Édouard?"

He started to speak, then stopped, shook his head.

"What is it?"

"I have figured out a way for us to always be together." He closed his eyes and blew out an unsteady breath. "It is a compromise, but one that could be the best solution for all involved."

My heart beat against my ribcage like a trapped dove. "A compromise, Édouard?"

"If you were to marry Eugène—"

I gasped. "You're joking."

He held up a hand. His throat worked. "Please, let me finish."

"Do not make light of it," I said.

"This is an unbearable, painful sacrifice to ask of you. But hear me out. It may be the only way. If you married my brother, you would become a member of the family. We would be united forever by respectable bonds."

I sat for what seemed an eternity in stunned silence. I could not believe he would ask this of me. That he was willing to give me away to his brother as Édouard himself took on Suzanne, his father's mistress.

A vision clouded my thoughts—it was of Édouard that day in Mirande when he learned of my possible engagement to Puvis. He could not tolerate the thought of me with another, yet he would send me to his own brother's bed. My insides twisted.

"Please, my love." He closed his eyes against the words.

"Please, consider what I have asked of you. It is our only option. Think about it—the very constraints that keep us apart will preserve us. If you marry Eugène, you will sign your name *Madame* E. Manet. We will see each other every day."

"And I will spend my nights in your brother's bed. Could you live with that, Édouard? Could you be content knowing you had bequeathed possession of my body to Eugène?"

He didn't answer me. Instead, he focused on the canvas he painted. While I sat trying to sort out what had just transpired.

What had just transpired? He tried to pawn me off on Eugène? Could Édouard really have me marry his brother for the right to keep me in his life? I shuddered at the thought. Why not just let me go? Let me fade into the horizon like the last light of a sunset. Édouard had watched his share of fading sunsets. The thought sent an uncomfortable rush of ire pumping through my veins.

"How is your friend, Victorine?" I asked.

He glanced up. "Victorine? I suppose she is fine. I haven't seen her in months."

Months? I wanted to ask how long she was in his life before she left him. I wanted to know if he offered his Olympia the consolation option of being his brother's wife. But I said nothing. If I brought it up, he might misconstrue it to mean I cared.

I'd come today for professional purposes. I would act as if nothing had happened because I had to talk to him about far more important matters.

"All right," he said, his gaze on the canvas. "I think I have accomplished something." He gave me a stiff smile. "Look at this and tell me what you think."

I stood, walked around the easel. It was the same black hat and dress. Only now the woman's sad green eyes had been transformed into sensuous brown pools. "Oh, Édouard. It's lovely."

"You are lovely."

His compliment made me tingle, but I braced myself against the sensation. "But my eyes—my eyes are green. You have painted them brown."

I noticed he'd also added a nice touch—he'd painted a small bouquet of blue violets into the bodice of my dress. My hand fluttered to my neckline.

In the painting, I looked stronger. Somehow more sure of myself. He had transformed the despondent, green-eyed girl from the earlier version into a confident—one might almost say sultry—brown-eyed woman. With violets.

What was art if not a revelation of what lived inside us?

"You like it?" he asked.

"*Oui,* very much."

We stood side-by-side, regarding the canvas. We were so close all one of us would need do was list slightly to touch the other. The moment was ripe to lose ourselves. To allow the beat of a heart to push us into each other's arms, into bed, head-first into the vicious cycle of love and obsession that would begin again only to end in the same way it always did—in misery.

I couldn't do it again. I was no longer the despondent, green-eyed girl. I stepped back to regard the painting from a safe distance.

Édouard shifted, too, away from me. "I have a gift for you."

"A gift?"

He opened a drawer in the chest and removed a small canvas. With a sad smile he handed it to me.

It took a moment for me to understand, but the charming and bittersweet pieces collided.

My hand flew to my mouth. I needed to sit down, but somehow, my legs held me upright.

The painting was a still life. It contained just three simple objects, mementoes of the portraits he'd painted of me: a bouquet of blue violets, the red fan, a note inscribed *Mlle. Berthe from E. Manet.*

For a moment I believed my heart would break into tiny pieces. Until his words rang in my mind . . . *If you marry Eugène, you will be able to sign your name Madame E. Manet.*

It knocked the wind out of me.

The name *Madame* E. Manet would not make me Édouard's wife any more than the marriage would bind my heart to Eugène. It would not be the same. It would not be fair to anyone involved. How could he think that twisted web would ensnare happiness—for any of us? It was almost too much to bear.

"It is lovely, Édouard. *Merci.*"

The look on his face seemed to implore, *Have you considered my suggestion? Marry Eugène.* I could not discuss it with him and decided to change the subject before he voiced it.

I set the painting next to my coat and prepared to discuss the business I'd come to talk about.

"Édouard, I wanted to see you today about an important matter. The painters who gathered at Degas's table that day—remember?"

He nodded, motioned to the divan and sat down.

I chose the chair across from him.

"What are the scoundrels up to now? No good, I presume."

"I wouldn't say that. In fact, they—er, *we*—have been

quite productive as of late. We have joined forces against the Salon."

Édouard frowned and pulled at his beard, but did not comment.

"We are finished with the Academy and are planning an independent showing to coincide with next year's Salon. I have come today with an invitation. We would like it very much if you would join us."

He stared at me, blinked several times, as if he could not comprehend what I was talking about.

I scooted forward on my chair.

"Édouard, haven't you grown tired of being bound by the Academy's strings? Dancing when they tug and dangling lifeless when they leave you hanging? I have endured my last Salon rebuff."

"The Salon did not reject you last time. You showed a wonderful little piece."

"A wonderful little piece that went all but unnoticed. It garnered me nothing."

"You're being dramatic."

"No, Édouard, you are the one who cultivates the drama with your larger-than-life paintings. I have simply been Victorine's successor in fulfilling your needs."

He threw his head back, but did not laugh, and slapped his lap with his palms. "Is that what this is all about, Victorine? I am happy to lessen your regrets by informing you that Victorine is not part of my life."

"What?"

A train rumbled by outside, and I had the strange, jolting sensation that he and I were two trains traveling different tracks.

"I am talking about my career, for a change. Not my private relationship with you. Édouard, I cannot wait for you.

I have decided to carve out a life for myself, and that life re-volves around my career. Pissarro, Renoir, Monet, Degas and I will exhibit together. Right now we call ourselves the Independents. Will you please join us?"

"And make a public stand against the Salon?"

I nodded.

"You must be out of your mind. You are making a grave mistake. Do you want to be branded subversive?"

Heat spread to my cheeks. "You of all people afraid of being different? Who am I talking to? I came to see Édouard Manet, the rebel, the revolutionary. Did I happen upon somebody's grandfather, instead?"

He challenged, "Rather than sitting there looking so for-lorn, talking about nonsense, why don't you stay with me?"

"*Merci,* no. I am quite disillusioned with the official system and would be happy to concede the privilege of con-ventionality to Eva Gonzalés or whomever you choose as your next protégé."

"Degas has put you up to this, no?"

"Degas has been instrumental in orchestrating this group, but no one has put me up to inviting a great talent to join us. Why are you behaving this way, Édouard?"

"After all we've meant to each other, how can you be so disloyal as to abandon me for a doddering old fool like Degas?"

I stood and glared down at him. His words were a swift blow, a carpet yanked out from under my feet. For a mo-ment I felt as if I might fall. But I did not.

"You can't seem to accept the fact that this is not about love or sex or anything other than art. But while you are on that subject, there is nothing more that I would rather do than be with you, Édouard. I have been a vast deal more than civil, but you are the one who dictated our fate by staying with Suzanne."

"You knew from the start I was not a free man. No, I cannot leave Suzanne and Léon. They need me. They would have nothing without me."

"And you like it that way, don't you? I am a free woman with desires and dreams. I am free to do as I please. Free to make a life for myself as you have made one for yourself. My life will include Degas and the Independents."

Standing in the middle of his immaculate studio, I set aside the small canvas—I would not accept it—and picked up my coat. Standing there, I had an epiphany—Édouard was so used to having everything his own way and on his own terms that there would never be hope for us.

I'd always prided myself on being open-minded. Yet my own modernity had been severely tested since meeting Édouard. I'd pushed myself to bounds I thought certain I was not prepared to traverse. Yet, as I stretched, I touched the outer realms of possibilities, pushed my limits far beyond what I fathomed possible. Doing so, I'd become the person I was that day. The woman he'd painted with the sultry brown eyes. A person far more forward-thinking than even the great Édouard Manet.

As I left his studio, the two halves of myself—Propriety and Olympia—melded into one whole person. For the first time, they both agreed I could no more back away from participating in this show than I could cease breathing.

# Chapter Twenty-Five

*I am in love with you. I have been thus since
the first day I called on you.*
*—Alfred de Musset*

"I have received a nasty note from your friend Manet," said Degas to me at the next meeting of the Independents. "He said it is one thing for me to ruin myself, but quite another when my self-destruction spills out and taints the careers of others. He seems to believe I am corrupting you. Am I corrupting you, *Mademoiselle?*"

I rolled my eyes. "I can assure you, *Monsieur,* if you were corrupting me and I objected, I would tell you to cease and desist."

Degas's eyebrows peaked over his eyes. Yet he managed to maintain an expression that bordered somewhere between annoyance and boredom. "Yes, I thought as much. Manet will live to regret his decision. There must be a realist's alternative to the Salon, and that's what he does not seem to understand."

Sitting around Degas's kitchen table drinking coffee, Renoir, Degas, Pissarro and Monet frowned and nodded.

"He is more vain than intelligent," said Degas. "Let's move on. Any new business?"

Monet signaled the floor. "I'm talking to Nadar about the use of his space on Boulevard des Capucines for the show. It's on the second floor. Large. A nice space. I don't think we could do better. Try to stop by and see it when you get the chance."

"That's a good idea," I said. "Once we have secured the space, we will have a better idea how many artists we can recruit for the show."

"Which brings up a good point," said Pissarro. "What does a name like the Independents say about us?" He looked from face to face. No one answered. "It says nothing. I suggest we adopt something less radical and a bit more businesslike. Something more inclusive."

"Why do I have the feeling you have already come up with a suggestion?" Degas leaned back in his seat and crossed his arms over his chest.

"Now that you mention it, how about the *Société Anonyme des Artistes?*"

"Too long," said Monet.

"But it says exactly what we are," said Renoir.

I nodded. "He has a point."

"Think about it," said Pissarro. "We have time."

*Dear Mademoiselle,*

*I hope this note finds you well and working.*

*As your friend, I feel it my duty to express my concerns about your potential alignment with the artists' group calling themselves the Société Anonyme des Artistes.*

*You possess such talent. I beg you consider what involvement with such a radical group will do to your fine reputation and subsequently to your career. I know at times you experience frustration with the official system. We all do, Mademoiselle. Please believe me when I say, it will be far worse for you should you tread the less traveled road.*

*Your faithful servant,*
*Pierre Puvis de Chavannes*

*February 1874*

My beloved Papa was dead.

How would we ever be the same? What would become of our family now that he was gone?

Financially, he left us quite well off. It was more a dearth of direction that concerned me. This loss shook the very foundation of our lives.

Tiburce was off chasing rainbows. Edma and Yves had families of their own. It was just Maman and me. Sometimes I believed Papa was the glue that held us together. Now, I feared we would come apart at the seams, scattering each of us in our own direction.

Maman endeavored to sell our beloved home on the *rue* Franklin. All my memories were there. My studio. My flowers and trees. I could not fathom someone else living in our home, but she found an apartment on the *rue* Guichard and was preparing to leave. There was no turning back.

Poor Papa had such a hard time of it. Three days before Christmas his declining health forced him to retire. One month later, he was dead.

Now Maman leaned on me for strength. Over the years, I'd caused her more than her share of heartache. Now I would stand strong for her, keep my woes to myself, and put forth a countenance resilient enough for both of us.

"Berthe, dearest." She sat across the breakfast table from me, looking ashen in her black paramatta and crepe mourning dress. "I have learned the hard way I cannot tell you what to do. You are much too headstrong to listen to me. I respect that you have your own way of doing things. But my *Bijou*, I fear I am not capable of weathering this storm on my own."

I reached across the table and took her frail hand.

"Maman, please do not worry. I am here for you."

She squeezed my fingers, released me and wiped a tear from her watery eyes.

"I must ask something of you. I know it will not be easy; nonetheless, I must prevail upon you."

"Anything Maman."

"I shall receive the Manets today."

This news jolted me. Édouard and I had not spoken since Papa's funeral. I was sure Suzanne was no worse for my absence. She'd gotten her way. In fact, I was sure she was quite happy. However, Eugène and *Madame* Manet had done nothing to deserve my silence.

"I beg you to mend your differences with the Manet family. We need our friends around us now. Please do make peace with them before we lose their friendship forever."

I thought about the ups and downs Édouard and I had experienced over the past six years. It gave me pause to consider where we should go from here. Where do you go when you've tested a relationship to its outer limits and blown holes in it whilst trying? Would attempts at friendship simply leak out through the wounds and scars?

Alas, perhaps it was our chance to heal. A tiny voice inside warned against hoping for too much.

"Of course, Maman. I should be happy to receive them with you today."

They arrived less than an hour later. Édouard, Suzanne, Eugène and *Madame* Manet.

Édouard carried a small package, which he handed to me. "Please open this later."

He did not smile. His gaze did not linger about my face as it used to. He took Suzanne's elbow and helped her to the sofa. She limped, and I suffered a pang at the tender way he assisted her.

Maman gave the package a curious glance, but did not belabor the matter. I excused myself and delivered it to my bedchamber.

I set it on the foot of the bed and turned to go, but my curiosity got the better of me. I tore off the plain brown paper. It was the small still life Édouard had presented to me that last day. The fan, the bouquet of blue violets, the note with that inscription. Above the letters I traced the words *Mlle. Berthe from E. Manet.*

My heart filled with a hollow longing, the likes of which I believed would never be quenched.

All this emotion brewed inside me like a storm rolling in from the sea. *Merci Dieu,* it did not slip past the iron barrier I'd erected.

I rejoined our guests in the drawing room. As I entered, I saw them all sitting there as they had so often during our visits and weekly soirées. I was overcome by a sense of loss that ran as deep as Papa's death. I could not imagine the memories of so many good times just fading away, and was overcome by the feeling that long after Maman and I vacated our house on the *rue* Franklin, our laughter and tears would remain imprinted on these walls, ringing throughout the rooms of our beloved house.

"Berthe, dear, the brothers Manet have expressed an interest in visiting your studio. Would you be so kind to take them?"

Out of courtesy, I cast Suzanne a glance.

"Would you care to join us?"

"*Merci, non.* I have twisted my ankle and the doctor has advised me to stay off of it as much as possible. But thank you for asking."

A vibration passed between Suzanne and me. It was hard to explain—she was not completely smug, not entirely warm. An understanding somewhere in the middle, possibly out of respect because I was in mourning.

I donned my black mantle and led Eugène and Édouard to the snow-covered garden with its leafless trees and frozen ground, toward my sad little studio that sat all alone.

I blinked at the brightness of daylight. After living with the blinds drawn for the weeks since Papa's death, it was a shock to the senses to venture out of doors. The naked trees stood dark and barren, silhouetted against the gray sky. I had always wondered at winter's light. The sky looked like a seamless quilt of gray-white clouds that hung so low it seemed possible to reach up and touch them. I'd been trying my entire life, yet they'd always managed to remain just beyond my reach.

The men's footsteps crunched the frozen ground as they walked behind me, and I sank deeper into my cloak. Something in the air reminded me of my childhood, made me wistful. This garden contained so many memories of our family, when we were whole—the sound of children laughing somewhere on the other side of the garden wall; the smell of hot brioche drifting from a nearby home; the steady puff of gray smoke escaping from the surrounding chimneys that wisped up to the winter sky. Households so alive, and so unaware that time was a bandit that prowled in the night, stealing lives and beauty and purpose.

I opened the studio door to admit the brothers Manet as snowflakes began to fall from the sky.

The men shook them off before they entered.

"Please excuse the mess." I rubbed my hands together to warm them. "I have already started packing. Everything is in a bit of a disarray."

"No need to worry, *Mademoiselle,*" said Eugène.

I was surprised to hear him speak up like this. While Édouard, a bit sullen, hung back, for once allowing his brother to take the lead. My mind raced back to the day Édouard asked me to marry Eugène.

"If you require assistance with the move," Eugène said, "I should be obliged to be at your service."

"*Merci, Monsieur.* I might accept your generous offer closer to the date of our relocation."

"And when will that be?" Édouard asked. His back was to us as he looked out the window.

"A fortnight yet."

"And what will you do for a studio?" he asked, still gazing through the condensation on the windowpanes at the frost-covered lawn.

"There is an extra bedchamber we will convert. Not as spacious as what I am used to." I sighed. "But it will do."

Édouard walked to the center of the studio and looked around.

"How is the *Société Anonyme des Artistes* shaping up? I should very much like to see the work you are producing for the show."

A bolt of ire zagged through my veins. "*Monsieur,* I have lost my father. I am in mourning. I have had no time to work, as my mother has required all my devotion."

Édouard bowed his head. "Of course, how thoughtless of me. I beg your pardon, *Mademoiselle.*"

"It is a shame you will not participate," said Eugène. "From what I hear the *Société* sounds dynamic, but I do respect your situation."

Édouard's glance was a poison dart that bounced off Eugène without effect. I was intrigued. Eugène was aware of his brother's dislike of the *Société.* Yet he was bold enough to have an opinion to the contrary.

"I would like to get involved with the group myself," he said.

Édouard snorted. "What, pray tell, would you show?"

Eugène faced his brother square. "I would not show anything. You know that I am not the artist of the family. I should offer help on the business end. Promotion, tickets, hanging the show. I suppose there is always next time."

"Perhaps," I said.

Hmmmm . . . perhaps.


In March, Maman encouraged me to submit two of my finest pieces to the Salon. Her suggestion took me by surprise, because scarcely two months after we buried Papa, I did not think it proper to attempt such a public display. Alas, she insisted. I must admit I was quite eager to oblige.

When each piece was rejected, the blow hurt all the more.

That was the last straw. I was tired of having my hopes dashed, bending and kowtowing to the whim of the Academy.

Idleness did not suit me, and it was plain to see if I did not do something constructive with my time, I would be of no good to Maman or myself. She was as disgusted with the Salon jury's rejection as I was, and since she had given me her blessing to show in the official exhibition, I decided to take a leap of faith and forge ahead with the *Société*'s show.

I feared Maman would be none too thrilled, but I would break the news to her gently. She was resilient even in her fragile state of mind. I was certain she would see it was the best recourse for both of us.

If I acted quickly, I could gather a sampling of the work already completed, as it would be futile to try and produce new canvases. The tricky part would be prevailing upon

Édouard to loan me the canvas of Edma at the Lorient Harbor. But it was time he and I settled our differences once and for all.

# Chapter Twenty-Six

*My queen, my slave, whose love is fear*
*When you awaken shuddering,*
*Until that awful hour be here,*
*You cannot say at midnight dear:*
*I am your equal.*
*—Baudelaire, Les Fleurs Du Mal*

*LE CHARIVAR—BY LOUIS LEROY—April 25, 1874*
*"Exhibition of the Impressionists"*

*Oh, it was indeed a strenuous day, when I ventured into the first exhibition on the Boulevard des Capucines in the company of M. Joseph Vincent, landscape painter, pupil of the academic master Bertin, recipient of medals and decorations under several governments! The rash man had come there without suspecting anything; he thought that he would see the kind of painting one sees everywhere, good and bad, rather bad than good, but not hostile to good artistic manners, to devotion to form, and respect for the masters. Oh, form! Oh, the masters! We don't want them any more, my poor fellow! We've changed all that.*

*Upon entering the first room, Joseph Vincent received an initial shock in front of the Dancer by M. Renoir. "What a pity," he said to me, "that the painter, who has a certain understanding of color, doesn't draw better; his dancer's legs are as cottony as the gauze of her skirts."*

*"I find you hard on him," I replied. "On the contrary, the drawing is very tight."*

Berlin's pupil, believing that I was being ironical, con-
tented himself with shrugging his shoulders, not taking the
trouble to answer. Then, very quietly, with my most naive
air, I led him before the Ploughed Field of M. Pissarro. At
the sight of this astounding landscape, the good man thought
that the lenses of his spectacles were dirty. He wiped them
carefully and replaced them on his nose.

"By Michalon!" he cried. "What on earth is that?"

"You see . . . a hoar-frost on deeply ploughed furrows."

"Those furrows? That frost? But they are palette-scrapings
placed uniformly on a dirty canvas. It has neither head nor
tail, top nor bottom, front nor back."

"Perhaps . . . but the impression is there."

"Well, it's a funny impression! Oh . . . and this?"

"An Orchard by M. Sisley. I'd like to point out the small
tree on the right; it's gay, but the impression . . ."

"Leave me alone, now, with your impression . . . it's neither here nor there. But here we have a View of Melun by M.
Rouart, in which there's something to the water. The shadow
in the foreground, for instance, is really peculiar."

"It's the vibration of tone which astonishes you."

"Call it the sloppiness of tone and I'd understand you
better—Oh, Corot, Corot, what crimes are committed in your
name! It was you who brought into fashion this messy composition, these thin washes, these mud-splashes against which
the art lover has been rebelling for thirty years and which he
has accepted only because constrained and forced to it by your
tranquil stubbornness. Once again, a drop of water has worn
away the stone!"

The poor man rambled on this way quite peacefully, and
nothing led me to anticipate the unfortunate accident, which
was to be the result of his visit to this hair-raising exhibition.
He even sustained, without major injury, viewing the Fishing

*Boats Leaving the Harbor* by M. Claude Monet, perhaps because I tore him away from dangerous contemplation of this work before the small, noxious figures in the foreground could produce their effect.

Unfortunately, I was imprudent enough to leave him too long in front of the *Boulevard des Capucines*, by the same painter.

"Ah-ha!" he sneered in Mephistophelean manner. "Is that brilliant enough, now! There's impression, or I don't know what it means. Only, be so good as to tell me what those innumerable black tongue-lickings in the lower part of the picture represent?"

"Why, those are people walking along," I replied.

"Then do I look like that when I'm walking along the Boulevard des Capucines? Blood and thunder! So you're making fun of me at last?"

"I assure you, M. Vincent—"

"But those spots were obtained by the same method as that used to imitate marble: a bit here, a bit there, slap-dash, any old way. It's unheard-of, appalling! I'll get a stroke from it, for sure."

I attempted to calm him by showing him the *St. Denis Canal* by M. Lepine and the *Butte Montmartre* by M. Ottin, both quite delicate in tone; but fate was strongest of all: the *Cabbages* of M. Pissarro stopped him as he was passing by and from red he became scarlet.

"Those are cabbages," I told him in a gently persuasive voice.

"Oh, the poor wretches, aren't they caricatured! I swear not to eat any more as long as I live!"

"Yet it's not their fault if the painter . . ."

"Be quiet, or I'll do something terrible."

He gave a loud cry upon catching sight of the *Maison du*

*Pendu by M. Paul Cézanne. The stupendous impasto of this little jewel accomplished the work begun by the Boulevard des Capucines—Père Vincent became delirious.*

*At first his madness was fairly mild. Taking the point of view of the impressionists, he let himself go along their lines:*

*"Boudin has some talent," he remarked to me before a beach scene by that artist, "but why does he fiddle so with his marines?"*

*"Oh, you consider his painting too finished?"*

*"Unquestionably. Now take Mlle Morisot! That young lady is not interested in reproducing trifling details. When she has a hand to paint, she makes exactly as many brushstrokes lengthwise as there are fingers, and the business is done. Stupid people who are finicky about the drawing of a hand don't understand a thing about impressionism, and great Manet would chase them out of his republic."*

*"Then M. Renoir is following the proper path; there is nothing superfluous in his Harvesters. I might almost say that his figures . . ."*

*". . . are even too finished."*

*"Oh, M. Vincent! But do look at those three strips of color, which are supposed to represent a man in the midst of the wheat!"*

*"There are two too many; one would be enough."*

*I glanced at Bertin's pupil; his countenance was turning a deep red. A catastrophe seemed to me imminent, and it was reserved for M. Monet to contribute the last straw.*

*"Ah, there he is, there he is!" he cried, in front of No. 98. "I recognize him, Papa Vincent's favorite! What does that canvas depict? Look at the catalogue."*

*"Impression Sunrise."*

*"Impression—I was certain of it. I was just telling myself that, since I was impressed, there had to be some impression*

*in it . . . and what freedom, what ease of workmanship! Wallpaper in its embryonic state is more finished than that seascape."*

*In vain I sought to revive his expiring reason . . . but the horrible fascinated him. The Laundress, so badly laundered, of M. Degas drove him to cries of admiration. Sisley himself appeared to him affected and precious. To indulge his insanity and out of fear of irritating him, I looked for what was tolerable among the impressionist pictures, and I acknowledged without too much difficulty that the bread, grapes and chair of Breakfast, by M. Monet, were good bits of painting. But he rejected these concessions.*

*"No, no!" he cried. "Monet is weakening there. He is sacrificing to the false gods of Meissonier. Too finished, too finished! Talk to me of the Modern Olympia! That's something well done.*

*"Alas, go and look at it! A woman folded in two, from whom a Negro girl is removing the last veil in order to offer her in all her ugliness to the charmed gaze of a brown puppet. Do you remember the Olympia of M. Manet? Well, that was a masterpiece of drawing, accuracy, finish, compared with the one by M. Cézanne."*

*Finally the pitcher ran over. The classic skull of Père Vincent, assailed from too many sides, went completely to pieces. He paused before the municipal guard who watches over all these treasures and, taking him to be a portrait, began, for my benefit, a very emphatic criticism:*

*"Is he ugly enough?" He shrugged his shoulders. "From the front, he has two eyes . . . and a nose . . . and a mouth! Impressionists wouldn't have thus sacrificed to detail. With what the painter has expended in the way of useless things, Monet would have done twenty municipal guards!"*

*" 'Keep moving, will you!' said the 'portrait.' "*

*"You hear him—he even talks! The poor fool who daubed at him must have spent a lot of time at it!"*

*And in order to give the appropriate seriousness to his theory of esthetics, Père Vincent began to dance the scalp dance in front of the bewildered guard, crying in a strangled voice: "Hi-ho! I am impression on the march, the avenging palette knife, the Boulevard des Capucines of Monet, the Maison du Pendu and the Modern Olympia of Cézanne. Hi-ho! Hi-ho!"*

*PARIS-JOURNAL—by ERNEST CHESNEAU—*
*May 7, 1874*
*"Le plein air, Exposition du Boulevard des Capucines"*

*A young group of painters has opened an exhibition on the Boulevard des Capucines. If they had had the complete courage of their convictions or strong enough backs to run and bear the risks they might perhaps have managed to strike a considerable blow.*

*Their attempt, very deserving of sympathy, is in danger of being stillborn because it is not sufficiently emphatic. To have invited the participation of certain painters who are shuffling around the edges of the official Salon's latest batch of inanities, and even artists of unquestionable talent, but who are active in areas quite different from their own, such as MM. de Nittis, Boudin, Bracquemond, Brandon, Lepine and Gustave Colin, was a major mistake in both logistics and tactics.*

*One must always reckon with the inertia of public judgment. The public has no initiative. Initiative has to be taken on its behalf. If it has to choose between two works presented to it simultaneously, one in conformity with accepted conventions, the other baffling all tradition, it is a foregone conclusion that the public will declare itself in favour of the conventional work at the expense of the work of innovation.*

*That is what is happening at the Boulevard des Capucines. The only really interesting part of the exhibition, the only part worthy of study, is also the only part whose curious implication eludes the great majority of visitors.*

*This rapprochement was premature, at the very least. It may work in a few years' time. So it is possible that it may offer a lesson and, in certain conditions, may provide the opportunity for a triumph for the "plein air school."*

*For this is what I would like to call this school—which has somewhat oddly been christened the group of the Intransigents—as that pursuit of reality in the plein air is its clearest objective.*

*The plein air school is represented at the second-floor studio in the Boulevard des Capucines by MM. Monet, Pissarro, Sisley, Degas, Rouart, Renoir and Mlle. Morisot.*

*Their leader, M. Manet, is absent. Did he fear the eccentricities of certain paintings? Did he disapprove of the compromise that allowed into so restricted an exhibition pictures conceived and painted in a spirit quite different from that of the school? I do not know. Was he right or wrong to hold back? I offer no answer. But there is no doubt at all that a selection of his paintings would have provided this exhibition with a more decisive, or at the very least more complete, statement of intent.*

*It is also possible that M. Manet, who has a fighting spirit, prefers to fight on common ground, that of the official Salon. Let us respect each man's ideal freedom to prefer one course of action to another.*

*It may be helpful to inform the visitor that none of the pictures exhibited here has been submitted to the scrutiny of the official jury. As the exhibition opened on April 15, it is by no means an exhibition of Refuses. But those who have seen it do not need to be told that not one would have been accepted, had they indeed been subjected to that trial. Why? In my eyes, that is their merit, for they break openly with all the traditional conventions.*

*But let the Limited Company—since that is what it is, indeed it might even be described as a cooperative—take stock. Its current organization opens the door to all the inept painters, all the laggards of the official exhibitions upon application for a share. This is the kiss of death.*

*If the company does not alter its status, does not affirm a common principle, it will not survive as an artistic company. That it might survive as a commercial one does not interest me at all.*

"Impressionist." Maman scoffed. "Is that how you wish to be known?"

"I can think of worse things to be called than an Impressionist."

"Is spinster among them?"

I sat still, staring at my hands, weighing my words because I did not want to fight with my mother. I did not have the energy. The move, the exhibit. Nearly the half the year was gone and so was my will to forge headlong into battle.

"What people think is very important to you, isn't it, Maman?"

She frowned at me as if I'd just uttered a riddle or posed a trick question when she was in no mood for games. But what I said was clear and true.

The showing of the *Société Anonyme des Artistes* was a disappointment in many ways—not a single sale, mediocre attendance, mixed reviews tilting toward bad—

Maman was mortified. She'd been spoiling for a fight since the reviewers' first snide words appeared in print.

I couldn't fight with her because I didn't even know what I wanted anymore.

At least Maman had conviction.

What kind of existence was I leading? Waiting to live, waiting to be happy, believing better days would befall tomorrow, when tomorrow never came.

"I took the liberty of contacting your former teacher *Monsieur* Guichard and asked him to view the show and render his opinion of the horrors in which you involve yourself."

She pulled a letter from her pocket and held it up. "I almost chose not to share it with you, but then thought better of it. My dear child, you are thirty-three years old. Well beyond marriageable age." Her voice cracked with the raw emotion I saw swimming in her eyes. "My *Bijou*, I am not well—"

"Maman stop this nonsense, you are as fit as I am."

She waved the letter to silence me. I fell back against the cushions on the divan and threw my arm over my eyes.

"I worry about you," she said. "I worry what will happen to you when I am no longer here. Who will care for you, what fate will befall you?"

I bit the insides of my cheeks because I wanted to remind her that I was the one who took care of her. That I was capable of existing on my own. As she was so fond of reminding me, I was thirty-three years old and I'd had quite a while to grow comfortable with my own company.

"It is with these reasons in mind that I have decided to share *Monsieur* Guichard's words," she said. "I hope you will take them to heart."

I sighed. I was so tired of this back and forth, push and pull. She was tolerant when the reviews were favorable or the sales large, but the moment the sky clouded, she ran to escape the rain. I realized, as I sat there, that my own mother was more of a fair-weather source of support than even the critic Louis Leroy.

She unfolded the letter, and I braced myself for what I was sure was to be the evidence of my mortal failure.

*Madame, the kind welcome you gave me this morning touched me deeply. I felt younger by fifteen years, for I was transported back to a time when I guided your girls in the arts, as teacher and as friend.*

*I have seen the room at Nadar, and wish to tell you my frank opinion at once. When I entered, dear Madame, and saw your daughter's works in this pernicious milieu, my heart sank. I said to myself, "One does not associate with madmen except at some peril. Manet was right in trying to dissuade her from exhibiting."*

Maman paused and glanced at me, to make sure the dart landed squarely where intended. Yet what baffled me was how *Monsieur* Guichard learned of Édouard's feelings toward my participation. I did not tell Maman—

*To be sure, contemplating and consciously analyzing these paintings, one finds here and there some excellent things, but all of these people are more or less touched in the head. If Mademoiselle Berthe must do something violent, she should, rather than burn everything she has done so far, pour some petrol on the new tendencies. How could she exhibit a work of art as exquisitely delicate as hers side by side with Le Rêve du Celibataire? The two canvases actually touch each other!*

*That a young girl should destroy letters reminding her of a painful disappointment, I can understand; such ashes*

*are justifiable. But to negate all the efforts, all the aspira-*
*tions, all the past dreams that have filled one's life, is a*
*madness. Worse, it is a sacrilege.*

*As painter, friend, and physician, this is my prescrip-*
*tion: she is to go to the Louvre twice a week, stand before*
*Correggio for three hours, and ask for forgiveness for*
*having attempted on oil what can only be said in water-*
*colour. To be the first watercolourist of one's time is a*
*pretty enviable position.*

Maman glanced up at me to see if I was still listening. I
was not so happy at his deeming the members of the
*Société*—the Impressionists—madmen. It did not sit well
with me. But the moniker Impressionists was starting to
grow on me. The more I considered it, the more I liked it.

His letter surprised me in that it had not proven to be as
harsh as I feared. It was quite complimentary.

"Berthe, are you listening to me?" Maman said.

"Yes I am, Maman."

"Good, this is the most important part."

*I hope, Madame, you will be kind enough to answer*
*this devoted communication, which comes straight from*
*the heart. For I am greatly interested in this promising*
*artist; she must absolutely break with this new school, this*
*so-called school of the future.*

*Please forgive my sincerity,*
*Joseph-Benoît Guichard*

Maman slapped her leg with the letter. "There, you see?
If you will not listen to me, will you not heed the warning of
your former teacher? He sees it as a monstrous association."

I scratched my head and a strand of hair broke free.

I appreciated *Monsieur* Guichard's flattering encouragement toward my talent, but I wondered how it was he could be so blind to the fabulous talent of the likes of Monet, Renoir and Degas. If they were madmen, then he must brand me as demented as they, for I resided in excellent company.

"Berthe, will you give up this nonsense and settle down? I insist you settle down."

It was clear to me that the beauty of his letter escaped Maman. "All you can read in his words is that he wants me to give it up?"

"You might as well if you insist on carrying on in an unbecoming manner. You are too old for such antics."

I was stunned silent. Aghast at her narrowness. She would rather see me the idle spinster, sitting at her side with needlework in hand, rather than making a happy, independent life for myself.

"Are you suggesting I should quit painting so I will stop drawing attention to myself and the fact that I have chosen not to marry?"

Maman grunted. The sound might as well have been an affirmative, but she considered my question for a moment before making the verbal commitment. Then, as if sent by the heavens, Amélie entered the room.

"Pardon, *Madame* and *Mademoiselle*. *Monsieur* Eugène Manet calls. May I show him in?"

"*Oui, Merci.*" Maman brightened and straightened in her chair. "Bring us some tea, *s'il vous plaît.*"

I was not at all disappointed to see Eugène. He'd become a good friend in the six months since Papa died. Eugène was gentle in offering his condolences and quite indispensable assisting with the administration of the Impressionists' showing. All this despite his brother's vocal stance against us.

My newfound friendship with Eugène was quite refreshing. He'd even painted alongside me on several occasions. He didn't possess the talent of his brother, nor the sparkling personality, but it was nice to not feel the burn of competition that simmered beneath the surface of my relationship with Édouard.

What had I expected? With Édouard, I'd built the beast that nearly consumed me.

I tucked the piece of stray hair into my chignon just before Eugène entered the room.

*"Bonjour, Madame* and *Mademoiselle."* He bowed to Maman and me, took a seat on the divan next to me as Maman suggested.

Maman made the appropriate small talk before she excused herself, leaving me alone with Eugène.

A beat of awkward silence hung between us as we stared at each other.

I smiled. He smiled back, flushed, glanced away.

"Your brother received as much press from our exhibit as the *Société* members. It seems we shall forever be tied to him."

Eugène frowned and blinked. "Yet he is dismayed at the lack of attention his paintings received in the Salon."

"At least he was accepted by the jury. I guess it's human nature to always want, despite one's accomplishments."

A rueful expression washed over Eugène. He was a handsome man. He didn't wear his good looks as comfortably as Édouard donned that self-possessed, determined suit of armor. But Eugène was a good man. There was sincerity in the set of his jaw, the gentle notes of his quiet voice, and honesty in his gray eyes.

Gray.

Yes, they were indeed gray. I'd never noticed the color

of his eyes until that moment. He held my gaze for a moment, laced his fingers in his lap and glanced down at his large hands. I sensed he had something on his mind.

Amélie carried in the tea tray and set it down on the table in front of the divan. Eugène shifted his knees out of the way and it dawned on me how much smaller the room was than the drawing room in the house in the *rue* Franklin.

"May I get you anything else?" she asked.

"No, *merci,* this is lovely."

I lifted the pot and poured two cups of tea.

Eugène settled back against the cushions with his cup in his hands before he spoke.

"*Mademoiselle,* my family has secured a house in Fécamp next month. We would be delighted if you and your mother would accompany us."

I wondered if Édouard would be in attendance, but I did not ask. The earnest note in Eugène's voice and the manner in which he presented the invitation wouldn't permit me.

"Thank you for thinking of us. I shall talk to Maman."


Society cast women in a rather unfortunate role. We were daughter, wife, mother—beyond those perimeters our very person was diminished. Society expected us to find love. Yet finding love was the most difficult challenge a woman faced.

That's why it was much easier to funnel all of my devotion into my career. It was the safe existence, as Eros had not smiled kindly upon me in the arena of love.

I could blame the poets for creating an impossible standard. We were all Juliet, the devastated lover who would rather plunge a knife into her heart than live a moment without the love of a man.

Perhaps I should've blamed Maman for bending me to

the breaking point. Perhaps I should've blamed Édouard for making me love him; for loving me so intensely and letting me go. Even after all we'd been through, in my heart I knew the true depth of our feelings.

Perhaps that was all that mattered. Perhaps it never mattered. Perhaps it was time to let it go.

On the Fécamp shoreline, I fashioned a boat out of paper. Into the tiny vessel I released all the misgivings I held inside and set the little boat out to sea.

The tide pulled it out. Pushed it back. Consumed it in one frothy bite of azure wave.

The tidal dance was much like my on-again-off-again six-year relationship with Édouard. Much like his on-again-off-again summer plans. In the end, he opted to travel to Argenteuil rather than joining us in Fécamp.

How symbolic.

Light glinted off the water. The little paper boat lost its shape during its tumultuous journey in and out of the sea. How much easier it was to glide effortlessly along the calm, quiet floor of the ocean rather than fighting the waves to keep from being sucked under.

After being knocked about on the surface and flattened, the little boat succumbed to the pull of the tide and ducked under for the last time.

Eugène offered me his arm and a vow to make me the most cherished woman in the world. I accepted both, and we began our journey together down the beach.

# Chapter Twenty-Seven

*The night has a thousand eyes,*
*And the day but one;*
*Yet the light of the bright world dies*
*With the dying sun.*
*The mind has a thousand eyes,*
*And the heart but one;*
*Yet the light of a whole life dies*
*When love is done.*
*—Francis William Bourdillon,*
*The Night Has a Thousand Eyes*

*January 1875*

*My dear Tiburce:*
*Eugène tells me this is the day the mail goes off and for fear of missing another opportunity of writing to you, I am scribbling a few words in haste. The thought of you has obsessed me for several weeks, mon pauvre ami. Where are you? What are you doing? I should give a great deal to know these things and even more to be able to contribute in some small way to your happiness.*

*As for myself, I have been married a whole month now; it is strange, isn't it? I went through that great ceremony without the least pomp, in an ordinary dress and hat, like the old woman that I am, and without guests.*

*Since then, I have been waiting for events to take shape, but so far fate is not in our favor. The trip to Con-*

stantinople, so definite, so certain at first, is no longer certain at all. However, I shall not complain. For I have found a very nice garçon, whom I think genuinely loves me.

I have entered into the positive side of life after living for so long with foolish chimeras that did not make me very happy, and yet, thinking of my mother, I wonder if I really fulfilled my duty. These are all complicated questions and it is not very easy, at least not for me, to distinguish clearly right from wrong.

Your loving sister,
Madame E. Manet

# Author's Note

When my husband and I set off for Paris in May 1999, little did I know the trip would change my life. I'd lived in France and longed to return to Paris; it was my husband's first trip to this magnificent country. Our main focus (besides food) was art. From the Louvre to the *Musée* d'Orsay, to the *Musée* National de l'Orangerie, we immersed ourselves in the works of the great masters.

I was particularly interested in the French Impressionists. I'd always loved their work and was anticipating a day-trip to Giverny, Claude Monet's home and famous gardens. Before we boarded a train at the *Gare Saint-Lazare,* to make our way to Giverny, we stopped Paris's *Musée* Marmottan to gaze upon Monet's infamous *"Impression, Sunrise"* (*Impression: Soleil Levant*), the image that launched the French Impressionist movement.

On the second floor of the *Musée* Marmottan, I met Berthe Morisot for the first time. Not literally, of course, but her essence permeated her luminous paintings on display. Even though I'd been a fan of the Impressionists, I wasn't familiar with her work. I was immediately captivated by her style and drawn to a photograph of Berthe and her family. Something about the photo haunted me and urged me to research her life. In doing so, I discovered the tale of a deeply complex, richly talented woman who bucked nineteenth century convention to become one of the world's greatest artists. It also became exceedingly clear she was likely very much in love with the great painter Édouard

Manet, the brother of the man who would become her husband.

Very little is documented about the depth of Édouard and Berthe's affinity for each other. Biographers recognize their intense *friendship* and acknowledge hints of romantic fancy in her correspondence. Also telling are reports of Berthe's extreme jealousy of Manet's wife, Suzanne, and his pupil, Eva Gonzaléz. Most revealing, though, are the eight portraits Édouard painted of Berthe between 1872–74. In the span of his career, Manet did not paint anyone as often (fourteen portraits of her total), nor as passionately as he portrayed her.

It's well documented that the Manet brothers doted on Berthe. Some biographers have implied a bit of sibling rivalry ensued over her attention. Alas, Édouard was a married man. Eugène was not. For all intents and purposes, Eugène won when Berthe became his bride on December 22, 1874.

Upon the announcement of her engagement to his brother, Édouard painted Berthe one last time. The portrait prominently showed off her engagement/wedding ring. Once she married Eugène, Édouard never painted her again. According to documentation, Berthe took her marriage vows seriously, and settled into a close platonic relationship with Édouard, but it's unclear to whom Berthe's heart really belonged.

While I have attempted to portray the documented facts of Berthe Morisot and Édouard Manet's lives as accurately as possible, the book, *With Violets*, is most definitely a work of fiction. I have drawn on her correspondence—several letters are reproduced within the pages of this book. Although, some of the "letters" in the book are strictly fictional. I have attempted to "paint in" the missing pieces of Berthe and

Édouard's relationship, exploring what *might* have happened between them during the years prior to Berthe's marriage to Eugène. It is with great awe and respect for Berthe and Édouard and their nonconforming, artistic spirits that I have asked the question "what if" and sketched a love story with the deepest honor intended.

# About the Author

Award-winning author Elizabeth Robards formerly lived in France and has studied art and writing. Currently residing in Orlando, Florida, she dreams of living in Paris and living the life of a bohemian writer with her husband, Michael, their daughter and three cats.